L e Duc let his eyes stray to the altar and the head, sitting motionless as if it had been carved from stone. Lifeless as it now was, it had the the appearance of something stolen from a grave. Le Duc was outraged at the blasphemy, but he couldn't help being curious at the same time. He'd seen that thing *move*!

Santos followed his glance, and the dark priest's smile deepened.

"You saw, then. You know that the head is more than it seems. That is the first of your lessons. You will find that there are many things in this world that are more than they seem. Never take anything at face value. That head is no head, but a window—an oracle. There is no secret it cannot ferret from the vaults of history, given the proper preparation and ritual."

Le Duc was about to ask a question in an attempt to buy time, but at that moment Santos stiffened and turned toward the door. The odd, faraway look returned momentarily to his face, as if he was listening to a voice from within his mind; then it passed, and the fire blazed even more brightly in his eyes. Le Duc would have given a lot to have known what Santos had seen, or thought, during those few short moments.

"Bring him," the priest said, gesturing at Le Duc. "We must make our escape more quickly than planned. It is as we were warned—flight is once more upon us."

TO SIFT THROUGH BITTER ASHES

THE GRAILS COVENANT TRILOGY

BOOK 1

By David Niall Wilson

ACKNOWLEDGEMENTS

I'd like to thank John Rosenman, Richard Rowand, Jacqueline, and the others for their wisdom and criticism. I'd like to thank Mark Rainey, Rich Chizmar, and Karl Wagner (whom I miss) for their editorial wisdom and continued support of my work. I'd like to thank Kathe Koja, Poppy Z. Brite, Peter Straub, and Stephen King for inspiration. (Not necessarily in that order.)

Thanks to the crew, Beth, Wayne, Brian and Dollie, Jeff, Von, Barb and Charlie. Thanks to my mother-in-law, Mary, who supports my history-book habit, and my sister-in-law for her bad taste in sports teams. Thanks to Kevin Fowler—his bookstore supported me, and he proof-read and collaborated with me. Thanks to Andrew Burt and the on-line Critters SF workshop for the crunch-time critique sessions. Also, thanks to Stewart Wieck for believing in me, and Rob Hatch, Rich Dansky, Justin Achilli, and Anna Branscome for putting up with my panic attacks and helping me see this through.

This book is dedicated to my brother, whom I have wasted a lot of years not being close to.

And, of course—to the blood. The power is in the blood.

ONE

The villagers scattered as the huge black stallion thundered into the square. The tall, broad-shouldered rider reined in outside the *taverna* contemptuously, sliding from the saddle like liquid darkness. He was standing beside the master of the stable before the horse had fully calmed.

The old man took in his late visitor in quick, nervous glances. This was no rough mercenary, or country lord. He wore the finery of a noble, and his sharp, aquiline features and the glittering arrogance in his eyes were those of a warrior. A formidable pairing, and not one to be taken lightly. He tossed the long black tresses of his hair over his shoulder and stepped closer.

"Yes, Lord?" The stable master said in hushed tones, as though afraid anything he might say, or any stray movement he might make would bring this dark man's wrath. He'd seen such as this one before, more times than he could count, and their temperaments were as unpredictable as the winds. He'd seen friends and relatives who hadn't the wits to learn this lesson and live.

"I am Montrovant," the dark one said softly. His words carried forcefully despite the softness with which they were spoken. "You will care for my mount," he ordered. "You will watch him throughout the day, and I will call for him tomorrow evening. I am not certain of the hour of my return. Have him ready and keep him ready. Your head rests on his condition, your future depends on my pleasure."

The old man bowed his head, accepting the reins without question, and led the magnificent animal off toward the stalls in back. He had not grown old by being a fool, and there were some men it was better to obey and be done with. He'd never seen this noble before, and he hoped never to see him again, beyond his return to retrieve his mount. The less known, the less risked. They were dangerous times, and danger not faced was the best sort encountered, or so his Pa had told him.

There was a shuffle of feet beyond the door, and the sound of hushed voices. The old man had known they'd come. He'd also known they would cower in the shadows, uncertain of how to approach, but too curious to stay away. He wished that they had grown to more wisdom. One of them was his own grandchild, and he'd hoped to see that young one grow to adulthood.

Montrovant ignored the sound; at least he gave no indication that he'd heard it. He strode toward the door without once looking back. It was as though he believed that his words, once spoken, could never be denied. He didn't turn toward the *taverna*. Instead, he turned toward the cliffs overlooking the village, where the bright, waxing moon outlined the monastery against a backdrop of cloudy darkness. The squat, severe lines of the stone edifice sat like a short silk cap on the mountain's peak. The monastery brought its own fears. Stories had circulated about the place for years, dark stories, but there was no proof, and the Church cared well for the people of the village. None pressed the issue.

The whispered voices grew bolder. The stranger seemed to pose no immediate threat, but somewhere deep in the pit of his stomach the old man knew it was a mask. He wanted to call out to the young ones, to send them away, but he found that his voice would not function. Not this time.

He saw a young boy creeping up along the side of the wall, moving closer to the dark one. The lad was holding his breath, measuring each step carefully. He was nearly to the door of the stable at the stranger's back, and the stablemaster prayed for one long second that he would make it. He could see the boy's eyes, wide as saucers. In the dead silence of the night he believed he could hear the youngster's heart slamming waning courage through his veins.

Suddenly the man was not watching the mountains. He

had spun, and the boy was held aloft before him, screaming in terror. The dark one had a hand gripping the lad beneath each shoulder. He held him above his head as easily as a mother might hold her infant. He drew the boy close, so close that their faces nearly met. His captive was struggling. The scent of his sweat fell away to the acrid aroma of fresh urine, and the silence that had echoed in answer to his scream gave way only to a ragged, rasping sob.

The dark one stared at him for a moment longer, then threw back his head. The laughter that poured forth rang from the rafters of the stable, and to his shame the old man took another step back into the shadows.

Montrovant lowered the boy as swiftly as he'd lifted him.

"You should not make a practice of slinking through shadows, boy," he growled. His voice was still tainted by the unholy laughter that would not quit banging about in the old man's mind. From one side a woman appeared suddenly, kneeling to take the boy in her arms, her wide eyes upturned to Montrovant's in awe.

"Take him and clean him, lady," the dark one said softly. "He showed more courage than most. He will be quite a man one day."

Without a word the woman bundled the boy into her arms and fled into the shadows. Turning, Montrovant leveled his gaze at the old stablemaster contemptuously.

"I hope you will care for my mount better than you do the children."

Without warning, the man was gone. One moment he'd filled the doorway, the next, as the old man turned for a discreet glance over his shoulder, that doorway was empty, but for the darkness and the lingering taste of danger, soured by the taint of death. Turning away from that emptiness, this time with a shiver transiting the arthritic, bent lines of his back, the stable master led the horse to the largest, warmest stall available. Waving away the young man he'd hired to help with the animals, he left the stallion for a moment and went for his personal gear. This was an animal that required his best effort.

The shadow of the monastery was clearly framed in the

small circle of light from the stable door. For some reason the long-familiar sight of the holy place disturbed him at that moment more than it had at any other in the long years of his existence. The shadow seemed to be creeping down the side of the mountain and reaching for him. He shivered again.

Pulling the heavy doors shut, he closed his eyes for a long moment, banishing the images from his mind and shutting out the spirits of the night. He heard the horse shuffling behind him, and he returned to his work, for the first time in years wishing he'd left for his home before dusk.

Silk vestments hissed across stone like passing serpents as Bishop Claudius Euginio made his way swiftly across the top of the stone wall. The moon painted the scene in shades of silver and grey, catching the white locks of his hair and reflecting wetly off the scarlet and gold of his robes. He was not a tall man, but there was an aura of authority and power that surrounded him that was unmistakable. His movements were sure and graceful, and the set of his shoulders spoke of confidence bordering on arrogance. These were traits he fought to suppress. They were not seemly in a man of God, well-placed as they might be.

He stopped suddenly and stared into the distance in silence. Far below he could see the glittering lights of Rome. Nearer were the softly glowing fires of the village, and it was there that he directed his concentration. They feared him in the village, he knew. It was an integral part of the security he'd set up about himself. They feared the knowledge of why he frightened them even more.

He let his senses broaden. Those sights, sounds, and smells nearest to him grew fuzzy as he focused on the homes and hearths below. He could hear voices faintly, and he could sense the beating of the communal heart of the villagers as they went about their lives. It was all familiar, and he brushed it aside in annoyance. He placed his hands on the stone rail and breathed deeply. The control of the moment was exquisite, his mind linked to theirs, their fates lying in his hands. The village, even Rome itself, were his kingdom, albeit that his monarchy existed in the shadows and behind the scenes. It was enough that *he* felt the control.

The monastery at his back was silent. Each of the brothers he'd indoctrinated and trained was in the cubicle assigned to him, communing with God in his own way—some with their own God altogether. Claudius was not as demanding on the theological level as he was on matters of discipline. God was not one of his major concerns, since their final meeting had been indefinitely postponed. None of his followers would disturb him at this hour, and he spared them no thought.

He had waited days for Montrovant's arrival. Even for an immortal, patience is not infinite, and with Montrovant involved it could be outright difficult. Montrovant's message had not been clear, as they never were. Euginio was both angry and curious at the same time. The dangers of the two of them meeting publicly, complicated by the vows of the brotherhood itself, grated on his nerves.

Montrovant had always been too arrogant. It was a matter of age, and of maturity in the blood. He was not young, nor was he weak, but he lacked the discipline that would lead him into latter centuries. There were protocols for every occasion, deceptions that had to be scrupulously maintained. Montrovant recognized all of this, but he rarely acknowledged it. He lacked the plain common sense. It was, of course, part of his appeal.

Claudius took another deep breath and stiffened. He sensed Montrovant's approach, a breath of Kindred wind against the backdrop of the night. His progeny was moving along the ground below, faster than any mortal eye could have followed, only a blur to even Euginio's supernatural sight. He didn't need to see clearly—there was no mistaking the tug of the blood tie.

Bishop Euginio saw few of the others, and then only reluctantly. If the clan did not look to him for leadership—for the wisdom of his years and position—he would not have seen them at all. He had a perfect niche carved out for himself, protected, but controlled. He was not fond of putting his position at risk. On the other hand, he had to act occasionally to maintain his control, and to keep their respect. As dangerous as it would be to be discovered by the brethren, or the Church, to be stalked by his own would be the greatest danger. It was important that they understand his strength.

Although it was ill-conceived, Montrovant's message and subsequent visit were an opportunity to make that necessary contact. If it were truly foolish, it would give him a chance to show his strength.

Montrovant moved with uncanny swiftness. Claudius nodded in momentary approval, pride, even, though he'd never have admitted it. At least the fool had not come charging up on a war horse, waking the entire complex. That had been the first image to surface in Claudius's mind, and it was one he gladly discarded. Montrovant was the strongest, and eldest, of his remaining progeny, but for sheer audacity and disregard of reality, he mocked that ancestry each moment of his existence.

Montrovant closed on the wall and never hesitated, scaling the vertical surface with ease and grace, his form a dark ripple on the shimmering, moonlit surface of the stone. Claudius stepped away from the wall and slipped into the shadows, waiting.

The younger vampire crested the wall and landed easily, silent as a cat. He hesitated for just a second as he took his bearings, then turned toward the shadows, a slow smile working its way across his elegant features. Both of them knew that the hesitation had been sufficient to end his life for a second time. He had extended his trust in his sire. The lines between them had been drawn.

Claudius waited and watched as Montrovant drew near. He didn't speak. He wanted to hear what his protégé had to say before he committed to any particular response.

"It has been too long, Claudius," Montrovant began. Even in whispered tones, his voice was full and rich, born to power. Claudius resisted the urge to smile. That voice, the long hair, and the incessant energy had been the qualities that had drawn him to Montrovant in the first place. That meeting had occurred so far in the past that the rulers, even the face of the land itself had changed, as had both of their names, and yet Euginio could still remember his first sight of that smile—the arrogant inner strength that was Montrovant's core.

There was also the tall, slender build and the ripple of muscle beneath cloth that spoke so eloquently of strength. Others had made the mistake of believing Montrovant too emaciated for real physical strength. It was a deception that Claudius approved of.

"It is rarely too long between such occasions," he answered at last. "What is this thing that has brought you to me, at such risk? What is it that you cannot decide or undertake without chancing the corruption of all I have created? I find it hard to believe that it was but a moment of my company that you sought."

Montrovant's smile never wavered. He continued to move closer, tilting his head enigmatically and taking in his sire's countenance with a cat-like grin.

"You are no more at risk than the mountains, old one. If your velvet-lined throne and army of "brethren" deserted you, you would merely slip into the shadows and build a new world. It has happened before. I know you too well to think you fear these mortals."

"You know so little that it is frightening," Claudius growled. He was unable to hide his smile this time, however, a weakness that nearly drove him to sudden anger. Montrovant took his hand, moving yet closer.

"It is good to see you."

"You have not traveled all these miles to comment on my health, or to flatter me," Claudius sighed. "If you only wanted my company, you never would have left in the first place. Tell me why you have come."

Montrovant hesitated again, looking pained.

"You know I could never have survived here," he said softly. "It is too much like a cage."

Claudius waved his words away. "Why have you come?"

Montrovant's countenance grew serious and intense. His smile clouded over in a frown and his deep green eyes were suddenly miles away. He was obviously giving a lot of thought to his choice of words. It was a thoughtful expression—rare to Montrovant, but not unheard of. Claudius tensed—he'd seen that expression before, and it had never boded anything but ill.

Taking both of his sire's hands in his own, Montrovant began.

"You are old," he began slowly, "and you have seen things I have not. You will remember. I too have seen great things, but I do not have the base of knowledge that I desire. I need your guidance, and your blessing."

Claudius remained silent, waiting.

"On the night when Jesus of Nazareth last dined with his disciples, he was served wine in a particular cup," Montrovant began, his eyes burning embers in the deep shadows. "He took that wine, and he blessed it, and he made of it his blood—bidding all who followed him to drink of that blood, and to taste of his flesh, that they might never die."

"I need no lessons in Holy Scripture," Claudius grated. "What is your point?"

"I seek that cup," Montrovant whispered. "The Grail. I want to find it, and to bring it back to you. It is the key, the answer to all the petty, endless struggles for power between clans. It, if it itself exists, has held the blood of one not of this existence. How powerful would that blood be? What would it be to drink from such a vessel—such an object of power? None could stand before us if we had it in our possession."

"This is what you believe?" Claudius asked, stepping back and barely stopping the sardonic grin that engulfed his features short of a sneer. "This is why you have come to me, risking my position and the power we have striven generations to achieve? A quest for a holy talisman? I knew that you were rash, that you didn't comprehend things the same way that I do, but I never dreamed that you were so naive.

"What makes you believe that this 'Holy Grail' exists? A better question—what makes you think that, if it exists, and it stands for all that you believe that it must, that if you found it you would not crisp and burn at its touch?"

"There are tales of others," Montrovant continued, his voice unwavering under Claudius's disdainful sarcasm, "others who have touched—even fed from the chalice. Kli Kodesh…"

"Kli Kodesh," Claudius spat the words back at Montrovant, backing away, his eyes blazing. "Now you want to tell me fairy stories. I know the legends as well as you—I told them to you. They are only that, legends. I am disappointed in you,

Solomon, truly. You are beginning to make me wonder at my own judgment in presenting you to the darkness."

Montrovant flinched at the use of his true name. He'd lived in so many places, behind so many guises and ruses, that he sometimes forgot that there were those who'd known him as a man. He also forgot, from time to time, that he was not omnipotent. It was traveling among humans that did it to him. In their world, during the hours of darkness, he was invincible. Here he was at risk, and the enormity of that risk was not lost upon him as Claudius glared at him in growing anger.

"I mean no disrespect, Claudius," he said quickly. There was no compromise in his voice, but his tones were less assertive. "I have not come to this course of action lightly, nor would I disturb you for a fool's quest. I have not been sitting back, waiting for eternity to swallow me. I have been seeking, learning. Surely after all these years you know me better than that?"

"I am uncertain if I know you at all," Euginio grated. "You appear to have taken leave of what little sense of our reality you may have achieved in the many years of your existence." Claudius had begun to pace slowly, picking up speed and volume as his anger grew.

"You ask too much. I cannot risk myself, nor can I put such a burden upon the others without their knowledge or consent. You should have called a council, made your case to the clan..."

"I have spoken with the others." The words were out before the thought was fully formed, and Montrovant took a step back, realizing his mistake. Claudius's brow furrowed, and his eyes darkened. He had been ready to forgive Montrovant's disrespect, but this was a different matter. It challenged his own control of the clan. It was not the place of one such as Montrovant to consult the others—not without coming to Claudius first.

Claudius came to a stop and stood as still as stone for the space of several moments, a span that he knew would be growing to an eternity in Montrovant's mind. When it finally slammed through the silence, his voice cracked the air like the sound of ice on a frozen pond.

"You have spoken to the others? Please tell me that I have not heard you correctly, or that it is some sort of joke. If it is true, you have not only compromised my own position, but you have risked theirs, and you have done all of this because—what—you wish to die the final death? You are ready to cast in your lot in life and take a chance on finding your lost soul in the next world? You are insane? Or perhaps the cub thinks it is time to challenge for the pack? I can think of no other reason you would do what you claim to have done, then come to me and admit your guilt."

Claudius turned to face Montrovant fully, eyes blazing, and he took a step forward. His words carried the weight of strength and the promise of a challenge met. Montrovant took half a step back, then stood his ground.

"I meant no disrespect." Montrovant said at last. "I knew how you would react, but I wanted you to know how they felt before you made a decision, and I knew you would call no council for me on this matter. I went to them first because I have heard rumors—because I believe I know where the Grail is kept, and because I believe I can bring that power back to you. There is no challenge. I only felt the request deserved an honest chance."

Claudius didn't answer him, and he went on quickly. "The others believe, as well. At least, they think the matter worth investigating."

"I cannot risk our position, even if you know the very door to which we could ride up and make off with this 'Grail' of yours without incident. Do you understand that? Do you comprehend what I'm saying to you? Somehow the reality of the world that rejects you is also rejected by your mind. We cannot romp about the countryside, seeking this or that treasure without regard to others of our kind, or to those who would put a final end to us."

"There will be no risk to you, or to the clan," Montrovant said slowly. "I am not asking for your assistance, only your blessing. I need to know that I will act without fear of your anger or retribution. I will do this thing alone, and I will bring the power back to the clan. I will do this, or I will never return, and you may continue as the fates guide you. That is my oath."

"So arrogant," Claudius whispered, moving closer to where Montrovant stood beside the wall. "So full of your dreams and aspirations you can't *see*. What makes you believe that I will not 'continue as the fates guide me' despite your request? What makes you believe I will not send you to your final death here and now for your impudence? What makes you think in your misguided, twisted mind that you are destined to lead us to new power?"

"I see more than you believe," Montrovant answered, standing his ground. "I see others gathering, growing in power, moving among the cities and the churches and taking what is rightfully ours. I see my own brothers slaughtered in the daylight by hordes of fanatic mortals, ripped apart by the sniveling followers of the Wyrm, dying of decadence and sloth. I see us slipping into corners and caverns and hiding away, hoping that it will all pass us by and just let us be. It will not.

"The world is not a static thing, and it is not meant to be met sitting back and waiting, but head on. There are none more fit to lead the clans into the future than we. It is in our blood, and I know you feel it, for all your caution and doubt.

"All this I see, and I see a way around our troubles, as well.

"I see a new world, a new era, and I see a way to attain that dream. You may accuse me of many things, but do not accuse me of not paying attention to what happens around me. You know more than you are saying. It was you who first planted the knowledge of the Grail in my mind. It was you who met the madman, Kli Kodesh, who told me of the legend of how he had walked the earth since the days of Jesus himself. You cannot tell me it was all just an amusing story. We are closer than that. I felt the power in your words. You might not want to risk anything in the search for it, but you know more of the truth I seek than any other being on the planet."

Claudius turned away. "It is not that simple. If it were, don't you think I'd have gone after it myself? Don't you think I'd have that fool Kodesh's head dangling from a spike on the wall of my keep, rather than huddling away during the day while my pious "brethren" pay homage to a God so far removed from my mind that it is difficult to remind myself I once believed in him? There are factors you don't understand, risks you don't bother to see."

"Then make me see, Claudius!" Montrovant lurched forward, casting caution to the winds and placing his hands on his sire's shoulders. He moved in closer, bringing his eyes so close that he could see his own reflection in the icy depths of Claudius's own grey orbs. "Tell me what you know."

Claudius pulled away and turned toward the wall in silence, but Montrovant persisted.

"The Grail is kept beneath the ruins of the Temple of Solomon," he proclaimed. "I have spies throughout the Holy Land, informants in the Church. They have seen the vaults, and they know the secrets within the walls of Jerusalem. There are rumors of great treasures and holy talismans, and the Grail is reputed to be one of them. It is *there*, Claudius. It is there, and I mean to have it."

"Solomon's temple?" Claudius asked, whirling back to face his progeny once more. Once again he began to pace. His ire had melted into a grim mask of concentration, and Montrovant could see that he was making headway. "How can that be? The Grail was one of the great treasures of the Church. It was rumored to have left the Holy Land long ago—Kli Kodesh himself claimed knowledge of this. He said that it was being watched—that it was safe, but he would never reveal its whereabouts, and I assumed this to be because he truly knew nothing.

"Then there were the Turks—they would never have left such an object to the Crusaders, even as they surrendered the holy city. They built a mosque above that accursed temple, how could such a thing as hidden treasure have escaped them? The Pope would have *known*, our people would have known."

"Very few know," Montrovant stated firmly, "and that is hardly surprising. It is just a cup, to the Turks, Claudius. It would not glow in the dark, and it wasn't made of gold. It came from the home of a poor man of great faith, and it held magic; but, to one who does not believe, what is it? An old cup. Such is the way of the truly great objects of power.

"There have always been those within the priesthood who, for the security and sanctity of the church, controlled the relics. Urban II did not know of the Grail's presence when he took the temple and the city back from the Turks, and even had he known, the secret died with him before his goal was carried out. I was there.

"I rode with de Bouillon. I walked the halls of the temple, and I saw the guardians. They were there. No one could explain them. No one knew their names, or how they came to be in the temple the moment it was in our hands, but no one questioned *why* they were there. But they were. They inhabited the tunnels beneath the temple—a labyrinth of passageways and hidden rooms. They were sent by someone with power, and they were sent there for a purpose. They guard the Grail."

"They?" Claudius asked, stopping his pacing to fix Montrovant with an icy glare. "Who are *they?*"

"I'm not certain," Montrovant admitted, turning to stare out over the wall and into the darkness below. "Their leader is old. Not Kindred, but old, all the same. I could sense his power, even from outside the temple itself. I met with one of his followers in a corridor of the temple, just in passing, and he looked into my eyes. He did not know what I was, exactly, but he knew that there was more to me than what met his eyes, and he was curious, not fearful."

Claudius's eyes hadn't wavered.

"He tried to read me. He reached out with his mind, and had I not thrown up mental walls and made my way out of that place, he might have broken through and found all of the answers he sought."

Montrovant spun to meet Claudius's gaze head on. "He *smiled* at me, Claudius. He smiled, turned, and walked away.

"The Grail is there. It is there, and I mean to have it."

"If this guardian you speak of is so old, so powerful, how will you get past him?" Claudius wondered aloud. To himself, he thought, *and why don't I know about them? If they know you, do they know me? Can they reach me through you?*

"I will use their own guise against them," Montrovant answered. "I will approach those with power in the Church, and I will find a way to become the chosen defender of the Grail. With their backing, I will supplant the authority of these— guardians. Once I know who they are, and to what lengths they will go, I can plan for their deaths. If they bleed, I will feed on their souls. If they do not…well, dust is dust."

"Interesting." Claudius replied. "I assume you have a plan? I assume, in fact, that you have a plan that will set my heart to rest on how you will end the existence of one as old as you claim this guardian leader to be? You know nothing of him, or his followers, and yet already you are 'feasting on their souls.'"

Montrovant grinned at him in answer, his expression half amused, and half wary.

"You know me too well to question that, in truth. My men are in place, they await only my word. I have worked for many years toward this moment."

"*Your* word," he corrected quickly, as the fire leaped suddenly back into Claudius's eyes.

"You will be set apart from us completely until this is finished." Claudius said finally. When Montrovant moved as if to speak, the Bishop held up a hand to warn him to silence. "You will not contact me. You will stay clear of all of the others. They will know what you are doing, but unless their aid comes freely and safely for us all, it will not come at all. You will never ask for it. You will be an entity unto yourself, and if you fail, you will be hunted down and hung from the very walls of this monastery for the sun to feed on your bones and wretched flesh. Am I clear?"

"You are," Montrovant answered, lowering his eyes to the ground so that the fierce grin would not give away his emotion. "It will be as you say. If it is a year, or a hundred years, you will see me again, and I *will* have it. On this you have my oath."

"I have no need of your oath," Claudius whispered. The force behind his words nearly drove Montrovant to his knees. "You are mine, as you have ever been. I cannot control your mind every moment of every day, but I can call you home, and I can put an end to you for eternity. Never let that bit of information slip from your mind. Never."

Montrovant nodded, not trusting himself to answer. Without a further word, he leaped to the wall and over. His shadowy figure was making its way across the grounds and toward the forest beyond almost before Claudius noted his passing. So swift. So arrogant. So full of passion. Of the three, only swiftness was a virtue among their kind.

Turning, Bishop Euginio lowered his eyes to the ground beneath him. Even after so many years it seemed that he could still be surprised. The Grail, hidden beneath the stone of Solomon's temple? He'd walked those halls—perhaps his steps had crossed the very ground where it lay. It was ironic that his progeny bore the name of that great king. Solomon's temple. Perhaps it would be so again, before all was said and done.

And these guardians, he'd never encountered anything like what he'd just heard. Montrovant's words had reminded him vaguely of tales he heard out of Egypt, but he couldn't place the facts. Had he been blind, or had they always been there, behind the scenes? Were they another factor he would need to expend valuable resources on, or were they a figment of Montrovant's overactive imagination? One thing was certain, if they existed, they were a threat, and Claudius did not allow threats to go unchallenged. He would have to send out some eyes and ears of his own. Just because he was granting Montrovant no help didn't mean that he wasn't interested in the outcome.

And that was another question. Could Montrovant handle them? There were others he might have sent along who had clearer heads, but Montrovant was the eldest. Short of going himself, it seemed he had no choice. Too many questions. Claudius made his way through the halls of the monastery and into his own cell silently, encountering no one.

He couldn't shake a sensation of anticipation. Perhaps the century to come would not be without its amusements.

TWO

Montrovant eased his mount into a slow canter, scanning the shadows as he made his way through the tree-lined forest toward the abbey. Claudius and his monastery were miles behind him, but the image of Euginio's eyes in that single moment when he'd slipped and admitted going behind his sire's back had been etched into his mind. There had been other such moments, but none so intense, and not for many years.

Montrovant had known the risks of his actions, but only in those eternal seconds had he *truly* understood what it was that he'd risked. He had walked the earth for a long, long time, but somehow the span of his existence had compressed to the span of an instant when the termination of that existence had stared him in the face.

Dust coated his cloak, and his mount was lathered and panting. It had been a long ride, and there was not much time before daylight. As he'd counted on, the old stablemaster had taken good care of his mount. It was fed and well-rested, as he'd known it would be. There had been no sign of the child or his mother—no sign, in fact, of any life in the village at all.

He'd met no one on the road. It was just as well. His mind was awash in plans and questions, and there had been no time for distractions. Now that he had Claudius's blessing, he wanted to waste no time in setting his plans into motion. Pressing hard, he'd made the journey to the abbey in less than a week. He'd feared that his mount would give out and that he'd have to continue on without it, or steal another, but the animal had proven strong and resilient. A fitting companion on the road.

He'd fed only once, and rested as few hours as the killing

bite of the sun would allow. This last night he'd pressed on mercilessly. He wanted to reach the Abbey without the necessity of seeking shelter on the road again. It had seemed a prudent decision earlier, but the longer he remained in the saddle the closer the dawn, and the greater the risk to his own well-being. Not for the first time he found himself considering Claudius's words more carefully. Perhaps he could do with a measure of caution.

He had to make it the last few miles to Bernard's abbey unseen, and he had to count on the door to the cellars and vaults beneath being left open, as he had ordered. Bernard had never let him down, but where was the sense in taking such chances? Bernard was human—a remarkably reliable and intelligent human—but human all the same. It was not a good practice to place one's future in the control of an unknown factor. That was what Claudius had tried, once more, to warn him about—his reckless disregard of danger. Montrovant grinned.

Without a little risk, what would be the point in living, such as it was? He spurred his mount to a faster pace and broke through the line of trees into the fields surrounding the abbey. None of the brethren were in sight. He knew they would be making their way to morning mass soon. Bernard had three passions: God, rules, and enforcing the rules.

Montrovant let his thoughts slip ahead of him. Bernard had proven a remarkable ally, all things considered. Small and slight, sickly from birth, Bernard's future had spread out before him in bleak contrast to those of his boisterous, powerful brothers and domineering father. All of that had changed as Montrovant had trained the young man's mind to compensate. Given a modicum of civilization to back it up, the mind would always win out over the sword, if properly applied. Bernard was, if anything, better at applying that axiom than Montrovant had been at teaching it.

The one fault the young priest showed in abundance was an insistent faith in the Church. Montrovant had carefully worked his deceptions and teachings around this, putting on the face of piety, such as he could muster, but at times he wondered if it were truly enough. He could intimidate Bernard into acting on his wishes, but it was more important to win the man's trust, however tenuous. Humans and their faith were not things lightly to be trifled with, however harmless they might appear.

Montrovant slipped around the back of the building toward the stables. He led his mount into the shadowed stalls and secured him to one of the posts. The horse was damp and breathing heavily, but he gave it no thought. Bernard would see to the animal soon enough. Without a backward glance Montrovant slipped back out into the predawn grey of the dying night. He could see lights through low, square windows, moving down the inner halls toward the chapel.

It was a low-cut building, as were many others of its time. It seemed to grow from the stone of the mountain at its back, rather than to have been built up from the ground, as though it had been a part of the earth all along, only waiting to be revealed by the hands of men. Beyond the small ring of fields, where the brethren cultivated their meager crops, the forest cut the abbey off from the world, save for a single road that wound through the center of the trees.

The numbers of the brethren had grown steadily since Bernard had founded the abbey, and the building itself had grown as well. Montrovant had stood by the young man's side through it all, watching, coaxing, exerting his own will and strength whenever possible, but careful to remain in the shadows. It was no easy task to create a saint, even less simple when complicated by nocturnal hours and the necessity of safe haven during the hours of daylight. The danger was always there that Bernard would see through his deception and attempt to "set things right."

The door opened easily, and he slid inside with a quick indrawn breath of relief. He hadn't really expected treachery, but it was calming to know he had judged rightly once more. He would go to Bernard when the sun had set, and they would talk. It was time that his plan was set in motion, and even the threat of the coming sunlight nearly failed to drive him below ground before he outlined that plan and got Bernard started on it.

He descended a steep set of stairs, passing directly by the

lower storerooms and into the wine cellar beyond. There were barrels and casks neatly arranged in rows against the walls, held in place by wooden frameworks that stood easily the height of a man. The brothers were seldom inactive. To waste even a moment of God's day would be a sin. They made some of the finest wine in all of France.

Though the fields surrounding the building were not large, the vineyards that populated the mountain behind the abbey were another story. Carefully cultivated and blended from some of the finest grapes available, the fruit of "God's vines" was truly plentiful.

Behind one of the older frames that supported the casks, Montrovant felt along the wall until his hand slipped through a large metal ring. He pulled on it sharply, and a stone slab separated itself from the wall, allowing a cool wisp of musty air to escape. He pulled it a bit farther open and crawled inside.

The doorway was an addition that only he himself and Bernard had knowledge of. It had been constructed by a small team of stonemasons, late at night. Somehow, each of those men had met a horrible fate soon after the project's completion. Montrovant had used outside agents on that one. There would have been too much risk in killing them himself. Bernard, if he'd noticed the men's disappearance, or made the correlation between their labor and the loss of their lives, had said nothing. Wisely.

There was no need to wait for his eyes to adjust. Darkness was much more natural to him than light. He quickly pulled the stone back into place and checked the seal. Perfect. No danger, and even if one of the curious monks, or three, for that matter, were to discover the metal ring, they would never be able to move that stone from the entrance. He was secure and safe, for the moment.

He moved wearily to a stone slab in one corner of the dark little room and lay back. He wasn't really tired, but the lethargy brought on by the sunrise was beginning to grip his limbs. He felt the familiar tug of the earth beneath him, the slow torpor creeping through his mind and wiping it clear of thought. For once he was thankful it was so. If he'd had to lie there with his plans raging through his senses while he was helpless to act, it might have driven him mad. That is, if he was not already. The immensity of the task before him was not lost on Montrovant's mind, despite Claudius's doubts.

As it was, the darkness was comforting, and he slipped away quickly and completely. A matter of hours, no more, and he would put things into motion. He hoped Bernard was up to the challenge.

Above the vaults and wine cellar, the brothers made their silent way into the chapel and lined up, row upon row of down-turned eyes and shuffling feet. Each carried a single candle, which he placed on the raised stone shelf surrounding the room as he passed inside. The humility was palpable in the air. Moving toward the front and center of the room, they spread out, forming around the altar in long semi-circles, each falling to his knees as those of the man before him touched the stone. Like macabre human dominos they fell into place, and from above and behind them, Bernard watched. He stood secluded in a small, shadowed alcove, a grim smile masking his face.

As each of his followers entered the room and knelt before the altar, the aura of strength and purpose in the room grew. It was a calm, peaceful sensation, but it held the tingling promise of spiritual energy as well. Each candle added a bit more luminescence, and the shadows lengthened and danced about them. It gave the impression that those shadows were being held at bay by their silent prayer.

Bernard was a man of great faith, but his passion and personal vision cried out for action. So much ungodliness, so heavy the burdens of spirit and flesh. These men were his small answer to the problems of man in God's world. He was fashioning them, teaching and strengthening them in their faith. He was making a difference.

The men in the chapel before him were evidence of this. They were faithful, God-fearing men. They saw the gift of God's voice working within Bernard, and they heeded his words. Already there were others, other abbeys—other followers who'd gone into the world and brought his message to new ranks of the faithful. They were like an army, spreading out to conquer in the name of the Lord. It was not the same sort of army he'd dreamed of leading as a small boy, but the implications and power inherent in the spirit were immense.

Bernard's own father and his older, healthier brothers had sneered at his condition, his frail body and slender hands. He had overcome their taunts and their beatings, their snide remarks of "womanly ways" and "weakness." He'd given his life and his heart to the Church, and God had granted him the strength to win them over. What he couldn't accomplish on a battlefield of dust and blood, he could more than make up for in a community of spirit and faith.

Among those kneeling before him were the very father and brothers who'd doubted him. They waited, as did the others, for the benediction. They waited to share in Bernard's wisdom. He knew that pride was a sin, but in the face of what had come before, he thought the Holy Father might forgive him this one failing. It felt good to be vindicated, and he was happy to have brought his own family to God so completely.

His mind slipped to the dark angel, Montrovant. Bernard thought of him as an angel because any other correlation his mind could make would have been less than holy. Odd and enigmatic as Montrovant had proven over the years, Bernard had convinced himself, or reconciled himself to the illusion, that God had sent him. There was no way to question the difference the dark, brooding man had made in Bernard's existence—in the validity of his faith and the answering of his prayers. If God had chosen to test Bernard's faith by masking his messenger in darkness and shadows, denying him the light of day and the communion of the brotherhood, who was Bernard to question? And in questioning, he knew he would lose it all—this had no small weight in his decisions.

In truth, it was another small failing of his faith. He would not have given up Montrovant's support had he known the dark one to have been sent by the Devil himself. What Montrovant offered had done wondrous things for the Church—if these things were not the direct goal of the messenger, did that make listening to the message wrong? Bernard didn't think so. He had spent his share of brooding meditation contemplating the world through Montrovant's glass, darkly. What had shone through was worth the cost.

There were other things that troubled him, though, and among them was the notion that, at least in part, his father had been right. Might of arms was a God-given gift as surely as prophecy or wisdom, and there were causes that deserved their champions. There were things that Mother Church might be doing more completely, more efficiently. Montrovant had hinted at the same thing, recently. Though Bernard could never be a strong force physically, he knew there were roles that he could play in such an arena, all the same. He yearned to discuss it all with his mentor. It would be good to talk with him again. It was always good to talk with him.

The Holy Land had been taken back from the infidels, and after a stretch of time, godly men had taken charge of the spoils. The Crusades had been a brilliant stroke—masterful and effective. They had freed the holiest of cities, the city of Jesus's death and rebirth, no less, and yet they had not been enough.

They had delivered the prize, but it was becoming increasingly obvious that those involved were now seeking personal gain before that of the Church. The hold Rome had over the cities of the Holy Land was tenuous at best, and the defense of those lands was fragmented between the desires, goals, and egos of a large group of noble houses. The Church, in theory, controlled all of this, but in reality the nobles did as they wished. There was no formal control. As often as not, a pope who dared to disagree with whatever monarch was in charge at the moment would be exiled, tortured, or even killed before he would be heeded.

Montrovant had promised Bernard an answer to this problem, a solution worthy of a saint, and Bernard prayed that his odd advisor would appear with that answer soon. He also prayed that he would be able to live up to the intimation of Montrovant's words. There were few enough of saints remaining to the Church. He felt deep within his heart that everything that had happened to him was in the interest of a higher purpose. He felt himself pre-ordained as a leader, but with the limitation all men possessed as the obstacle between himself and success. That obstacle was freedom of choice, and the ability to choose wrongly. Most of Bernard's prayers included a cry for wisdom.

For the moment, he had his followers, his duty, and his God. It would suffice. As the last of the brethren fell obediently into place, Bernard made his way down the winding stairs that led to the chapel and passed through their ranks in silence.

With all of the candles in place, their light dancing and playing in the shadows, Bernard's robed form seemed to slide across the stone floor, an eerie apparition of holiness. Just for a second, as he mounted the short steps to the altar, a chill wind blew through the room, sending the candle-flames dancing madly to and fro. Bernard hesitated. It was not a good omen for the beginning of Mass. It passed, and he turned to begin.

Change, he told himself. *It was the breath of change on my neck.* Deep within his heart, shadows mocked him.

He raised his powerful voice, letting it combine with those of the brethren as they chimed in with the responses to his litany. The sound echoed through the small stone chamber until all thought of anything save God and the sacrifice of his only son were washed from Bernard's soul. As always, the Mass cleansed him, revitalizing his spirit and re-orienting his thoughts to align more closely with the Almighty.

Far below, Montrovant shifted in his repose, as though he felt the vibration of their voices, or the glow of their faith pressing down through the stone walls and floor to drift over and around him. His body tensed, pressing more tightly into the stone, but his face remained impassive. The daylight passed.

Bernard sat alone in his chamber. Candles, as always, lined the walls, lending a false air of day that held the encroaching shadows at bay. A half-full flagon of wine stood before him, and a great leather-bound book lay open beside it. He was trying to concentrate, to bring forth something of the wisdom of the words on the pages—a commentary from Rome on the Epistle of St. Luke, but his mind wasn't cooperating. Somehow the commentator's words rang empty, and even the magic of the gospel itself seemed weak and without vision. Dangerous thoughts, but he was unable to push them aside.

He'd tried kneeling on the cold stone of the floor. He'd scourged himself with a leather whip until blood flowed in rivulets down his back and his breath came in heaving sobs. He hadn't eaten since early that morning, the beginning of several days' fast. His faith had slipped before, and he knew how to bring his recalcitrant mind under control.

He nearly jumped from his skin when a deeper bit of darkness passed across the night beyond his solitary window, sending the flames of his candles jumping madly about and nearly extinguishing them. Then Montrovant was there. No knock on the door, no sound, but he was there.

The dark one might be angel, or demon, but a man he was not. That Montrovant did the work of the Lord Bernard truly believed; the only question was whether or not Montrovant was aware of it. *It is better to be cold like ice than lukewarm.* The quote was not exact, but Montrovant fit the image. His touch had that chill—the chill of death, the cutting breath of a winter's wind. No man, but a blessing all the same. It was this knowledge that enabled Bernard to go on. As always, he shivered in Montrovant's presence.

"You have come," he said simply.

"I bring news. Good news," Montrovant replied. "I have word from Bishop Euginio in Rome."

Bernard raised his eyebrow sharply. Euginio was one of the eldest and most revered leaders in the Church. His piety and the vows he'd dedicated himself to were legendary—vows that had inspired many of Bernard's own beliefs and been written and enacted into the rules of those who worshiped and studied in his abbey.

"You were not gone long, to have ridden to Rome and back," Bernard observed, rising from where he'd been kneeling painfully on the floor. He made his way slowly to the single stone bench in the room and sat, leaning gingerly back against the wall.

"You would be surprised what proper faith can achieve," Montrovant grinned, his smile enigmatic as ever. Bernard could never judge the depth of sincerity in the man's words. He spoke all the right phrases, had the aspect of one of the great saints, but there was a taint of darkness about him, the taste of danger and death so close to the edges of his essence. That taste was bittersweet to Bernard. It was the closest to death and adventure he was likely to come.

When Montrovant was near, the temperature in the room seemed to drop. And there was the way he controlled men with his eyes that disturbed Bernard the most. It was uncanny—possibly unholy. More than once, Bernard had had to question whether his own actions had been controlled in that fashion.

In the face of the good that had come from Montrovant's presence, Bernard believed the aspect of darkness to be an illusion, a test. He had set himself on the road to passing that test long years in the past, and now was no time to challenge the veracity of his own faith.

"I have come with a plan," Montrovant began. "It will require a great deal of commitment, but it may be the most important undertaking of the Church in the next hundred years—possibly the most significant accomplishment in all the years of history that have come before us."

"Great words," Bernard whispered, trying to hide the slight tremble in his voice. "Great men have come before, and will come again. What is this thing that we can do that will create new legends?"

Montrovant stopped dead in his tracks for just a second. The softness died in his features, and his eyes glowed with a light of their own, like those of a wolf. It was an intense, frightening light. His face was momentarily supplanted by that of a great, predatory beast, and his height increased with a suddenness that nearly stopped Bernard's heart. Then the illusion—if illusion it was, and not revelation—passed, and he was himself again. Bernard felt the urge to pinch himself on the arm to prove he hadn't been dreaming that image. He hadn't convinced himself either way before Montrovant began to speak again.

"We must form an army. Not a Crusade, but a guard for all things holy."

Suddenly he was scant inches from Bernard's face, those burning eyes so close that the younger man could see himself reflected in their depths. It was like a glimpse of himself, burning in the fires of hell. A warning?

"Would you like to return the Grail to the Church, Bernard?"

A long silence followed as Bernard tried to take in the two things that had just been thrust at him. What did an army have to do with the Grail, and what did he, a man of peace and spirit, have to do with an army? And could it be possible? And wouldn't it be grand?

His mind whirled with images and memories, stories and legends. He knew of the Grail, of course. He'd seen many other such relics, held more than one in his own hands and felt the power of the One God emanating from their depths and reflected in their essence. He waited, not trusting himself to make the correct response.

Montrovant spun away, and began to speak again. "When the infidels were driven from the temple, there were secrets still buried there that were never discovered. There are those in Rome who knew, those who have always known, and when it was safe, they returned. They are the guardians of old, the guardians who have failed. I have seen them."

He turned to Bernard then, as if to check for signs of doubt.

"I walked those halls, Bernard, and I saw them. They are old, and they are wise, creatures—men, perhaps, but older than time itself—guardians from some time before ours. I doubt that even the Pope himself is fully aware of them, their origins or their purpose."

Bernard almost spoke then, almost voiced his disbelief, but Montrovant's eyes stopped him. This man alone was reason to believe in things beyond the natural world he'd been born to. He held his silence, and Montrovant continued.

"They have the task of guarding the most sacred relics, the treasures that even members of Mother Church believe lost or too powerful to be handled. They have been at this task for too long, and they have grown weak. They did not hold back the invading armies of the Turks, and they did not get the treasures free of the temple. They abandoned them. They can offer no better protection now. Not without our help. If the

Crusades had not freed Jerusalem, those relics would still lie waiting for whoever first ventured beneath the temple.

"Every day our people travel to the Holy City. Every day Muslim bandits and slavers strip them from the roads, killing, robbing, and selling them into servitude, while the Church, and King Baldwin in Jerusalem, do nothing." Montrovant had begun to move slowly closer, and Bernard fought to hold his ground and not back away.

"They are cutting us off," Montrovant continued, drawing even nearer and letting the full strength of his gaze seep forth, washing over and through Bernard, "and we must do something before that rift is complete. The leaders in Jerusalem as often refute the directions of Rome as they follow them. Even the Patriarch sent to represent the Church in those cities has been infected with corruption. Something must be done."

"What has this to do with me?" Bernard asked, finally finding his voice, "and what do you mean by mentioning the Grail? It is a legend, nothing more."

"It is fact," Montrovant asserted, his face now so close to Bernard's own that they could have kissed. "Do you doubt me?"

He moved back and continued, never missing a beat, but allowing Bernard the return of his breath. "It is a fact that they keep these treasures in a vault beneath the ancient temple of Solomon. I have seen the vault, and I have met its guardians. Why would you refute its existence? You yourself have held and communed with the Relic of the Cross."

"They told you all of this?" Bernard asked, unable to hide the skepticism in the tone of his voice, despite the sensation of imminent danger. "These guardians spoke with you?"

"They had no need to tell me," Montrovant replied curtly. "I have eyes, and a mind of my own, and I am no fool. You are not accusing me of being a fool, are you, Bernard? I know things about the Church that your father's father would have forgotten, were he alive today. I know of what I speak."

The menace returned so swiftly to the tall, gaunt man's eyes, and Bernard felt himself giving in to the pressure and retreating slightly, pressing against the stone at his back, though the action shamed him. He'd never seen Montrovant so intense.

His responses were no more impertinent than usual, and yet he felt himself on the defensive.

"Of course not," he replied at last, regaining his voice. "I have never doubted you."

"Then you must listen," Montrovant grated, "and you must act. Everything may hinge on the speed of our actions. Here is my plan."

Bernard did listen. Long into the night he listened, and after a while, he began to ask questions, and to add thoughts of his own. The vision that unfolded before him was vast and wonderful, and he could feel God at the base of it as surely as he'd felt the call to the priesthood. Before the dawn had dusted the horizon with the gold of another sunrise, letters had been drafted and plans laid firmly in place.

The rest is history.

THREE

The keep of Hugues de Payen stood alone, starkly outlined against the light of a moon three days short of full. The stone walls were overgrown with vines and damp near the base. It was an old structure. Many generations of de Payen blood had matured and fallen to dust within its halls. Hugues was not a great lord, but he was not without his followers, or his property, and the history of his family stretched into antiquity. Montrovant made his way carefully along the road, scanning the area for movement. Nothing stirred.

The walls were steep, but to Montrovant they might as well have been a stairway. He slipped from the shadows, having ridden as close as possible on horseback and made the last few miles on foot. He could move more quickly without the animal, but it was important, as openly as he acted, that he maintain appearances. Had he made a practice of rushing about the countryside on foot, covering ground at impossible speeds, eventually someone would have noticed. Even Bernard's credulity had its limits. The priest's faith in Montrovant's goodness was no more solid than the evening mist. If it hadn't been for Bernard's desire to lead, to prove his worth as a man, he would long since have declared his mentor a demon, leading the witch hunt himself.

Montrovant couldn't risk any notice of this visit. In this instance, approaching on foot was the answer; the horse was more likely to be noticed than he. If things went as planned, he would be in, make his mark, and out without even the man he sought comprehending where he might have come from, or where he'd gone. He needed to play the part of a night spirit.

With the chill wind and the low-lying clouds as a backdrop, he certainly looked the part as he scaled the pocked stone.

Though there was no imminent threat, there were sure to be guards on the walls. He had no fear of them. The entire garrison of de Payen's men would be no real threat. If anyone spotted him, however, months would be wasted. Too much depended on the perfection of this one facet of his plan to risk it all in some unfortunate guard or serving woman's untimely death— or twenty such deaths. He needed to keep this night clean and pure in the eyes of the master of the keep. This night Montrovant was not Death—he was an angel.

It had been one thing to win over Bernard, whom he'd counseled since young adulthood. It was quite another to win the respect and obedience of a grown man, a pious man. De Payen was no fool, and Montrovant had to remind himself constantly to re-align his approach as the moment drew near. It wouldn't do to burst in and start ordering the man about—he would have to speak with the voice of God.

He sensed a movement to his left, and without thought moved to the right, slipping over the railing of a balcony and into the shadows beyond. He waited for a moment to see if there would be an alarm sounded, but all was silent. He didn't believe that he'd been spotted, but he wasn't willing to take the chance. It wasn't too late, at this point, to retreat without cost, but a few more moments and all choices would be irreversible.

As he stood, he let his senses expand, scanning the walls and the interior of the room beyond the balcony. The guard he'd heard on the wall was still moving lazily toward the far end of the keep. There was no immediate threat of war in the area, and such guards were largely for show. Montrovant felt a slight movement of air against his cheek, caught the scent of lilacs. A serving woman, or one of the ladies of the tower. He wasn't certain who inhabited the room he was about to enter, but whoever she was, she was up and about at a very late hour.

He heard her slip through the doorway and make her way stealthily down the hall. Montrovant froze, waiting until the woman was clear of the room to make his move. It appeared that his luck was holding. Had she remained in the room, he might have had to seek another entrance, taking further risk of discovery. Perhaps it was a sign.

Still, he hesitated. What if she were making her way to the very bedroom he sought? It would put a quick end to everything he'd planned, not to mention the lives of any who saw him. He remained in the shadows of the balcony, considering the risks. There would be other nights, but his heart told him the time to strike was now. Bernard was convinced, and the wheels were turning. If he failed to come through on his end of the agreement, how could he be certain the others would not, in turn, back out on theirs? Bernard's loyalty was dependent, at least in part, on the infallibility of Montrovant's actions. As long as nothing he did directly opposed Bernard's faith, then everything else could be rationalized.

He slipped through the room and into the hall, moving slowly past stout wooden doors and sliding along the brick wall to the stairs he knew lay at the back of the keep. As he passed the second door from the stair, he paused. The lilac scent was strong, and he smiled. It was not de Payen who had a late-night visitor, but his steward, Montclaire. More information to file away for what was promising to be an intriguing future. Montrovant didn't know at what point he might require Montclaire's cooperation, but it was wisest to be prepared for any and all occasions.

No one else moved within the walls of the keep, and he mounted the stairs without incident. He'd visited this keep more than once, though not on such auspicious business, and never with the knowledge of the lord. Hunger had brought him, but even then he'd been attentive. He remembered each turn of the layout of stairs and halls...his memory was serving him well. It had proven to be one of his greatest tools since his death.

The entire upper floor belonged to de Payen. He had servants during the day, but he banned them from his presence at night. A religious man, de Payen took his nights to be alone with his wine and his Lord. There were rumors of a lost love, dead before her time, but they were vague. De Payen was a secretive man, and his pious nature did not call gossip like the wayward habits of some of the other local lords.

Montrovant was certain that these stairs were not entirely free of the scent of flowers and lust, but de Payen was a discreet ruler. Rumor even had him devout. It was that devotion that had led Montrovant to this keep rather than a dozen others he might have visited in similar fashion. What was to come depended greatly on the humans he chose to carry out his plans. If he chose wrongly, a greedy man, or one easily deceived by others, then all would be wasted. De Payen might have his faults, but if he did, they were hidden well enough to fool the man's peers, and that was an indication of the perfect tool.

The door opened silently, and Montrovant breathed yet another sigh of relief. He had no intention of exiting through that doorway, but if it had given away his entrance with a sound, his charade would have been undone. Angels were not generally perceived as requiring doors or stairs. He let it close behind him with a soft click and made his way into the inner chambers. Not for the first time since leaving the monastery, he wished he'd been just a bit more certain of the location of de Payen's own balcony.

There were candles burning in the back room, and incense as well. Montrovant moved forward slowly, watching the shadows and listening for any sign that his presence had been discovered. It was unlikely that de Payen's senses were that acute, but there was no sense in testing them.

A low, mumbling chant floated out to him from that back room, and the light of many candles sent shadows dancing along the walls. As he approached, he realized that de Payen was praying. Words tumbled from the man's lips in an endless stream, combinations of scripture and rambling pleas for forgiveness. Though the words themselves were all but incoherent, there was an air of mystery and power in the sound of those rhythmic syllables. It reminded Montrovant of Bernard's monastery, the air of holiness that permeated both the air and the walls, despite the shaky foundations Bernard's faith was built upon.

There was no time for hesitation. Montrovant moved forward. He used every ounce of the incredible agility and speed granted him in that motion, and it was quicker than human senses could comprehend. It was several moments after he'd come to a halt directly in front of de Payen that the man took any notice of his presence.

Rather than jumping up, or showing signs of fear or bewilderment, de Payen allowed his eyes to rise slowly, taking in every inch of Montrovant's large, muscled frame. He didn't stop until their eyes locked, and Montrovant could feel the energy in the air—the questions waiting on the tip of the man's tongue. Montrovant found himself envying de Payen's control and his faith. He was also a bit disconcerted by the thoughts he plucked from the big man's mind. He wasn't entirely used to being considered the direct answer to a prayer.

Despite their longing and begging for miracles, few men could have remained so still in the face of a physical manifestation such as de Payen now faced. Montrovant had been prepared to restrain him, or to take control of the man's mind if he bolted or sounded an alarm. What he hadn't counted on was this eerie control. De Payen was not afraid. If anything, he seemed to gain confidence from Montrovant's sudden appearance.

"Who are you?" de Payen asked finally. "Lord, who are you, and why have you come to me during my prayers?"

Montrovant didn't answer immediately; he held the man's gaze with his own and let his thoughts sink into de Payen's mind, sorting the man's thoughts quickly and molding them to his will. It was simple. De Payen sought help, and his mind was a blank slate, waiting for Montrovant to scribble in the answers. He couldn't have asked for a more perfect vessel into which to pour his mind. There were dark recesses he could not quite make out, but it didn't matter. The foreground of de Payen's mind was all that concerned him, and he took over swiftly and completely.

"I have come because you have called. Your prayers have not been in vain, Hugues de Payen. You seek a purpose—a chance to prove your faith in the light of God. I am here in answer."

De Payen's expression was rapt. He never moved to rise from his knees, nor did he attempt to speak further. He drank in the sight of Montrovant, letting the words he heard sink in slowly.

"The Holy Land needs champions, Hugues," Montrovant intoned. "Not all of God's enemies are sin and spirit. There is a need for a strong arm, even in the army of the Lord. Will you be that arm?"

Eyes glittering with pride and sudden purpose, de Payen answered. "I will. Lead, and I shall follow, Lord. Ask, and I shall answer your call. I have waited all my life for such a moment as this. As Jesus laid down his life for me, I will do so for you."

"It is not for me, Hugues. It is for the people of God, and it is leadership you are called upon to provide, not servitude. Go tomorrow to the monastery and seek Bernard. He will guide you—you and a few others—good men, godly men that you will choose. It is for Madeline."

The name had come to him suddenly, and he spoke it without thought. De Payen stiffened as he spoke it, but if anything the desire and faith in the tall knight's eyes burned brighter and hotter than it had before. Another fact—another name—to be pushed aside but remembered.

There was a long moment when it seemed as if de Payen might speak. He searched Montrovant's unwavering gaze for something—didn't find it, or did, then dropped his eyes to the floor in prayer. He had been given his direction, and it was all he required. It had been too easy, Montrovant thought. The fool had had such faith in his own prayers, in his own concept of God, that he hadn't had the sense to fear treachery when those prayers were answered so directly. Standing there, with de Payen's head bowed before him, he considered for a moment how easy it would be to crush the life from the fool and leave him there. The notion passed swiftly, but the image was somehow satisfying.

Then, for just a second, Montrovant found himself envious. He'd had such a faith once, a faith in something beyond himself and his hunger. It might be imprudent to name de Payen a fool in the face of such courage and commitment.

Montrovant turned slightly toward the window, then hesitated. It seemed he should say more. The few words he'd spoken hardly seemed a foundation upon which to build an army. He glanced down once more, opening his mouth to speak, but de Payen was already lost in prayer, concentrated and focused on the stone at Montrovant's feet. Enough or not, he knew that it would be unwise to break that trance.

With a sigh, he backed toward the window. De Payen never looked up, and with a shrug, Montrovant leaped out and upward, clearing the sill of the window and launching into the night. He willed the change—taking on the form and substance of the bat with practiced ease.

It cost him a great effort, but for effect it was worth it. He doubted that de Payen had stopped his praying to note his passing, but if he had, he'd gotten quite a show. Montrovant swooped toward the woods beyond the keep where his mount was waiting, and as the ground approached swiftly, he let out a keening cry, orienting his senses with the echoed image of the earth beneath him. As he settled, he changed, his legs and feet re-forming beneath him in time to break his fall into a swift run.

He knew that the bat was a darker form than most would attribute to an angel, but in his heart he felt it more appropriate than any other. The great artists and bards painted glowing images of benevolent angels, granting eternity and peace to man. The angels of the Bible, the angels of legend, had been warriors—uncompromised by morals or guilt. They had done the dark work of the Lord since the beginnings of time.

His mount shied away violently at his sudden appearance, but he reached out with his thoughts, calming the beast. He could have made better time leaving the animal behind, but time wasn't an issue for once, and things were going too well to risk problems at this late point. Bernard and de Payen might prove loyal followers of his suggestions, but that trust was based on their faith. If they thought him a demon, or an agent of darkness, or if reports of a strange, powerful creature of shadow began to circulate among their people, they would prove equally dangerous enemies—Bernard in particular, though Montrovant knew that the young priest saw Montrovant's very darkness as a test of his faith, of his vision.

There were hours of darkness left to him, and the hunger was beginning to eat at Montrovant's concentration. His mission complete, he followed his instincts, letting them spread and sweep the countryside before him, seeking release. He did not have long to wait.

She was young—maybe seventeen, returning by shadows to her home. He concentrated, focusing on her scent—the pulsing heat of her blood. Her thoughts floated to him on gossamer threads of emotion and he drank them in greedily. Such innocence was a rare treat.

She'd been out to meet a young man—a young man her father did not approve of. The sheen of sweat that coated her flesh reached him, and he breathed deeply. Lust and passion leaked from her like nectar and he spurred his mount onward. He did not sense the young man's presence, so there was no danger of being spotted unless he let her get too close to her home. That was a mistake he didn't intend to make.

As he approached her, he melted from the back of his mount into the night air, pushing off and upward with all his great strength. The horse shied, letting out a scream that he knew would chill the girl's heart. He felt her stop, momentarily paralyzed with fear, and in that instant he fell upon her.

There was no time for subtlety, no lingering glances or seductive speech. He dropped from the darkness and took her in his arms, locking onto the vulnerable softness of her throat before she could cry out, drawing her to him and into him in heaving, convulsive gulps.

He felt her flesh pressed wantonly against him, shared the myriad images of fear, lust, and confusion that warred in her failing mind. Her warmth flooded him. As she iced over, releasing her essence to his thirst, his strength returned. His vision cleared, and he fed more slowly, savoring the last of her—drawing her inward and welcoming the visions.

Her long hair fell back over his arm, and the scent of her perfume, mingled with the musk of her desire, drove all thought from his mind, save that of satiation and fulfillment.

She was beautiful. Now that he was in control of himself once more, he could see this. She—Monique—had grown to a young woman, fallen in love, and come to her end in darkness. So much potential had walked away from that young man's arms. He almost regretted having taken so much from her.

She'd been a piece of the world's art, in progress toward completion. With one deft stroke, he'd made her a bit of history. So sudden.

Completion. How he longed for that impossible state. So much hinged on the days to come, on his dreams and his plans. There was nothing to separate him from a fool at that moment but his passion. He wanted things to come to completion, to follow the logical lines of power and time full circle, but at the same time he wanted to hurry that process along.

Bernard, de Payen, they were just pieces in a grand puzzle that he was trying to construct from his own visions. He had grown to maturity in a world that worshiped a single God, and he'd seen that church evolve through faith to madness to evil and back again. The power to control men's minds was in their faith. The power to control worlds was in the past.

The Grail was more than a symbol. The blood that had rested in that cup, short as the duration of that stay might have been, was powerful beyond reckoning. Kingdoms would be risked in its recovery if it were certain. Lives and loves would be cast aside on the mere notion that it could be possessed. It would bring him to the power he craved, would bring Claudius to supremacy, and why not? Of all their kind, who was more deserving? Certainly not the cave-dwelling Nosferatu, or the pompous Ventrue. It was Claudius, ancient and powerful, who should rule, and the Grail could do that. It could bring back the sun, and anything that could return that was worth the risk of a second death. It was worth any risk.

He let Monique drop to the ground and looked around carefully. No one was near, but it never paid to be less than certain. One stray traveler, taking the story of the 'demon in the forest' to Bernard's monastery, and months—years—of work might be undone.

Working swiftly, he gathered branches and large stones from the surrounding forest and piled them carefully around the girl's still form. Before he covered her he took the dagger from his belt and slit her throat. The slice was clean, and it erased all sign of where he'd fed. She would not be found anytime soon, and by the time she was, there would be little evidence of the true manner of her death. It would be attributed to some passing vagrant, or bandit.

When he had finished, Montrovant turned toward the forest once more. He sensed his mount about half a mile away, and he took off at a run, letting the night-wind flow through the ebon locks of his hair and trail it behind him wildly. He felt powerful—invincible. There was an energy in the air and it blended with the fresh young blood flowing through his veins to lift his spirits.

Dawn was making its way slowly to the horizon, and he needed to get back to the abbey in time to get below without causing a stir; but for the moment what remained of the night called to him. He felt a kinship with the beasts that were abroad. Slinking wolves, owls soaring freely and swooping in upon unsuspecting prey. The freedom was splendid, and he let it soak through his being. It was good to let the cares and responsibility slip away, even if it was only for a fleeting moment.

He was nearing his horse when he sensed the other. He knew it was kindred, there was no mistaking the sensation. This time it was different from any other encounter in his experience, very different. This one was old. Older than Euginio. Older than anything, anyone Montrovant had ever encountered. The very essence of this being had the taint of grave dust and the magic of antiquity imbedded within it. It was a vision of his future.

Montrovant came to a full stop, letting his senses sweep the area and trying to pinpoint the source of the intrusion. He sensed no animosity, no imminent danger, but he knew better than to let his guard down in such a situation. He felt himself trembling, and his nerves were as taut as harp strings. Here was real danger, danger that could end him as swiftly as the snuffing of a small candle. Here was the thrill that came so seldom now that death had stolen his lifeblood.

A being as old as the one he was now seeking was powerful beyond his comprehension. Valuable in the same degree. The blood of such a one could make him little short of a God among men, were he to find a way to make it his own. The impossibility of attaining that blood without a serious element of surprise and luck did not stop Montrovant's mind from considering the implications.

"Who are you?" he asked aloud. There was no need for speech, but somehow the forming of the words, the sound itself, made him a bit more comfortable.

His answer was the same deep silence he'd addressed.

"What do you want? Why do you follow me?"

There was a movement to his right, silent and swift—beyond his ability to track. There were words hanging, suspended in the breeze caused by that movement, words whispered so silently that he could barely make out that they *were* words. He strained to grasp them, to decipher their cryptic message, but they slipped away, and the essence of whatever—whoever—it had been dissipated into predawn shadows.

"...the blood. Jerusalem...awaits. You..."

He lost the connection, and found that he'd been standing, listening and still, for too long. The words had somehow fogged his mind. It had begun to grow light, and the dawn was approaching too swiftly. He shook his head violently, trying to orient himself.

What had happened? He knew it had not been so late when he'd sensed the other's presence. How long had he stood there? How long might he have stood there, had he not come to his senses? What had been done to his mind, and what did it mean?

He found his mount, grazing contentedly a few hundred yards distant. Running to the horse's side, he slid easily into the saddle and wheeled quickly toward the abbey. No time to waste on conjecture. There would be plenty of time after darkness had returned, and after Bernard had informed him of what took place with de Payen. He would have ample opportunity to ponder this new development. Dangerous as this other might be, he would not be much of a threat during the daylight hours.

As he disappeared into the shadows, a form melted from the trees in his wake. Standing, staring after Montrovant's retreating form, a tall, slender man stood framed against the rising sun. He made no move to hurry from those rays. He watched until Montrovant had disappeared from sight, then turned slowly, making his way back in among the trees. With a sudden blink of shadow, he was gone. The forest awoke to solitude and silence.

FOUR

The dawn and de Payen arrived at once, just as Montrovant had predicted. Bernard, amazing the brethren, had rearranged their schedule in anticipation of the local lord's arrival. It was the first such deviation in their schedule in the memory of any among them, and the stir it caused was of equal rarity. Something was obviously afoot; something important.

While devotion went on as always in the chapel below, Bernard remained alone in his chambers, standing and staring out over his balcony toward the forests and fields. It was a rare opportunity to spend the early morning in the light of the sun rather than the close, emotionally charged confines of the chapel. He'd often stood there in the evening, waiting, wondering where the Spirit would guide him next, but for once it was pleasant to be there at the beginning of a day, perhaps at the birth of his greatest challenge.

It was a drastic contrast. Where the night had left him wondering about the future, he now found himself waiting for it breathlessly. He longed to be a leader—a voice of spirit and reason that could help to arrange the affairs and lives of others. He wanted to provide the answers they sought. It was a heady sensation, and he forced himself to his knees on the cold, hard surface, letting his head fall against the stone wall. Pride was not a luxury a servant of the One God could afford. It was also not conducive to clear thought.

He had known that de Payen would come. Montrovant had told him that it would be so, and in all the years of their odd partnership, he'd never known Montrovant to speak anything but the starkest truth. At times that truth did not follow the lines of theological conservatism, but it was always clear and straightforward. This time the dark one had spoken of the birth of an army, and that vision had filled Bernard's mind throughout the long hours of the night. It had not prepared Bernard for this moment. It was one thing to plan the formation of an army, and it was quite another to watch the general to whom you would entrust that army riding up to your front door.

His trust of Montrovant, the relationship they shared, was difficult to understand, even for Bernard. Montrovant himself did not give the impression of godliness. He was too quick to anger, too often given to curse, and yet there was a power leaking from him that soaked into any situation in which he was involved. Bernard had prayed to his God all his life, had lived each and every moment of that life in service to his faith. That faith was based on his personal relationship with the divine. Bernard had prayed for guidance where Montrovant was concerned, but there had been no answer more forthright and believable than the man's presence.

Though Montrovant did not glow with the light of holiness, he also did not stink of evil, and that made all the difference to Bernard. He believed he would know his enemy when he came across him, face to face, and he knew that Montrovant was no devil. Over the course of time Bernard's work for the Church, and for his Lord, had progressed. Montrovant had aided that progress time and again, often against what seemed impossible odds. Time—dependability—strength—these had made him an ally to be trusted.

It would be easy to take the low road, the road most would have taken, and name Montrovant an emissary of the devil. There were too many things about the dark one that Bernard could not explain in any rational manner. If it were true, though, Bernard would have to name himself both fool and worthless. It had been Montrovant, looking much the same as he'd looked only two nights previously, who had come to Bernard when he'd been but a sickly, frail lad of fifteen years and set him upon his present road. It had been Montrovant, tall, straight and proud, a knight in the very essence of the word, who'd seen the strength and commitment in Bernard's mind, and in his faith.

It had been Montrovant who'd shown him that faith was the stronger weapon, that the barbs and insults of his father and his brothers were only poor attempts to set themselves above him.

Now he knew his own strength, and he knew a wondrous relationship with his Lord, and all of that was owed to Montrovant. It was not a debt Bernard took lightly. He would, in fact, have liked to have been freer to pursue his own mind, but it seemed that this would be putting his own feelings before those of the Lord. He couldn't explain Montrovant's behavior, his insistence on walking only at night. His barely controlled passion that could be so quickly replaced by a controlled, icy calm.

Bernard had decided that the man's seeming disregard of things holy was a test of his own faith. Perhaps when one was closer to the divine, the relationship changed. In any case, Montrovant's coarse manner was a worldly shield that he was meant to see through, a divine attempt to assure Bernard's own sincerity. Each added curiosity, each mystery associated with Montrovant that itched at his desire to condemn was another layer of the test.

A lesser man, or a man more closely aligned with the standard teachings of Mother Church, would surely have mistaken Montrovant for a demon. It would have been a mistake. There was a greatness to the man that emanated from his actions and his words, his bold countenance and unchecked passion. Whoever he was, Bernard trusted that he had not been sent by Satan. He wasn't content with the notion that Montrovant was an emissary of God, either, but he had long since decided this was unimportant. What was important was faith, and the furthering of the message of salvation.

If Montrovant was not a holy man, he could be a holy tool. It was through Montrovant, "as through a glass, darkly," that Bernard had come to the knowledge and wisdom men attributed to him. If he were to turn from that now, what kind of man would that make him? And if he were wrong about Montrovant, if the man were purest evil and he'd been misled all along, then there would be little reason left for life. Choices are sometimes made at a very young age and maintained at great cost. Montrovant was as much a part of Bernard as his own family—more since he'd grown to adulthood.

Now destiny called. De Payen's solitary form, which had appeared on the horizon a few moments before, was drawing near. Bernard rose, feeling the pain in his knees and the chill where the stone had pressed against his bone through the thin protection of his skin. He straightened the simple brown robe he wore, stretching to return circulation. He didn't want to make an impression of weakness on de Payen as he approached. No more so than he usually did, in any case.

Bernard and Hugues de Payen were related by blood, but had had little contact in the years of Bernard's life. He knew de Payen as a man of solid moral fiber and indomitable courage. Bernard's father had spoken well of the lord, and nothing Bernard had heard since had contradicted this. On the battlefield, de Payen was near unstoppable, and the tales of his courage were so widespread that Bernard could not believe them all to be fabricated.

De Payen, on the other hand, would have conflicting stories of his sickly nephew. For the first fifteen years of life, Bernard had been little more than a nuisance, an excuse for ridicule and a point of shame to his father, whose other sons were tall and strong. It would be up to Bernard himself to set the seeds of truth in de Payen's mind, and to win his trust. That was a task he intended to accomplish. He needed this man's trust.

In his favor, the few memories he had of de Payen from his childhood were pleasant ones. The tall, powerful man had never spoken an ill word to him. He had never joined his voice in ridicule, at least not while Bernard had been present.

De Payen dismounted in the garden before the front gate of the abbey, and Bernard watched as brothers Miguel and Philippe made their way out, heads bowed low, to meet him. De Payen wore full armor, and it gleamed in the morning sunlight. It seemed that the man must have spent the entire night in preparation for this meeting. Glittering as he was in the light of the morning sun, de Payen's form took on an aura of purity and light that struck Bernard momentarily breathless. A moment of vision.

De Payen's mount was as tall and proud as its rider, black with stockings of white around three of its four hooves. It stamped and pranced, alert and ready for action. The two seemed joined as one, horse and knight, and it was a magnificent sight.

Once out of the saddle, de Payen dwarfed the magnificent beast. He was a giant of a man, and he stood, staring earnestly up toward the balcony where Bernard stood observing him, both questions and an open sense of wonder filling his gaze. Bernard remained hidden behind the lip of his balcony. De Payen's expression spoke equally of pride and humility, a perfect balance of the traits that made him the ideal choice to lead God's knights.

Bernard felt a pang of jealousy as his cousin disappeared beneath him, entering and ascending the inner stairs to where he waited. De Payen's long, raven hair, twisted into a single braid in back, his deep-set eyes and classic features, were quite a contrast to Bernard's own thin, bookish countenance. Bernard had spent his childhood in the shadows of active, warrior brothers, and friends who were able to push him around and ridicule him at will. He knew that those days were behind him, that the Lord had gifted him with words—with strength and power all his own to lessen the physical odds fate had stacked against him, but it was hard not to wonder what life might have been like had things worked out differently.

There was a light knock on his door, then Philippe pushed it inward and de Payen entered, ducking his head to clear the wooden framework. Without hesitation the big man dropped to one knee, lowering his wild, questing eyes to the stone floor. Bernard's heart sped. Such power and grace, and yet the man had the respect of one of Bernard's own brethren.

"Rise, cousin," he said quickly, moving forward to extend his hand and help the bigger man to his feet. The strain was great, but Bernard managed to stand fast, his grip firm and his stance steady, until de Payen stood before him once more. He gave a breath of thanks when the pressure was released not to have shown any sign of weakness so early in their encounter.

The two men spent a long moment studying one another, then Bernard spoke.

"You are a godly man, Hugues. I have heard this from those who serve you, from my father, and now it is revealed to me in my prayers. The Lord has a great purpose set aside for you. It is an honor to serve as his messenger."

"The honor is all mine, cousin," de Payen answered earnestly. "I have prayed long hours for a purpose, for some sign of what my life might mean. I have waited, serving as I might, but I had begun to fear that those prayers were to no avail, that I had no purpose to my Lord beyond that which had already been set before me."

De Payen hesitated for a moment, as if suspecting he might have said too much. Then he continued. "I would have served as I have," he added softly, "leading my small forces and solving the petty squabbles of those set to follow my own humble leadership. I would have married, eventually, and raised sons, teaching them of God's love. I would have done whatever the Lord called upon me to do, but I have prayed for this moment."

He stared at Bernard in sudden intensity, moving half a step forward. Bernard nearly took a step back, but managed to hold himself steady.

"I felt there was more to my destiny." De Payen's words came fast and furious now. Bernard elected to remain silent, letting the man vent feelings he'd obviously kept to himself for far too long.

"I have heard the bards speak of the glory of the Crusades, of the taking of the holy city of Jerusalem. I have heard the atrocities that plague the followers of our Lord, even now, and I have waited. I have prayed. There are those among my followers who think me mad, though they would not say as much to my face."

"Your prayers are answered, Hugues de Payen, and your vision was true. You will be the strong arm of the Lord, though it will take strength and courage beyond anything you have known."

"I would lay down my life in such a service," de Payen grated, lowering once more to one knee. "Tell me what I must do."

"First, cousin," Bernard said, almost playfully, "you must

get out of the habit of kneeling before me. I am not your lord, and I am certainly worthy of no man's worship. My wisdom comes largely from the same source as your destiny came to you. The dark angel has visited you, and I have spoken with him as well."

De Payen rose slowly. "'The dark angel.' Fitting. I have thought of nothing else since he left me. I feared he was sent by the Other—by demons. I feared that Satan merely mocked me, sending his servant to dangle this before me.

"But he came to me as I prayed, and I knew in that moment that my time had arrived. He sent me to you. If you can give my life the purpose I seek, I will revere your name and praise your glory until the last breath exits my body. This I swear."

Bernard grew silent for a moment, thinking. De Payen's spirit was strong, almost disconcerting. The man's piety was a weapon to be used, but it would take tact, and no small share of wisdom, to set the man on the right track. Bernard did not want de Payen to be a sheep, following his every movement or word. What he needed was a leader, a man who would take the fight to the roads and byways of the Holy Land itself—a war Bernard himself was not fit for. He wanted a man led by confidence in his own spirituality.

"We have both lost a cousin, recently," Bernard continued, changing tacks. "You may not be aware of it yet, but our cousin's son, Ferdinand, left his home less than three months ago to make a pilgrimage to Jerusalem. He took gifts for King Baldwin, and he took offerings for the temple. It was something he felt the desire to do before he took his rightful place as heir to the lands and titles of a de Montfort. He was the eldest son, but our Lord touched him in some way, and he felt that he must first show his deference to God before asserting his control over men. He was a wonderful boy.

"He never made it to Jerusalem. He made the journey on foot, wearing the robes of a peasant and taking only a small entourage of servants and like-minded young warriors. He died on the road."

"What happened to him?" de Payen demanded, rising suddenly. "I knew Ferdinand—I have hunted with his father."

"His party was set upon by Turkish bandits," Bernard continued, letting his eyes fall to the floor and losing himself for a moment in remorse. "He wanted nothing more than to show his love of God and the Church, and this is how his short life is ended. No honor. No glory. No protection from his homeland, or his Church."

"I will avenge him!" De Payen was pacing now, his hair tossing wildly about, the animal strength behind his serious visage shining forth brightly as his anger grew. "I will search them out, slay them as the dogs they are. I…"

"Stop." Bernard did not speak loudly, or with particular force, but something in the tone of his voice halted the older man's tirade. "You do yourself no justice, Hugues, nor do you any good for our dead cousin. Listen, first, then act. This is my message to you."

De Payen grew silent, but not still. He continued to pace the room, and the anger behind his eyes had not dimmed. Bernard was grateful, in that instant, that the anger was not directed at him. It was a flame that burned more brightly than any Bernard had ever sensed. The faith that drove de Payen was a palpable aura. It emanated in intimidating waves from his eyes and his gestures, from his stance and the set of his jaw.

"I feel as strongly as you about the death of our cousin," Bernard continued, forcing his voice to remain steady. "Indeed, I feel the greater pain. It was my teaching, my suggestion, that led him to place God before family and make his way to the Holy Land. Had I not intervened in the name of Jesus, he would walk and breathe and fight to this day. It is not to be so.

"The roads between Mother Church and Jerusalem must be open. There must be a pathway between God's people and God's land, or what is the purpose of controlling that land in the first place? There is a need for discipline, and for order.

"Many of our leaders have armies—armies of strong, dedicated knights such as yourself. These are God-fearing men, and yet they falter when the cost to themselves, or their families, outweighs their faith. This is not what we require, Hugues. The Lord, your God, requires total obedience and utter support. Are you willing to grant Him that? Are you willing to repay the sacrifice of His only child with your life, your strong arm, and your faith?"

There was no real reason to wait for an answer, but Bernard grew silent, waiting.

Instinctively, de Payen began to fall to his knee once more. Seeing the look in Bernard's eyes, he hesitated, then rose to his full height. "You know the answer to that, cousin," de Payen answered grimly. "I will serve with every ounce of strength, faith, and passion granted to me. It is what I have lived and breathed for—prayed for—all of my life. Tell me, what shall I do?"

"You must go to Jerusalem," Bernard replied. "It must be your own venture, not decided by me—not engineered by myself, or any other, but from you. You must go to the Holy City with an entourage of godly men that you trust unto death, and you must offer your service. Knights for God, warriors of the Holy Temple, your purpose should be to guard the roads between Rome and Jerusalem, to make the pathways free for all men who would seek the birthplace and vacated tomb of their savior. You can become the lifeline of the Church."

De Payen's eyes were glowing, and Bernard knew he'd won the day. Montrovant had chosen well. The faith of the man standing before him caused Bernard a moment of humble self-recrimination. De Payen's belief was intense—overpowering. He was focused and powerful, a weapon of flesh, blood and faith, guided by the spirit and the word of God.

"Cousin," de Payen began hesitantly. "I...I don't know who else to speak of this to, but the angel who came to me in the night, I know it must have been an angel, for he came during my prayers, and he sent me to you. How can such a thing be? How could I be worthy of such an honor, such a visitation? And how can I be certain from whence he came?"

"You will see him again," Bernard replied, nodding. "He is known in this time and place as 'Montrovant.' Trust him in all things. We...I...owe him much. He is a force for the Lord as surely as I am, and he will not lead you astray. Never let what your eyes or ears tell you interfere with this understanding.

"He is not as you or I. His ways will not always seem God's

ways. Do not be fooled by this. He is sent to lead us on the path
to righteousness, and to teach us to use our hearts, not our ears
or our superstitious fears. His message is that we must focus
our own faith. I believe he will bless you upon your journey to
Jerusalem."

"It would be a great honor," de Payen replied.

So dramatic, Bernard thought. *So full of energy and passion.*

"Gather your men, Hugues de Payen, and choose well.
You must leave as soon as possible, carrying nothing with you
but armor, weapons, and faith. Take only a small force, but a
righteous one. There will no doubt be times when you will
need to trust your life, and your mission, to each and every
one of them. When you arrive, you must convince the king in
Jerusalem to bless your actions. It is a beginning.

"Ours is not a passive God. He will not stand by and let the
Turkish animals overrun our world. You will form the wall that
will prevent this—you, your faith, your followers. It is a blessed
task, a holy mission, but I feel in my heart that you are the man
to accomplish this."

"I understand," de Payen replied. "I will not let God down,
or you, cousin. I thank you for your shared wisdom—for the
vision that will become my life. One thing…"

"Yes?" Bernard waited.

"I wish to take vows," de Payen asserted. "I wish the same
for each of the knights I shall choose to ride at my side. We will
take vows, even as you have done, and we will give up lands,
titles, and greed in this service. Without such commitment, I
feel it would be difficult to hold their loyalty, even with God and
an angel by my side."

Bernard almost argued against it. It seemed absurd—
knights curbed by the self-discipline and limits of holy vows.
The more he thought about it, though, the more sense it made.
He nodded slowly.

"It shall be so," he agreed. "You are a wise man, Hugues.
Montrovant has chosen well. Without hearth or home, there
will be no need of personal wealth. With lust set aside, there
will be no need of rape or pillage. An army of God should be a
model of righteousness."

De Payen nodded. Nothing remaining to be said. He departed the chamber and descended through the stone passageways and stairs to the front of the abbey. Bernard did not follow him, nor did he make any move to summon any of the brethren to do so. De Payen would find his own way out, and Bernard had much to think on—much to plan. It was a monumental day—a day to be recorded in the annals of history. It would require prayer and a clear mind—particularly since Montrovant would be joining him that evening.

He watched de Payen's retreating form until the line of trees surrounding the main garden cut him off from sight, then he sank to his knees and returned to his prayer. The hunger throbbed in his stomach, and he moved with the pain, letting the visions carry him away.

"It is good," Montrovant said at last, having listened attentively to Bernard's account of his meeting with de Payen. "It is as I expected. He is a man of passion and iron will. He will be the perfect foundation for our plan, and he is a leader that others will respect."

"Your plan, you mean," Bernard replied softly. "I have had little to do with this, other than the passing of words from one to the other. I feel almost dishonest in this, since it will be perceived that I am behind it all."

"You know better than that, my friend," Montrovant replied, smiling slowly. "You are great among the men of God, Bernard," he continued. "There will come a time when the very forces in Rome will be at your command. Faith brings strength, and few can match you in that regard. It is your destiny.

"Mine lies in another direction. I will follow de Payen, and I will watch over his journey to the Holy Land. We will both return."

"I will look forward to that day," Bernard breathed.

Montrovant held the man's eyes with the strength of his own gaze—held him until the silence grew heavy with tension, then released him.

"As will I," he said softly. "I will go now. It is a long journey, and I doubt your cousin will waste any time in preparation. I will ride out tomorrow night to join with him, though I will not make my presence known at once. He will need time to establish his authority, and I would not undermine that. You will hear from me. I will write, and I will send messengers. No part of what is to come will be kept from you."

Bernard glowed with pride. He knew such a sensation was sinful, but there was time enough to scourge the sin from his flesh when Montrovant had gone. At the same time, the jealousy he'd felt only moments before shamed him. He might have his doubts about Montrovant, but once again it appeared that the doubts were unfounded. He could see no wrong, no darkness, in what they were setting out to do. He hoped that it was not a lack of vision on his own part.

"Godspeed," he said softly.

"I thank you," Montrovant grinned. There was so much emotion behind that expression, so much left unsaid, that in that moment Bernard believed the man capable of anything, and it left him breathless. Turning, Montrovant disappeared into the shadows beyond Bernard's door so quickly that one moment he stood framed against the deepening shadows and flickering candle light, and the next there was nothing.

Bernard returned to his window, staring into the vast darkness and concentrating on the far-distant glitter of the stars. "God's will be done," he whispered, dropping once more to his knees. "God's will be done..."

FIVE

The group that wound its way through the gates of Jerusalem was not an impressive sight. They walked their horses closely together, watching the streets and people as they passed with wild, wary eyes. Dust matted the long, tangled locks of their hair, and their garments were simple—devoid of color and belted at the waist. At their head rode a giant of a man. His eyes swept the scenery with what could have passed for awe in any lesser of a man. He rode with his head held high, and the strength in his enormous frame was evident in his every movement.

The only thing that set them apart from the poor pilgrims who made their way to the city nearly every day were their mounts and their weapons. Long, polished swords, axes and daggers hung from saddles and belts. Shields rested at their sides, within reach, and a close inspection revealed that many of the packages tied onto the pack animals they led behind them held armor. Despite their inauspicious appearance, none questioned them or disturbed their steady progress.

Without hesitation, the lead rider turned his mount down the central street and headed straight for Baldwin's palace, sending women, children, and merchants alike scurrying in all directions to make way. Questions filtered along in their wake as the bustle of the city closed in behind them. Hushed comments were whispered in shop doorways and dark alleys. There was nothing to lend any particular significance to the small band's arrival, and yet their slow parade toward the palace spoke volumes. Though they looked like beggars, they rode like knights, and any arrival of knights in the city was worthy of note and thanks. Particularly if those knights were ready to offer their service to the king.

They approached the smaller gates of the wall surrounding the palace. It was not the gate that a visiting lord would use, but that through which patrols and guards entered and exited the grounds.

The leader dismounted, leading his horse forward. Stopping just short of the gates, he hailed the guards.

After a short conversation, one that brought much speculation to the tongues and ears of the citizens of Jerusalem, the small group was admitted a few moments later, the gates closing solidly behind them.

A few of those who'd watched approached the gates, calling out questions and trying to get a glimpse into the palace court itself, but all they got from the guards were more questions and shrugs of indifference, and there was no sign of the small party beyond the wall.

Baldwin admitted the nine almost immediately. He hadn't had word from France in months, and it might be that these men brought important information. The circumstances of their arrival were odd, and the description his guards had brought him drew questions to his mind, but not enough to wait another moment if there were news to be had. Baldwin had enough worries on his mind for ten kingdoms, and the best hope for relief of those worries was support from the Church, and from the various kingdoms of Europe. He hoped that this would be some sign that this support was to be granted.

The city was surrounded by the Turks, the Egyptians; and on the sides that were held by his own men, dissent and treachery brought their own prices. What had begun as a holy war to free the most sacred of cities had degraded quickly into feudal wars and political back-biting. Somehow the throne had seemed a much more desirable honor to attain before he'd fully understood its ramifications.

The king was slightly taken aback when de Payen strode forcefully into the room and knelt quickly at his feet, his long, bedraggled hair and beard nearly brushing the floor. The man looked as if he'd been without food or drink for days, and his eyes were as wild as the dark mane of hair that swept back over his shoulders.

"Rise, sir," Baldwin admonished him, "and tell me why you've come."

"I am a poor knight, Lord," de Payen began. As he spoke, the others who'd joined him on his quest filed in behind him, kneeling as he still knelt, their heads bowed. "As are we all. We have taken vows of poverty, faith, and chastity, and we have come to offer our services to the Lord."

This was far from what Baldwin might have expected out of a visiting knight, and he chose silence as his response. It would be best, he decided, to let this strange, grave man before him speak his piece.

"The road we have traveled to reach you has not been an easy one, Lord. We have fought long and hard along the way, and we have brought a small group of pilgrims to the city of our Savior. The Turks who would have taken them to slavery have been sent to their own dark god, and those we fought to protect have made it safely within the walls of the city. It is not enough."

De Payen rose, finally, and met Baldwin's eyes evenly. "We are here to dedicate our days to the safety of that road. We have formed a compact, a bond that can be broken by no blade in this realm, nor set aside by any who have taken the oaths. We will make the road to Jerusalem a safe one for our brethren."

Baldwin, thinking fast, rose to stand before de Payen, the steps leading to his throne giving him a foot or so of height advantage, despite the other's huge stature. This was a moment of destiny, somehow he knew it, and he drew forth every bit of royal pomp and arrogance he could muster to be certain that he remained in control of that moment. It was not an easy task, facing one such as de Payen.

"I will accept your service," he said, gesturing to the floor, "in the name of our Lord."

De Payen knelt instantly, bowing his head. In an uncharacteristically impulsive gesture, Baldwin drew the sword dangling at his side and brought it to rest on the knight's dusty shoulder.

"I accept your service, Hugues de Payen, and that of those who serve under you."

De Payen rose immediately, clasping the king's hand between his own and meeting the monarch's eyes once more.

"Thank you," he said simply. "You will not be disappointed."

That was the beginning.

Baldwin II was not a heavy drinker, but the night following Hugues de Payen's unexpected offer, he made an exception. A large urn of wine had been brought to his quarters and left there by his servants, and Baldwin lounged across a long couch, his goblet held easily in one hand, considering the implications of what had just taken place. He felt the need to get it straight in his own mind before consulting his advisors, or sending word back to Rome.

Knights were a valuable commodity at any price, but this was a singularly grand concept. Nine knights for the simple price of food, clothing, stabling and mounts—no lands or title desired—this was a gift of unprecedented good fortune. For all that, it was an odd gift, as well. Few things had come easily to Baldwin, and he was not in the habit of accepting things at face value. If there was a catch to this offer, something that de Payen sought to gain that was being kept hidden, Baldwin needed to discover that goal and find a way to make it work for his own greater good.

De Payen's men were a somber lot, and they had declined all his offers of hospitality save the night's rest and sustenance. They were eager, it seemed, to set themselves apart, and it would be necessary for Baldwin to find a means of accomplishing this. He thought for a moment of calling in the Patriarch, letting the influence of the Church aid him in his decision, but he decided against it. Any such act would be an admission that he wasn't fully capable of handling things on his own, and he had no faith in the godliness of Rome's messengers this far from the Pope. Likewise he believed it would be a mistake to consult his military advisors.

Daimbert, the patriarch, had already tried to ally himself with Jerusalem's enemies in the past, working toward a coup that would have put another in the palace. Baldwin had suffered him to remain in his position as spiritual leader of the city, and he did not publicly denounce or humiliate the man, but he did not believe that Daimbert had God's will in mind in all his affairs.

This new group, should it grow and prosper, would surely come to challenge the authority of those in Baldwin's armies. It was in their eyes. There was no compromise, no weakness in de Payen that Baldwin could sense. He was an imposing man, held in check, it appeared, by his own faith. If this was the case, then Baldwin needed a way to keep that challenge under control. Perhaps he could even use these newcomers as an example to his own men. Men who were governed by their desires and greed he was familiar with. These could be paid, bribed, or otherwise coerced. Men who truly lived by faith would be dangerous in many ways...particularly if that faith were ever crossed by Baldwin's own desires.

The hour grew later, the skies darker, and only the stars answered Baldwin's questions. The level of wine in the urn dropped slowly but steadily, and his thoughts began to drift. It was just as his eyelids were growing so heavy that he could barely force them far enough open to allow him to locate his drink that the first breath of—something—washed through his mind, and he lay back, forgetting the wine. The goblet clattered to the floor, forgotten.

A moment of clear, lucid thought wound its way slowly through the wine-fog and weariness. Images formed, and he found that he could fit them together as he wished—so obvious. The mosque. The al Aqsa Mosque. It was built on the very foundations of the temple of Solomon, ancient, consecrated ground, and yet he'd not made full use of the magnificent structure.

In truth, he'd hesitated to use the edifice for anything truly important. It was a leftover of the Moslems, a reminder that Jerusalem had not always been controlled by the Church. Now he had the opportunity to make a statement, to house God's own army within walls raised by their enemies. He would have to consult Daimbert, at least publicly make the gesture, but it was his decision to be made. A vision of hundreds of white-clad knights riding forth from the mosque washed through him, and he nearly cried out at the wonder of it. Then reality and the memory of nine bedraggled warriors with grim faces returned, and he began to sift through the visions for a plan.

There would be problems with the Patriarch, but Baldwin almost looked forward to that confrontation. He'd seen the slender, pale brethren who walked the halls of that temple, and he knew that there were guards on some of the chambers and temples within as well, guards he himself had not set. Guards supposedly ordained by the Holy Father in Rome. It had always bothered him that there were things going on in his city that he had only fleeting knowledge of, and no control over. Moving the knights into the mosque would give him a reason to assert that control, and it might provide some long-sought answers, as well. This would give him an excuse to pry into the Church's holdings in the city.

Baldwin was willing to risk the ire of the Church in the assumption that the Patriarch did not truly act with the full patronage of Rome. Baldwin's cousin, Baldwin I, had provided sufficient evidence of this in his dealings with Daimbert, former Bishop of Pisa. What was best for the kingdom was best for Baldwin, and that was the way he would have to look at it. What was best for the Church would have to follow in its turn.

He began to drift off again, and the images slipped slowly from his mind, but he carried it to his dreams. The mosque of al Aqsa would be perfect, and it would be the beginning of greatness for those nine poor knights. Knights of the temple of Solomon—Baldwin smiled as darkness engulfed him. Poor knights of the Temple of Solomon. It had a powerful ring to it.

Beyond the king's window, Montrovant chanced a glance around the framework to where the monarch lounged, now unconscious, on a couch beside the window. Baldwin looked anything but impressive at that moment, and Montrovant watched him in contempt.

So easy. So weak. He felt the urge to slip across the windowsill and sample the royal blood, but it passed as he launched himself backward into the night. Such actions would not aid him in his plan, satisfying as they might be. He needed to be gone before he was spotted, and he had needs of his own to be taken care of, needs that had little to do with either grail or king, but that had snapped back into focus as he'd sensed the warm pulse of Baldwin's blood.

Montrovant had walked these streets before, many times, and each time he was surprised by the enormity of the memories that seeped out to consume him, the tales and voices from his past that slipped through crevices of stone and whispered through the leaves on the olive trees. He knew there were others here who would remember, as well, but he did not think it wise to call their attention to himself.

He would have paid his respects to clan brethren, but he took Claudius's warning at face value, and those of the other houses would have little love for him. He was on his own, more so than at any point in his past, and the weight of humanity bore down upon him from all sides. He would have to find his own way, make his own luck, and trust himself totally. Even Bernard, whom he could trust to a point, was far removed from him in this place, and de Payen was still an untested element, despite the enormity and focus of his faith. Montrovant was not yet certain who would win in a test between himself and that faith.

There were others about, though, clergy and nobles alike, who could prove useful. He might need to introduce himself into their society, and before that could happen he would need to find a place that could provide safety until his plans bore fruit. He didn't have Bernard's abbey here. It had been a long time since he'd needed to seek his safety on a day-to-day basis, but the old instincts were kicking in and driving him to seek a hideaway that could provide shelter from both humans and sunlight alike.

The shadowed alleyways called to him, and he slipped from the main roads confidently. There were places here that could hide secrets for thousands of years. Among them, somewhere, it would be easy enough to add one more ancient relic. He smiled at the small humor in this. He might not be as ancient as the grail, or Euginio, but he probably qualified as a relic.

Many things had changed since the Christian occupation of the city. Where there had been groves and wells, open markets, there now rose homes and businesses. The Moslems had left their mark, their hand obvious in many of the newer structures. Jerusalem had always been a city of straight lines and simple structures, with the exception of the temples. Now minarets appeared among the smaller, stouter Hebrew buildings. There was a richer flavor to the city, more metropolitan.

Much of the power of the city had dissipated with these changes. The very simplicity that had once marked it had taken with it some of the purity. It was still the holiest of cities for the followers of Christ, but it wore new clothing. There were more merchants, more reasons to stay in the city rather than visiting it when you needed to trade at the market. Things he would have had to have sent for, or traveled for, were readily available on the street. Places he'd frequented in older times were closed, rebuilt, or simply gone. The only thing that was truly the same was the atmosphere of untouchable antiquity. He knew the streets beneath him had supported the feet of prophets and kings, Roman soldiers and Moslem hordes. Their spirits cried out from the stone, some for vengeance, others for release. History could be repeated, but it could never be erased.

He made his way through a small square, furtively keeping to the shadows. There was nothing untoward about his appearance, other than his height, but he was a man of striking features that were often too easily remembered, and he knew that the aura of power clinging to him would draw attention. He wasn't yet ready to announce his presence. There would be plenty of time for that once de Payen was firmly entrenched. He wanted no attention, and no distractions.

He found that, as his mind had wandered, he'd brought himself to the back of the mosque he meant to conquer. The spires and rough stone walls were a contrast against the surrounding buildings. It was a huge monument to the strength of the Moslem faith, even in defeat. He made his way to the base of the edifice, running his hands over the stone and taking in all the angles, doors and balconies, turrets and avenues of escape and defense.

He would need to know them all, before this was done. He knew he was not the only one present with power, or a purpose. There were others, within these very walls, who would not give their position up easily. He had named them guardians when speaking with Claudius, and to all intents and purposes that was what they were, but something about them itched at his mind. He wondered if they were truly present out of any deep desire to protect holy relics, or if there was even more to be learned than he'd imagined. The Church was not the only power on the earth interested in ancient secrets.

So many questions, so little time. He made his way along the wall, watching carefully for anyone who might be about at such an hour. A doorway loomed ahead, huge and ponderous, carved of wood and reinforced by iron and brass. It was closed, barred from the inside, he sensed, but he stood before it for a long moment. He considered forcing his way in and doing a bit of exploring on his own. Surely there were others who had broken into the holy places. One more would hardly be noticed if he took nothing and made his way out without being noticed.

He had his hand on the wooden frame when the presence of that other, the presence he'd felt in the forest near Bernard's abbey, fell across his back like a cold shadow. He spun, cat-like, and scanned the darkness, but there was no one to be seen.

"Who is there?" he called out.

Shadows shifted, moving away, and he followed. He caught a glimpse of deeper black against the shadows in one of the city's narrow alleyways and he slipped after it, heedless of the voices in his mind screaming for him to run, to leave it alone. He ignored the unfamiliar fear that ate at his thoughts and concentrated on following without being left behind. Surprisingly, it took all his concentration to accomplish this. The intruder was incredibly quick.

After only a few short moments, it became obvious that he was being led. If this other had not wanted him to follow, he would have been gone as simply and completely as he had appeared. It grated on Montrovant's nerves to be toyed with, no matter how powerful or dangerous the enemy. Though sanity dictated that he turn back, or escape, his pride would allow nothing but confrontation, if that was possible. If it all ended here, he would end it upright and in control of his senses.

They were passing near the Temple of the Holy Sepulcher, and Montrovant sensed that there were others still moving about the streets, despite the lateness of the hour. Most of them were merely old men, or penitents, praying or meditating. The soft glow of candlelight filtered out of cracks in the stone walls and uncovered windows. Montrovant ignored them. He sensed a small patrol of Baldwin's soldiers approaching to his left, and without a thought he leapt to the low roof of the building to his right and continued, crouching low against the stone.

Ahead, the other maintained a steady pace, moving toward the outskirts of the city and making his way toward the hill called Golgotha. Another place far too familiar to Montrovant. More memories. The dawn was still many hours away, but he still had the task ahead of finding a safe haven for the daylight hours. When the other passed into the desert, Montrovant hesitated.

"Who are you?" he whispered to the darkness. With a growl, he continued, leaving the lights and the pulsing heartbeat of the city behind.

There was no answer, but the other had stopped moving, and he sensed a presence, more solid than before, waiting ahead in the darkness. As he approached, he slowed his pace, scanning the shadows.

He need not have concentrated so hard. As he neared Golgotha, he saw a solitary figure standing atop the hill. The Patriarch had ordered that three crosses be raised upon the hilltop—monuments to the crucifixion that would remind all who saw them of what had come before. They were kept upright at all times, maintained by members of Daimbert's personal guard. On the hill, the figure stood like a sliver of jet black stone at the foot of the central cross.

Montrovant approached warily, watching for signs of a trap as he closed the distance between them. He knew there was no possibility of sneaking up on one such as this, but somehow the moment seemed to call for respect—concentration. He climbed the hill and came to a halt a short distance from the cross.

The man who stood there, staring upward at the cross, had long, flowing white hair and a hawk-like beak of a nose. His eyes were closed and his hands were clasped before him, as if in prayer. He took no notice of Montrovant's approach, and yet there was an energy in the air, an aura of expectancy. Montrovant chose not to speak, waiting for the ancient one to break the silence.

"It has been a long time since I last stood here," the man said at last. "It is not a memory I cherish, that last visit. It was a moment of destiny—for me a moment of change. You know of change, don't you, Solomon?"

Again Montrovant started at the use of his given name. It was the second time in a short period he'd heard that name uttered by another more powerful than he, and it set his nerves on edge. It was more control over him, more power than he wished any to have, let alone one so ancient. Euginio had known him since the moment of his embrace, but this one? Again, he chose not to speak. Better to know what he faced.

The man turned toward him, and Montrovant was shocked by the sorrow, the depth of pain and suffering, that shone from the depths of those deep, hollow eyes. He saw that his companion wore only the simple robes of a penitent, and he noted the pale luminescence of his skin, pearlescent as the light of the moon rippled across the surface of his arms and through the deeply etched lines of his face.

"You believe a cup can make you more powerful," the man said, the faint hint of a smile twitching at the corners of his lips. "You believe, as does Mother Church, that there is a strength in ancient things, that the power of a man, or a god, can be transferred to something so simple as a cross, or a grail...this is an odd thing to devote one's existence to the search of, Solomon, odd indeed."

"You know of the Grail?" The words escaped before Montrovant could halt them, and he nearly cursed himself aloud for his lack of control.

The other's smile widened. "I know things of the grail you couldn't even dream, Solomon. I know things that were only legend when your friend Euginio—Thomas—walked lands peopled by those long fallen to ash. I know of relics, have held them new in my hand, and again when they were legend. I know enough to know that you know nothing, and yet you seek the Grail."

Montrovant held himself in check. Half of him wanted to launch at this arrogant, grinning apparition, to tear that smile from ancient flesh and scream triumph to the night sky. The other half, the rational half, wanted to turn and to run, to take to the air and to seek the shadows, to put as much distance between himself and that damnable hill as the strength of his mind and form could carry him. He did neither. Instead, he answered.

"For one with so many answers, you have the aspect of a spirit doomed to sorrow. Why should I listen to one such as you? You admit defeat more readily than you explain your actions."

Another grin, this one less arrogant. "You are a credit to your sire," the ancient whispered. Montrovant saw that the other's figure was growing less substantial, his words wavering in the night breeze. "You must find a place to rest, and I must think. There are things you must know, if you are to complete your quest, Solomon. I can help you, if you can come to trust me. We will speak again."

"Wait," Montrovant cried. "Who are you?"

The other only smiled. His form wavered a final time, then broke apart in the breeze like so much mist and dispersed, leaving Montrovant alone beneath the moon, the crosses his only companions. He stared for a long time at the empty space before him, trying to find reason in the madness he'd just encountered.

His mind reeled. Turning, he made his way down the hill and fairly flew across the sand toward the city. Off to his right, he felt a sudden flicker of the other's presence, then it was gone. He diverted his path, following the sensation—once more—against his better judgment. There was no reason for that presence to present itself to him again if it were not meant to lead him to something.

He found himself in an ancient graveyard. There were stones and monuments, small caves carved into the face of the mountain beneath him. He moved among the resting places of the dead, and he came to a place where a slab of stone had been dragged aside, revealing what had once been the burial site of an important noble. The outside of the tomb was weathered, but the carvings and inscriptions spoke of wealth.

Montrovant entered the tomb and was surprised to find that there was nothing there. It was an empty pit, complete with a stone slab for a bed and the door that had been left open. It would be nothing for him to return that stone to its place and seal himself from the light of the sun. He wondered if the grave had been robbed, and what might have possessed the thieves to remove the body.

"You will be safe here."

The words floated to him on the breeze, and he started, again, growling his frustration as he sensed the other, then lost him in the vastness of the night.

It didn't matter if he trusted his tormentor. The dawn was approaching, and a more perfect resting place would be difficult to find, especially given the short hours remaining before dawn. Montrovant made his way to the door of the crypt and dragged the stone back toward the entrance. He found that handholds had been carved into the stone, handholds that would allow a man—a single man of great strength—to move that stone into position from the inside, sealing the entrance.

More to think about. He was not the first to use this resting place, that was obvious. The questions rose, one after another. Who was this ancient one, and why would he go out of his way to help Montrovant? How did he know the name Solomon, and what did that portend? How many others had slept where he was about to lay his head, and would they appear? If so, would they mean him help or harm?

The sun was rising outside, and Montrovant realized the questions would have to wait the night for their answers. Without further thought he reclined on the stone slab and let his eyes drift closed. If he were to be betrayed, it would be swift and final. If not, the darkness would bring him answers. It always had.

SIX

It had been some time since the al Aqsa Mosque had seen so much activity. Somehow, despite its size and central location, it had been overlooked by the growing Christian community. Overlooked, or possibly ignored for its Moslem lines and dark memories.

The palace and the main temple, where Daimbert celebrated the Mass, were the centers of activity and devotion. Pilgrims came and went through the doors of both with the regularity of the seasons. The mosque, on the other hand, was a grim reminder of days best forgotten. Though Baldwin and the Church held Jerusalem, the Moslem threat was never far removed from the minds of her citizens. Kingdoms had changed hands so often over the past decade that nothing could be said to be permanent. Despite the strength of their vision and their faith, fear was a way of life in the Holy Land.

This worked out perfectly for de Payen and his men. They did not have to fight with any other contenders for the space— no others wanted it. All that remained, after receiving Baldwin's blessing, was to clear away the detritus of those who'd come before them. This done, they set about creating what was to become their headquarters in the Holy Land. The mosque had not been a popular place, but it was large and well-built.

De Payen was strict in his orders. None of them were to have large quarters, nor were the rooms chosen to have anything within them but a bunk, a desk, a single chair, and a window. His thoughts on material possessions were the core of their creed. Allow no room for personal gain, and it would not be sought.

Given the austere construction of the place, this didn't turn out to be a problem. A large grouping of what must have originally served as servants' quarters lined two of the main halls. Plenty of space for the nine of them, and for those who were joining their service as well. Expansion would be difficult in the years to come, but for the present those rooms would more than suffice.

There was a small chapel built into the lower level of the mosque. Someone had come before them and laid it out, and though there were no magnificent altars or rich tapestries adorning the walls, it provided a link with God that de Payen found crucial.

Prayers were required morning and night of each of the knights, and a strict regimen of scriptural study was developed. De Payen proved swift with discipline and punishment, demanding as much from his men as he did of himself. They would form the core of his army, and they had to be trusted. He wanted nothing standing between them and their faith.

Distractions abounded, even in the Holy City, and these had to be weeded out of their lifestyles and wiped from their minds. They were a small group against impossible odds, and they would die facing those odds if they were not completely focused on the task at hand.

De Payen handled the entire setup with masterful insight. They had an armory and a small yard within the walls of the mosque itself where they could practice with weapons and horses, a mess hall where they ate the simple fare de Payen allowed them, and they set aside one very secure room in which they established their treasury. Baldwin was not without his generous side, and de Payen guarded each acquisition with a sharp eye toward building their worth. An army could count only so much on the assistance of kings...there had to be a source, within that army itself, of revenue and supply. This was the means to the end he sought—a holy army, self-sufficient and devoted to none but the Lord.

And they were a devoted group. Each had followed de Payen of his own accord. The one thread that bound them all, one to the other, was their faith. Each believed that there was more to their existence than women, fighting, and dying. They sought something to fill a void. For one it was a lost love, for another the dead-end hopes of a duke's fourth son. Each had found something in de Payen, in his words or his actions, that struck a chord deep within them.

They were also very private men. They shared their lives and their faith, but they kept their silence. Though each had, in his own way, been born to leadership, they bowed to de Payen for orders and instruction. He had that effect on men.

It was in the small chapel that de Payen first met Father Santos and learned that he and his knights were not alone in the mosque. He'd come in for morning prayer, kneeling on the cold stone before the altar and offering the sign of the cross as he did every morning, noon, and night without fail. His mind was full of the day's activities, and of plans for things to come, but he fought those images back. It was a time for worship, for prayers of forgiveness, for prayers of strength. He never prayed for himself, or for mundane matters he could handle on his own. God did not need to carry Hugues's burdens. That task he kept for himself.

He prayed for those he'd left behind. They'd never understood him. He knew he'd been strict—probably stricter than most situations dictated, but the fire inside him had raged since he was a very young man—the fire to make a difference in the world. Others never shared his enthusiasm, and his patience had worn thin more than once. He'd left his holdings to his nephew, Antoine. He prayed that the boy would take what he'd been granted and do something with his life.

Throughout his prayers, he never lost sight of why he was in the Holy City, never wavered in the faith he placed in his new-found mission. It drove him, day and night, and he cherished the weight of that burden. He'd lived too many years in the shadow of uncertainty to falter now that he'd been chosen.

He'd just lowered his head, closing his eyes and beginning to recite psalms, using the familiarity of the words to cleanse and release the contents of his mind. He felt a gentle light building within, felt the pain of kneeling on the cold stone transforming to a glow that worked its way slowly up through his body toward his mind. This was the time he felt closest to the divine. When Hugues prayed, the world dissolved, and he could feel the strength and light of his Lord flowing down and surrounding him. He drew his strength from it.

This time, however, he was only just beginning his ritual of prayer and devotion when he felt a disturbance of air. He was so concentrated that the accompanying whisper of sandals on stone echoed like the clatter of weapons. Starting from his trance, de Payen rose, his hand going immediately to the hilt of his sword. Even in the temple of the Lord, there were few to be trusted.

The man he faced wore the robes of a priest. He was not as tall as Hugues, and more slender, but his presence was powerful just the same. He had hawk-like features and intense, burning eyes that speared straight through to de Payen's soul. Though the intruder was obviously a priest, he did not have the aspect of any man of the cloth that de Payen had previously encountered. Instead he appeared arrogant, cold and calculating. Hugues did not release his grip on his sword.

"Who are you?" he asked bluntly.

The priest stared at him for a moment, as if gauging the danger he might represent, then dismissing it as minimal. Moving forward a step, his movements predatory and swift, the priest drew nearer.

"I have come, as you, to worship in the house of God. Surely you would not deny me this, my son?"

"I would deny no man his communion with God, Father," de Payen replied slowly, the word 'Father' rolling reluctantly off his tongue, almost an afterthought to his comment, "but this temple has been remanded to my care, by Baldwin himself. None but myself, my men, and the Patriarch himself are to be allowed access without permission."

"I have been in this temple since the day the city came back to Christ," the priest asserted. "I am Father Santos, and my assignment here comes from the Holy Father in Rome. I am sorry that King Baldwin did not mention my presence. I assume he did not mention any of the others, then?"

"Others?" A cold pit had opened in Hugues's stomach,

replacing the glow of moments before.

"I have several brethren under my supervision," Father Santos continued. "I have been assigned here on a, shall we say, special duty, for as long as the Church has controlled the city. I belong to a very old order—Hugues, is it?"

"It is," Hugues replied, drawing himself to the full, imposing height his bulk made so natural. "Hugues de Payen, Knight of Christ," he said proudly. "It is my sworn duty to protect the roads to and from the holy city. This mosque is to become the first temple of my order."

"A remarkably difficult and worthy cause," Father Santos acknowledged. His smile was oily, his words calculating. There wasn't the slightest touch of sincerity to any of it, and yet Hugues could not bring himself to be too disrespectful.

De Payen felt himself growing wary. It was the same sensation that accompanied a fencing duel with a new, untried opponent. He decided that he did not like this man, priest or not. He also did not like games of any sort that required deception.

"Each of us does what we can in our own way," Hugues answered at last. "When you say you have been in this temple, you mean the mosque, I take it? How is it that with you, your men, and my men all within the same walls, we have seen no sign of you? We have worked these last weeks dawn until dusk to make this place liveable."

"We keep to ourselves," Father Santos smiled. "Our quarters are below, in the cellars. My teaching takes up much of my time, and our order is one given to long periods of meditation and prayer."

"The stables are beneath the temple," de Payen observed. "I trust you will have no problem with our use of them?"

"Of course not," Father Santos answered. "I would do nothing to deter you in your mission." He hesitated, then continued, the fire in his eyes burning a bit more brightly. "If I weren't certain that it were otherwise, my son, I'd believe you thought us to represent different sides of some confrontation."

"I don't know you, Father," Hugues answered brusquely, "and though I respect your office, I withhold personal respect for those who earn it. I have a mission here, and you are an unexpected addition to the conditions of that mission. So long as we do not distract one another from our chosen methods of service to the Lord, then we will have no problem."

"I assure you," the priest replied, the lines of his face grown stern, "that I have no intention of interacting with you or your men in any manner at all. I have my own concerns, as I've explained. Now, if you'll excuse me, I have devotions to attend to."

Without waiting for an answer, Father Santos turned and walked a few feet closer to the altar, kneeling and lowering his head. The act had an air of finality to it that told de Payen their conversation, for the moment, was through. He turned and left the chapel, his prayers cut short for the first time in so many years he couldn't remember the last time he had failed to complete his ritual. That was an omen he could have lived without, and the fact that the moment was tied to Father Santos cemented his belief that there was something more to the man than the devotions of a simple priest of God. Something less, as well, in de Payen's estimation.

He made his way quickly to the chamber he'd set aside for his formal quarters. It was not where he slept, or took his meals—his private quarters were, if anything, more severe than those of the others. It was a large, circular room with a long table in the center, lined with enough chairs for his men to join him. It included a cabinet with wine and glasses, a desk with paper and pen ready, and the only two comfortable seats in the temple sat side by side along one wall for the purpose of entertaining important visitors.

He could have made a bolder statement, but he felt that the less wealth and distraction they surrounded themselves with, the less temptation there would be to make a mockery of their vows—vows Hugues felt very strongly about. The others shared his vision, and his faith, but he doubted the depth of their devotion. Each of them had come from wealth, and though they were handling the transition well thus far, it was difficult to believe that they would easily give up their heritage.

In his own case, that heritage had never seemed more than a prison. It was the ritual, the prayer and devotion, that spoke to Hugues most strongly. He felt closer to these men than he'd felt to any since his father. They didn't fully understand him, but they respected him, and that meant more to Hugues than any more intimate form of sharing ever could. He'd respected his father, who had made him the warrior that he was, and he'd learned of the scripture from his mother. It had set him apart as odd from childhood, this pairing of spirit and strength.

Hugues felt that he had been chosen for a reason, and the future of both his order and his men rested on the decisions he would make in the months and years to come. Among them, he was first to prayer and last to rest. He would punish himself as readily as any other for a transgression, and he prided himself on treating each of the others with equal consideration. Now he would have to make decisions about their security.

He had been set apart within his own mind for so long that it was odd suddenly to see it through another's eyes. Father Santos was so set apart that few seemed to know he existed at all. His existence within the walls of the temple threatened the privacy and purity of Hugues's plans, the training of his men. He and his followers would be a distraction, causing rumors and speculation that would drag his men's minds from training.

He poured a flagon of wine, another departure for such an early hour, and sat by the window to collect his thoughts. He would have to see Baldwin at the earliest possible opportunity, and he would have to try to get this priest and his followers removed from the mosque. The affairs of his order, their vows, disciplines and deployment, had to be kept confidential and private. It would have to be so if he were to make them an important force in the Holy Land and the Church. Men respected most what they could not understand. Mystery was one of the great keys to power, and Hugues meant to keep his own secrets, whatever the cost.

No one could be allowed as intimate a knowledge of their comings and goings as Father Santos would have. Strategically it could spell disaster of the worst kind. Besides that, the man left a bad taste in Hugues's mouth. It was one thing to wear the vestments of a holy man, but it was another to keep the light of the Lord in your heart. De Payen had known enough priests in his lifetime to trust none of them further than any other man without reason. Santos, thus far, had given him ample reason for doubt.

He downed the wine and rose, dismissing the priest from his thoughts. He would see Montrovant that evening, and he would present the problem. Normally he would have consulted the Lord in fervent prayer, but Montrovant was swifter and more certain. Not for the first time, Hugues felt thankful for the availability of such an agent of the Lord. He felt the pangs of guilt, as well. It had seldom proven wise to take the easier path, but Montrovant inspired him to that choice over and over.

Though it still made him nervous to talk to the man, the power and wisdom of the words they exchanged never failed to move him. Hugues believed that Bernard had been correct in his assessment of their benefactor. For the moment, he needed to oversee the moving of mounts into the stables beneath the temple. There had been no animals housed there for quite some time, and a full day's hard work awaited him. He met it with a wide, determined grin.

Father Santos rose almost as soon as de Payen left the chapel. The man had been more difficult than anticipated, and it was obvious that there would be more trouble to come. Santos hated being burdened with such trivial difficulties when the fate of so much depended on his concentration. He'd grown distracted once in the past, and it had nearly spelled disaster.

De Payen was a distraction of the worst sort. He considered himself a man of faith, and he expected the world to live up to the personal standard he'd set. Priests would not be excluded from this, and the furthest thing from Father Santos's mind was ministering the word of Christ. When he'd taken up the mantle of the priesthood, it had been as a shield for other activities. Now it appeared he would have to play the role convincingly.

The others who followed him were efficient and well-versed in their particular discipline, but Santos was the leader, and all things in their dark little world hinged on his decisions and his presence. He needed to solve this difficulty with de Payen and his knights before it became a major confrontation, and there was only one way to do that. He would have to be the first to act. The Patriarch, Daimbert, was a foolish fop of a man who had no more godly trait than that he returned the food he ate to the land for fertilizer. Once Bishop of Pisa, he'd been dispatched by Urban II to take charge of the spiritual leadership of the Holy City after the crusaders had wrested it from Moslem hands. The Pope, unfortunately, had not seen fit to live long enough to see the succession of spiritual leadership in Jerusalem change hands properly, and Daimbert had seen this as an open ticket to reckless abandon. After a long and sordid string of bad judgments and near fatal blunders, Daimbert had ended up throwing himself at the mercy of Baldwin II, upon his ascension to the throne. Baldwin had not removed Daimbert as Patriarch of Jerusalem, for reasons known only to the king himself. Now Santos was faced with Daimbert as his only ally, and the thought made him cringe.

He couldn't allow that buffoon of a spiritual leader to discover his true reason for occupying the lower levels of the mosque, but he also couldn't afford to be caught in a deception.

He wound his way down into the depths of the labyrinthine tunnels beneath the temple, heading as swiftly as possible for his own quarters. The tunnels stretched endlessly beneath the city. They'd been there since the old temples had stood, and they would remain, he imagined, after the city of Jerusalem fell to dust, buried beneath the debris. The antiquity of their walls spoke to him, and he let the familiarity of it all ease his mind.

He passed two of his followers at their posts, guarding the entrance to the section of the subterranean vaults that housed their order, and their purpose in existing, all in one. He nodded almost imperceptibly in their direction and kept on moving inward. They watched him pass stoically, eyes glowing deep red beneath the cowls of their robes.

He needed to make certain that he was presentable, then he needed to get to the main temple and confront Daimbert with the problem of de Payen before the knight made it to Baldwin with a similar request. It was a game of chess on a huge scale, and it was a game he meant to win.

There was no way he was going to be able to eject the

knights, and in truth, he had no real desire to do so. Handled correctly, they would become part of his shield. After a time he might even be able to influence them. Not only did they draw attention away from any other activity that might take place in the mosque, but they provided a measure of protection that Santos and his own men could not. It hadn't been so long since they'd been exiled from their charge—denied access to the city—and Santos remembered those days well. The agony of waiting, wondering if the Turks would find the vaults, and if they'd realize what they had if they did. Now they were back, and he had no intention of letting a group of ignorant fighting savages deny him his destiny.

Daimbert might be a weak ally, but now that communications had been restored with Rome, he would do as he was told. The Patriarch had no idea why Father Santos was protected, or what he did with his time and the men and funds allotted to him, but he was not fool enough to countermand orders from the Pope himself. He would support Santos in this, given the opportunity, and Santos intended to provide just such an opportunity. Baldwin would have to be approached, and Daimbert was the man for the job, such as he was.

The simple solution to the problem of de Payen and his knights was to support them openly. If he came out thanking Daimbert for allowing de Payen access to the upper levels, no request de Payen could make would sound other than ungrateful. The thought nearly made Santos smile.

The doors to his chamber closed behind him with a sharp snap, and the halls beyond returned to their silence. The stone passages were lit by torches that hung from the walls, and the air, while cooler than that of the upper rooms, was tepid and dank. The sun might rise and set and rise again, and none who strode those tunnels would be any the wiser.

The scent of antiquity, spiced with that of death, hung heavily in the air, and nothing stirred to drive it away. It was a scent that Father Santos found comforting.

The two guards, short, dark men in brown cowled robes, let their eyes meet for a moment, questioning, but they kept their silence. As they melted back into the alcoves that served as watch-stations, they all but disappeared, swallowed in shadow. When Santos exited his chamber again and brushed past like a cold breeze, they didn't even acknowledge his passing.

By the time Father Santos had completed his mission and returned, the shadows outside were growing long and the heat was beginning to fade from the stone walls and the street beneath his feet. The air still shimmered close to the surface, but the worst of the heat had melted away, and with the coming of the evening, he felt himself relaxing perceptibly. He preferred shadows to sunlight. When he was obscured from the view of those around him, that was when he felt safest, and that was when he was most effective.

His was a solitary existence. He lived for his studies and his duties, and there was little in the world that could sway him from either. Despite this he pursued any avenue that would serve to cut him off further from those around him. His followers knew only a small part of him. There were others, a very few, who knew more. He avoided these and kept the rest in the dark whenever possible. In his own little world there was no room for baggage.

The daylight journey to the chambers of the Patriarch had been a risk that brought the hackles upright on his neck. There were too many inquisitive eyes in the city, too many who knew more than they let on and saw more than they told. Santos did not try to fool himself into believing that he and his order were the only ones aware of what lay beneath the temple of Solomon. He might know more than any other, and yet there were those who knew more than he would have liked. There had always been others, and it was against these others that his preparations and secrecy guarded. Some were powerful enough to pose a threat.

They knew him, as well, and in open conflict none of them would test him. He had been guardian for so long that even he had lost track of the years, and he knew the faces and weaknesses of his enemies well. Some of them knew a part of his as well; others had died in that discovery.

Daimbert had been more compliant than he'd have believed

possible. Since learning of Santos's existence, and his ties to Rome, the man had been literally obsequious. It was almost unnerving, and it was dangerous as well. If someone saw the oaf fawning over a mere priest, word would certainly spread. It was not the behavior of a patriarch, and Father Santos had been forced to take great pains to explain this, under his breath, during the course of their conversation.

Daimbert was going to take up the issue of the chambers beneath the temple with Baldwin that very evening. He was expected to dine with the king, and it would provide the perfect opportunity for such a conversation. It was as good as Father Santos could expect. Still, he would make arrangements against another disaster. If they were forced from the temple another time, they would not leave anything behind. He had promised this to those he served, and it was best if he did nothing to disappoint them. They might not be as forgiving a second time.

He passed quickly from the streets and came up along the side of the temple. There were several ways into the place, most of which he knew, some so old and well-concealed that even he had forgotten them. He pulled aside what appeared to be a thick growth of brush and revealed a steel ring imbedded in the wall. The growth was attached to a carefully woven tapestry by an intricate structure of roots and threads. He slipped the stone free, slid inside, and pulled the door closed behind him. The carpet fell back against the outer wall neatly, concealing the entrance completely.

Santos hurried his steps somewhat, using main passages whenever it seemed prudent. He was passing the small garden in the central square of the temple when he heard voices and something made him stop to listen. His senses were more acute than most and there was a sensation in the air that itched at the back of his mind.

It was de Payen, and some other—a voice he hadn't heard before, though it reached out to caress his mind with a dark familiarity. It was none of the knights—none of them would use such arrogant tones with their leader. None of them had the power, or the age that Father Santos now detected. He cautiously approached the entrance to the garden and peered around the corner.

He could make out de Payen and another man, nearly the same height, though narrower of girth. The priest melted more closely against the stone, his heart quickening. This was no ordinary man. The aura of otherworldliness seeped from the garden and spilled into the passageway beyond. There was the scent of fresh blood and recent death in the air, even more strongly than in his own chambers below.

This was new. He'd had no idea that de Payen had alliances beyond Mother Church. It was a bit of information he might use, to be certain, if the need arose. His immediate concern was this other, though. There was a darkness about him that drew the eye, and the mind, a deceptive grace and swiftness to his movements. His voice didn't quite carry to where Santos stood, and in any case, the priest couldn't risk discovery. He would find out what the two were up to soon enough.

This was the type of thing he'd trained himself for. Such an enemy would be a true challenge. Santos had spent enough years in the spanking of children. There were preparations to be made. The time had arrived to see if his followers had learned anything from his teaching. Dropping back into the shadows, he found his way to the stairs and went below.

In the garden, Montrovant looked about himself, suddenly wary. De Payen watched him, alerted by the sudden shift in the darker man's posture. Something had happened, but the knight had no idea what it might have been.

"What is it?" de Payen asked quickly.

"I'm not certain. For just a moment, I thought I heard someone in the hall, but there is no one."

De Payen decided against questioning how Montrovant could know whether someone moved through a passage separated from them by a wall of solid stone. There were a great many things about this dark, powerful man that the knight had chosen not to question. He wasn't at all certain he was prepared for the answers.

"I will see what can be done about this Father Santos,"

Montrovant said at last, returning his attention to the matter at hand. "I don't like the secrecy, and I trust your judgment of the man. You must take your doubts to Baldwin himself—I cannot yet make myself known to him, though the time when I will do so is not far in the future. I have a destiny of my own, Hugues de Payen, and it may be that this Father Santos is an indication that the completion of that destiny is at hand. Great things are coming, and you are a part of them. Do you feel it?"

Hugues did, indeed, feel it. He nodded.

"It is well, then. Continue with your preparations, and soon it will be time to take your knights to the road and do battle. After so long cloistered in one place, it will be a welcome release."

"That it will," Hugues replied. "That it will. Will you join us when we go?"

"I may," Montrovant grinned. "I may do just that."

Without further words, Montrovant spun and was gone. The movement was so quick that he appeared to blink out of existence, and Hugues was left to stare dumbly into the shadows.

Strange times, he thought to himself, moving toward the halls and his own chambers in quiet amazement. *Strange times indeed.*

SEVEN

It was early morning, and the sun was just creeping over the skyline of the city. Merchants were wheeling their carts to market, and women scurried about fetching water and feeding animals. The late guard was just returning, winding its way lazily through the streets toward Baldwin's palace, ready to turn over their post to a fresh unit. It was a beautiful day.

Hugues led his mount through the gates on the south side of the mosque and into the street beyond, taking in deep breaths of the fresh morning air. The others followed, their steps punctuated by the slap of leather and the clatter of weapons and scabbards. It was a good day for battle, and Hugues, while he couldn't be certain they would find it, found himself anticipating the moment. He could find his Lord in the moments of silence he spent alone in the temple, or praying at the side of his bed, but the red haze of the warrior was his true mantle. If Bernard and Father Santos chose the vestments of the priest, that was well, but for a man such as Hugues, action was the purest form of worship. He was born to it.

That was a part of his strength. The knowledge that God was not always kind and soft was an important weapon. The further knowledge that, in God's name, a warrior could do no wrong was the key to his salvation. The anger and the violence had always come to Hugues, despite his desire that he could evade it. Red was the color of his faith, and it had been too long since he'd had a proper avenue for venting that faith.

Each of his men, in his own way, needed the escape that this first "campaign" would bring. Too many days spent within stone walls could drive a fighting man to insanity faster than any force of nature, and they were approaching that limit. Hugues had instituted an iron-clad system of discipline and training, and the very cloistered, separatist method he'd chosen for the building of his army led to the need for the venting of energy. They were knights, men of action and faith, and it was time to test that faith on the field of battle.

The control he had to exert over his own emotions had prepared him well for the instruction of others.

They left behind the small contingent of servants and pages that had entered their service. In the future, the pages would ride at their sides, carrying their weapons and armor, but for the moment Hugues had felt it best just to get on the road. He trusted that Montrovant, though he was not visible, would look after things while he was gone. In truth, there was little that could happen in the mosque that the servants couldn't handle. He didn't like leaving Father Santos and his odd, shadowy minions alone in the lower levels, but there was nothing to be done about it.

Baldwin had agreed to look into the matter of the priest, to try to find out the purpose of the man's "secret" mission, which Daimbert had assured them both had been assigned by the Pope himself. Baldwin had seemed put out by the notion that the Church had secrets within his own city, and yet he'd been equally reluctant to act immediately. The people were very sympathetic to Daimbert's ministrations and demands, and it would take good solid reasons for Baldwin to stand against him in a matter of faith.

When Hugues had called upon the monarch on the previous evening, the patriarch had been present as well. Hugues suspected that Father Santos had acted more quickly than he, and he cursed himself silently for waiting on Montrovant's word like a child.

The bishop had been sitting calmly at Baldwin's side, raising one eyebrow curiously at Hugues's approach. He'd worn a smirk that forced Hugues to concede the battle almost immediately. Never the war, though. One thing that Hugues did was to pay his debts. This was one that the patriarch would owe him, and it would be collected. There were more ways than one to influence a king, and Hugues was no stranger to any of them.

His mind returned to the moment. Many of the citizens of the city had gathered to watch them depart. Children gawked openly at the tall, armored knights and their magnificent mounts. In France it was a common enough sight, but here it was unheard of beyond the palace walls.

They mounted in silence, each lost in a world of his own thoughts, and turned their mounts toward the desert. Baldwin had informed Hugues during their short meeting the night before of a large group of merchants, accompanied by a contingent of French pilgrims, that were overdue along the road. Messengers had announced the company's approach days earlier, and they should have been in sight. They *should*, in fact, have been within the walls of Jerusalem.

De Payen prayed that it was not too late. He did not wish to start his service by burying the dead. There had been enough of the dark and negative since he'd left Father Bernard and taken up his vows. It was time that his work should begin in earnest. He had his own selfish reasons as well. He needed a good fight—particularly in the face of his futile attempt to expel Father Santos and his men from the temple. It was, he knew, a mosque, but he still thought of it as a temple, and it was thus his men addressed it.

They rode out, making swift time across the desert terrain. The gritty sand and the wind in his hair soon wiped all concerns from Hugues's mind except for the passing of time and the covering of the miles. They did not stop to rest themselves or their mounts, but continued on a straight line over the merchant road. It was not long before smoke appeared on the horizon, and Hugues spurred his mount to even greater speed, casting a prayer to the wind. It had begun.

They were surrounded. Pierre Cardin, his brow awash in sweat and grime, fought to keep his eyes clear and his leaden limbs in motion. If he and the others hadn't managed to reach the minimal shelter provided by the small outcropping of rock that stood at his back, they would all be dead. As it was, they numbered less than a dozen of the fifty they'd begun with, and most of the supplies had been burned or taken. What remained, barely, were the lives of the few strong enough and skilled enough to continue fighting. The Turks circled, their horses no good in the close quarters, waiting patiently.

There was no escape. The small group might fend off their attackers for a few hours longer, coming in only a few at a time as the close quarters dictated, but they were severely outnumbered, and they were tired. The Turks could bide their time, sending fresh men in every few minutes to take up where their companions left off in an endless circle of madness and death.

The madman, Le Duc, had been their saving grace. He alone must have sent a dozen or more of the heathen dogs screaming back to Allah, and his blade never wavered. He fought like a demon, endless strength and a burning desire to kill seeped from him like a red mist, swallowing any who came too near. A dangerous man. Pierre had not liked Le Duc from the beginning, but without him, Pierre himself would no longer have the luxury of apologizing for his lack of sensibility. Despite the help the small swordsman was providing, Pierre did not let himself stray too near. He wasn't certain the man's killing frenzy would contain itself to Turks.

A commotion was rising in the outer ranks of their attackers, and Pierre tried once again to wipe the grime-soaked sleeve of his robe across his eyes and clear his sight. He succeeded mostly in increasing the stinging pain, rubbing the grime and salt in deeper. There were cries and screams erupting at a distance, and he knew that even Le Duc was not capable of having won his way so far into enemy ranks.

A screaming Turk launched out of the swirling sand, and Cardin was forced to concentrate on the battle directly before him, ignoring the screams and curses that flashed from the enemy's ranks. He caught a quick flash of glittering metal beyond the choking cloud of dust, but he paid it no attention. If someone was coming to his aid, it would do him little good were they to find him dead, and if it were more of the enemy it would make little difference.

He parried the wild lunge of his newest adversary, letting

the man's momentum carry him forward and bringing his own blade back and overhead in an arc that met the man's neck cleanly, nearly severing the head from his shoulders. Pierre gave a push with his sword, dropping the Moslem's body behind him and down, and brought his blade steady before him again. He'd been ready to lunge, or parry, a cry of vengeance and fury on his lips, but there was no attack. There was nothing.

There were sounds of a struggle, and there was the pounding of hooves, but no more opponents presented themselves. He backed against the stone and finally managed to take a moment to clear his sight, though he didn't let down his guard for an instant. It could be nothing but a trick, or a regrouping before the final charge. When the dust cleared, he saw that it was not.

The battle was over. A group of knights, splendid in white robes and glittering armor breastplates circled the last of the Turks like beasts stalking helpless prey. The bulk of the Moslems had fled, those on horseback turning tail and abandoning their comrades in a cowardly display of terror. Those who remained cowered in the sand, groveling. As Pierre watched in amazed silence, a huge, bearded knight dismounted, tossed the reins of his mount to one of his fellows, and walked purposefully toward the Turkish prisoners. The man towered over them like a giant out of legend, Goliath come to put David in his grave. Even the horses looked small.

There was no hesitation. The man's long, gleaming blade rose, and fell. The first of the prisoners' heads rolled from shaking shoulders and, gibbering, the others began to scramble over the ground like insects. They saw that there would be no quarter, and like rats from a doomed ship they made their futile bids for freedom.

The huge knight took out a second, leaving three, and the others broke and ran. None of them breached the silent circle of mounted men that surrounded them. Blades swung out, and heads rolled cleanly free. The strokes were mechanical in their precision. It was over in a matter of seconds.

The tall knight stood staring down at the bodies that lay silent at his feet, then turned away in contempt. His features softened somewhat, and clarity returned to the depths of his eyes. He moved toward where Pierre still stood with his back pressed defensively against the stone.

"Hail, friend," the knight called out as he approached. "I am Hugues de Payen, servant of God. We will bring you and your companions safely to the Holy City. I am sorry we were so long in coming."

Pierre had no words for such a moment, and his knees gave way as the fatigue and tension roared up to claim his mind. He had been too long without water or food, too long with his sword in his hand and his life replaying before his eyes. The sudden release was overwhelming, and he gave in to the moment, letting it all wash over and through him as he knelt, weeping in the sand. The only word that had mattered in all he'd just heard was "friend."

Le Duc, whose eyes were just beginning to clear of the battle madness, staggered forward then, and through the haze of his pain, Pierre heard the man speak.

"Who are you, Lord?" Le Duc asked, his words gasped between tortured breaths. "Why have you come?"

"We are the Knights of the Temple of Solomon," de Payen replied. "We are sworn to make this road safe for all who would travel to the Holy City of Jerusalem. Our service is to God, the Church, and Baldwin."

"I have never heard of your order," Le Duc gasped, gaining control of his breath slowly, "but I thank you for my life."

Pierre raised his head, trying to muster the strength to add his own thanks. He did not like the idea of Le Duc speaking for them all, but the others, what few remained, were in no better shape than Pierre himself. He could barely raise his head from the sand, and his voice was lost to him.

He watched as Le Duc took in the remains of the small caravan, sweeping his gaze slowly from side to side over the carcasses of men and animals alike. What remained of the caravan of goods the merchants had worked so long and hard to bring to the Holy City was spread across the ground in ripped heaps. It was like seeing their dreams spread open and bleeding.

Le Duc's gaze swept back to the fallen Arabs. Moving

suddenly forward, he spat on the nearest Turk, slamming the toe of his boot into the man's face. He brought his leg back again and again, pummeling the fallen Arab until his breath came in short gasps and he nearly collapsed on the sand himself. Then he pulled himself together and stood, shuddering with fatigue, the hatred burning brightly in his eyes.

"We will help you to gather what remains," de Payen assured him, ignoring the sudden outburst, or approving it. "I regret that we were not aware of your predicament in time to prevent this..." Hugues swept his arm in a wide arc to include the carnage surrounding them. "I wish to God that Baldwin had told us of your approach sooner."

Le Duc gazed at their unexpected savior for a moment, as if taking de Payen's measure. He nodded, finally, turning to where Pierre was rising, at last, from the sand. This seemed to set the others into motion, and within moments, de Payen's knights were moving among them, helping those to walk who could manage it and tending to the injured and dying.

Graves were dug in the sand, quickly and efficiently, and the remnants of the supplies and belongings of both pilgrims and Turks were gathered and sorted. It was the most precise, efficient use of manpower Pierre had ever witnessed. So little like the raids of his childhood, or the war stories of his father.

He noted with interest the calculated manner in which these men inventoried what they took from the Turks, the way they moved to obey de Payen's orders without thought or question. They were like no knights he'd ever encountered. Not one of them slipped a gold coin into his own pocket, or bickered over a captured weapon. It lent an added level of surreality to the moment, and he was forced to shake his aching head once again to clear his thoughts.

Before they mounted to finish the journey into the city, de Payen gathered them all before the graves of those who had fallen, and he led them in prayer. Pierre took the moment to steal a glance at the huge man, kneeling devoutly with his head bowed and the sweat of battle soaking the white robes beneath his armor. For an instant the sweat that still stung his eyes met with the dying sunlight to form a prismatic halo over de Payen's lowered head. Pierre blinked, and it was gone, but the moment etched itself into his mind and heart. Such faith, combined with such awesome strength. Truly, this man must have been sent by God himself.

When they'd paid their respects to the dead, they mounted and rode out in a long column. De Payen's men had managed to round up nearly a dozen of their lost horses, and a couple that had belonged to fallen Turks. They'd helped Pierre and his comrades to mount, offering whatever support they could, as well as encouraging words and sympathy for their losses. It was like being herded home by solicitous parents, or older brothers.

Pierre rode in a daze, Le Duc keeping his mount close by his side. He caught the other man's gaze for just a moment, made contact with those dark, penetrating eyes. There was a new light burning in those depths, and a shiver transitted Pierre's spine at the sight. He wondered what was to come. He was comforted to have the man at his side, but he was no more comfortable in his presence.

For the moment, sand and sun, pain and the hazy line of buildings ahead—Jerusalem—filled his thoughts. He concentrated on them, fighting to banish the screams and the blood from his memory. There would be ample hours of sleep for nightmares, he had no wish to relive them while he was still awake.

De Payen's troupe had made quite a sight, ushering the wounded and weary pilgrims into the city. Hugues had directed his men to bring those they'd rescued directly to the palace. Baldwin's men had appeared then, helping the pilgrims to dismount and make their way to medical attention, baths, or hot meals.

Once he saw that things were in hand, de Payen had turned away, leading his men back into the street and turning toward the mosque. They had to tend to the few light wounds among their own ranks, and he had announced a formal prayer of thanks to signify the success of their initial foray. Even in victory, he had no intention of letting his discipline slip. They had won by God's grace, and they would give proper thanks for that gift.

They'd done well, also, in the acquisition of supplies and weapons, as well as a few Turkish horses that would be put to good use in the coming days. It was not the grand victory he'd envisioned when he first began his journey to the Holy Land, but somehow the reality of this day's work, the respect he'd seen in the eyes of those he'd saved, moved him more deeply than any battle on a grander scale might have done. It was real. It was happening. The Lord had called, and he, Hugues de Payen, had answered.

Before he could make his way to the chapel where the others awaited him, a servant appeared in the doorway of his chamber, head bowed and waiting for permission to speak.

"Yes?" de Payen said, more softly than his usual gruff baritone.

"There is a man here to see you, Lord," the boy said quickly. "He gives his name as Pierre Cardin. He pounded on the doors until we were forced to open them to quiet him. I have explained that you are not to be disturbed, but he insists. Lord..." the boy hesitated for a second before continuing, "he is kneeling on the front steps of the temple in prayer. He will not answer me when I speak. I do not think he will leave before he is allowed to speak to you."

De Payen hesitated. "He may wait, then," the knight said at last. "I will go to the others in the chapel now, as I have promised. None come before God in any temple where I am in control. Tell him, though he may not acknowledge your words, that if he remains when we have completed our devotion, I will see him then."

The boy nodded and was gone. De Payen departed the room immediately, a thoughtful smile creasing his normally austere and somber visage. A day to be remembered, indeed.

From a distance, Jeanne Le Duc watched his companion of many days, Pierre Cardin, as he knelt before the mosque of al Aqsa in prayer. Le Duc guessed at the younger man's purpose, and he found it intriguing. Similar thoughts whirled through his own mind, though he doubted very seriously that there were many similarities between his own motivation and Cardin's. There were few similarities between them at all.

De Payen and his knights had exhibited a strength and discipline that Le Duc had never before encountered. He was not a man that gave in easily to the control of others. In fact, his journey to the Holy Land, as mercenary guard to the caravan, had been an escape from one such attempt at structured obedience. It was the long story of his life, this rebellious flight from the control of others, and yet somehow de Payen brought warring emotions to the surface.

De Payen's knights were different. They did not appear interested in riches, or in women. There had been no motivation in saving the pilgrims other than faith and a desire to serve, yet they'd been disciplined and vicious. There was a beauty in that unity of purpose. Le Duc found that an empty place within him cried out for what he'd witnessed, even as his mind warned him that the personal price of such service might be more than he could handle.

The sun was setting, yet Cardin showed no signs of leaving the temple. He knelt on the stone as if he had not been half dead that morning, as if food and water meant nothing to him. Le Duc knew that the heat of the stone must be blistering the man's knees, and that the air so close to the ground would be suffocating. It was a show of strength for which he would not have credited Pierre with the ability to present. It was a show of commitment he was certain he could never live up to himself, yet the pull on his senses was strong. He had always been an outsider with no other to turn to or to be responsible for.

As the shadows grew longer, he found that he'd been standing, staring at Cardin for so long that his own legs were growing weak from the strain. He turned to slide back into the shadows, and that is when he saw the man watching him. It was the second time that day he'd felt dwarfed by the size of another man. This stranger was tall and slender, gaunt even, though there was no indication of weakness. He was, in fact, the most singularly powerful being Le Duc had ever come in contact with, though he had only his senses to base this on.

Being seemed the appropriate thought, rather than *man*, though Le Duc didn't understand why.

"Jeanne Le Duc," the man greeted him, speaking slowly, as though snatching the name from Le Duc's mind. "I have come to reveal the secrets you seek."

"Who are you?" Le Duc responded curtly. He was afraid, and more weary than he'd imagined, but he remained calm. He'd faced death enough times for it not to steal his nerve.

"Does it matter?" the man responded, stepping forward from the shadows.

"It does to me," Le Duc replied, his hand slipping down toward the blade at his side.

"There is no need for your weapon, friend. My name is Montrovant, and I come to you in the name of Hugues de Payen and his knights. I come to offer you a place in his service."

"And if I seek no such service?" Le Duc replied.

"I would not be standing before you if you did not," Montrovant said, his voice powerful and commanding. "It was I that set de Payen upon the road he now follows. I seek your service, not he. This part of our conversation must remain between you and me. De Payen must never know. I sense in you the strength for both the service and the deception I require."

Le Duc considered Montrovant's words carefully. If this Montrovant was truly all that he appeared to be, then why would he not wish de Payen to know he was asking after the services of another? Why would he worry about the thoughts of any other—what could it matter?

"Why not just tell de Payen what you need?" Le Duc asked.

"Hugues is a very devout man, as you may have noticed," Montrovant replied, smiling. "Not everything I do makes sense to him, and I have no time to explain each and every need. You are a man of quick thought and quicker action. I sense, as well, that your faith may lie in different directions than that of the knights."

Le Duc didn't answer, but he was becoming more intrigued by the second. At the same time, a strange lethargy was seeping through his limbs, and he was having trouble focusing on the reasons he had distrusted this man only moments before. He found himself nodding in sudden agreement. It all made sense. His own thoughts had been plucked free and repeated to him, and they were even more logical than when he'd thought them initially.

He turned suddenly to stare at the space where Pierre Cardin knelt before the doors of the mosque. The man hadn't moved since he'd looked last. He might have been carved of stone.

Montrovant moved to stand at his side. "Go to him, Jeanne, and wait as he waits. I will see to it that de Payen accepts you. You must win his trust; that I cannot do for you, but I can see that you get the chance. Once you are accepted, I will contact you again.

"There are things that I seek. De Payen's motives are of the highest order, but there are forces more powerful operating here, and there are things that must be done that he would not approve. I will need the help of an agent on the inside, a man who will draw less attention than myself."

Le Duc was going to answer. The words were forming, and his tongue was in motion, but somehow no sound escaped. He felt strong hands clasping his shoulders, drawing him into the shadows, but it was a disconnected sensation, like watching strangers through a window. He felt a sharp pain at his throat, felt the life draining from him slowly. At the same time, he felt the draw at his mind, the rearranging of his thoughts. A single word slipped free of his lips in a whisper of air—*Demon*.

When he came back to himself, he was kneeling beside Pierre Cardin, sweating with fever and shivering as the chill of the evening seeped in from the desert. He was weak, weaker than he'd ever felt in his life. That life seemed to have been drained from him, but he fought against the weary bondage his mind sought to impose. It was not long before the huge wooden doors creaked open, and they were ushered inside. Cardin said no word, and Le Duc followed his lead.

From the shadows, Montrovant watched. Nodding in satisfaction, he moved into the night, leaving events to fall into place. The shadows swallowed him whole.

EIGHT

De Payen had not offered his two guests food or drink. He'd stood by in silence as they were ushered into his quarters, eyes downcast. In fact, he hadn't offered to let them rise from the kneeling positions they'd assumed upon entering his chamber, though it bothered him that they would kneel before him. One lesson they would need to learn was that God was the only power worthy of their worship. He remained deep in thought and he knew that, if they had the strength for what was to come, they would endure his silence and the suffering incurred during their wait.

The problem he considered was a deep one, and whatever he said to them would make his decision irrevocable. He had been ordered to come to the Holy City, and he'd been entrusted with the founding of the order. That order was to have been comprised of nine men, himself and eight others. No mention had been made by Bernard, or Montrovant himself, of how this number was to be increased. On the other hand, he'd been instructed to raise an army.

Father Bernard had been the one to dream of that army—that much Hugues remembered. Those words had come from him. He hadn't spoken of where that army was to come from, but he'd told Hugues that he needed to be a leader, not a follower.

Now Hugues found himself faced with two penitent men whose lives he'd saved scant hours before. These men wanted to enter his service, to fight at his side in the name of the Lord. He did not know them by more than name, and yet it was difficult to doubt their sincerity. After so long kneeling on the hot stone, the sweat of fever and the pallor of hunger bleached their skin—Le Duc, in particular, seemed pale and bloodless. It was difficult to question either motivation or faith.

They would make perfect additions to his knights, and yet he hesitated. It was a big change, and one that could not easily be revoked. Once he allowed these two to enter the ranks of his knights, how could he deny others? *Should* he deny others?

Hugues paced to the window, staring out into the starry expanse of the sky, but there were no answers waiting for him there. Montrovant had been strangely silent since Hugues had returned from the road, and the weight of responsibility settled more heavily onto his shoulders. That weight did not bear him down, but sat comfortably, and he made his decision, making the sign of the cross reverently as the decision cemented itself in his mind.

There it is, then, he whispered to himself softly. *It is up to me, and as God is my witness, I can see no reason to deny them.*

He turned so suddenly that the breeze from the motion of his robe through the air startled Pierre into looking up. The shivering man met Hugues's eyes just for a second, seeking something and apparently finding it, then dropping back to the floor. De Payen spoke at last.

"You are welcome here," he said. "Your faith is strong, and I have kept you too long from food and rest. It is not an easy road that I have set for myself, or for those who would follow me. The war I fight is as endless as time itself, and the enemy we face is the ultimate test of physical and moral strength.

"There are many things you must learn before you can walk freely among us. We will speak of those things in the days to come, and you will speak with the others. You will find our order...demanding. There are reasons for everything we do; in that you will have to trust me."

He saw that Cardin's entire frame was shaking with the effort to hold his position, and Hugues's expression softened.

Gesturing to the doorway, where a pair of young servants had been waiting patiently, he indicated that they should enter and go to his two visitors.

"Go with Phillip and Barnabas," he said. "They will show you where you can clean yourselves, give you some fruit and bread, a little wine, and then you will be shown to your quarters. You will find that there is not much of comfort to be had here, but keep in mind that what is yours is equal to what is mine. None among us lives in luxury. Poverty is one of our vows, and I believe that for good discipline and purity of spirit, it is the most important."

Neither man did more than nod in acknowledgment. They could not have if they'd wanted. Le Duc was holding up better than Cardin, but he looked like Death himself, and not on a good day. His skin was so pale that he might have been a shade. His strength of will was incredible. He had reached out a hand to steady Cardin, who glanced at him with an expression half questioning, half grateful. *An odd pair,* de Payen thought to himself.

The two of them rose with the aid of the two servants, staggering to the doorway and steadying their balance a bit as they reached the passage beyond. Le Duc caught de Payen's interest most strongly. There was a strength to the man, something more than just another knight, that he couldn't easily put his finger on. He thought fleetingly of Montrovant, but it was different with Le Duc.

When de Payen and his knights had come upon Le Duc's party, the man had been fighting mindlessly, as though he were possessed. Unlike a madman, however, he'd been holding his own against nearly impossible odds. Hugues knew that frenzy, the red haze that descended and painted the battlefield in slow-motion reds and blacks—chiaroscuro in scarlet. It was his own burden as well. Until Montrovant had cemented the knowledge that violence was one of God's weapons, it had been a burden he could not reconcile.

Hugues sensed that Le Duc felt it too, though differently. There was none of God's light in the small man's eyes, but there was a void that might be filled with that light. It was a task Hugues felt himself uniquely qualified to tackle. It was important. Le Duc was a true warrior, and few could stand against such a man. The question was, could Le Duc stand against his own darkness? Hugues knew he would have his hands full with that one.

Cardin had made a good showing of himself, as well, but he'd not shown the uncanny resilience that marked Le Duc. He would not be the same sort of challenge. Such strength as Le Duc had exhibited would not bow down easily, even before God. It was another challenge—another beginning.

Turning to the window, Hugues returned his gaze to the stars. He knelt and lowered his head, and as the mosque fell slowly silent around him, he prayed.

Montrovant hesitated. He'd meant to go to Hugues and add his own blessing to the addition of the two new knights, but as the big man dropped to his knees in prayer, he drew back, making his way along the outer wall like a shadow. If Hugues were ready to take the yoke of responsibility more firmly onto his own shoulders, that was fine. It was, in fact, perfect. Montrovant had more important things to occupy his time.

Shifting his senses, he felt the heartbeats of those within, tasted the essence of each as he passed the walls of their rooms. He sought Le Duc, but he couldn't help hesitating by each to savor the scent of warm blood, some pumped by strong hearts after a successful battle—others caught in the throes of dreams even Montrovant couldn't snatch from their minds. It was a heady sensation to know that all that had happened that day had been a part of his own plan, and that much more was to come.

The pieces of the grand puzzle he'd envisioned were falling into place with an ease he hadn't anticipated, and he found himself in a rare mood for adventure. It was the sort of mood that most annoyed Euginio, and that had come close to ending Montrovant's fun eternally on more than one occasion, but he couldn't resist the draw of the moon. He remembered a saying he'd heard while alive—you only live once. For him, it was the second time around that held all the savor.

Le Duc's shallow breathing reached his ears at the same time that his senses locked onto the familiar touch of blood to blood. He hadn't taken all that the man had to offer—that would have been a waste of good resources—but he'd taken enough to begin the process of binding Le Duc to him. He wanted a man on the inside, but he wanted that man to know the power he served. The man's blood was an invisible chain, a chain Montrovant could tug on, twist, or shake any time he felt inclined. He'd heard the knight mutter the word "demon" as he'd fed, and the memory made Montrovant smile. He was no demon, but to be thought of as such was intriguing.

What he planned for this night was simple. Using Le Duc's room as an entrance, he would slip into the mosque himself. There were not enough of the knights for a true guard to be set, and he was fairly certain that he could reach the lower levels of the building without being detected. It was a perfect opportunity to scout his enemies on their own ground.

He was curious about Father Santos and his followers, curious enough to risk discovery. It was the few times he'd seen them slinking about the temple that had drawn him back to this place. They had an air of secrecy about them that was impossible to mistake, and Santos himself reeked of the decadence and power of antiquity. He was no priest, that much was certain.

It was the presence of these "guardians" that had led Montrovant to his conclusions about the Grail. They were protecting something, something valuable enough to the Church to allow their existence here, in the holiest of cities, without even the knowledge of the Patriarch of Jerusalem knowing their true purpose. There were other things the Patriarch did not, and could not, know. This was the knowledge that Montrovant sought.

Not many treasures or secrets would rate such protection, or such blatant disregard for protocol and canon. Montrovant had seen relics, the fingers and mummified hands of saints, stones said to have been used in the slaying of martyrs, slivers of the true cross, and water blessed by saints long faded to dust. Each item held power, a palpable, real energy that one could sense as they came under its influence. That sensation permeated the air in the mosque, as well, but it was magnified to levels Montrovant had never before encountered. It might be from one great artifact, or a number of smaller, yet potent relics. He didn't know which, but he meant to find out.

He reached Le Duc's window undetected, and he was

readying himself to slide through, when he felt his mind being tugged in a different direction. Grunting at the distraction, he cocked his head to one side, like a dog who'd picked up an odd scent. The ancient one was calling him into the desert once more. He hesitated. It was not in Montrovant's nature to come to another's call like a servant. It was also against his judgment to be distracted from a course he'd set for himself without good reason. He needed to strengthen the bond between himself and Le Duc before the knight came to the wrong conclusions and let something slip that could be damaging.

But the old one had given him a sanctuary against the sunlight that he might not have found on his own, and cryptic as they were, he'd given him some answers, as well. It might be that if he ignored the call, he would lose the one ally he had in this odd affair, and that might prove a fatal mistake.

With a longing look at the window, Montrovant launched himself from the wall and landed on the ground as softly as a cat. The side of the mosque that he'd leapt from adjoined an alley, walled in on both sides by steep vertical walls with few doors. There were windows scattered over the sides of those walls, but there were few candles lit at such an hour. It was only a few moments before he was able to ascertain that no one had seen him.

Without further hesitation he moved into the street, walking swiftly, fighting the urge to take flight, or to move at the pace he was capable of. There was no reason to draw attention to himself, particularly when his mission might require him to make his presence public at some point. Now that he'd left the safety of the alley he was plainly visible, and not everyone in Jerusalem was in bed. It wouldn't do to take off like a bolt of lightning, disappearing and leaving a witness with a story and description with too close a resemblance to a night spirit slinking about the city. Besides, though he was responding once more to this old one's call, he was in no hurry to reach his destination. That would have seemed too obedient for his taste.

Despite his lack of haste, it did not take him long to find the one he sought. The ancient one stood alone at the very edge of the desert, watching Montrovant calmly as he approached. The ancient wore the same white robe and sad, far-off smile that Montrovant remembered, but there was something more urgent in his expression. He seemed troubled somehow, or confused.

"You called?" Montrovant stated. There was no question.

"You are rash," the old one began, turning his back and beginning to walk away from the city across the sand. Montrovant had heard those words before—from Euginio. From others, all older and 'wiser' than he. He was in no mood for another lecture.

"Why does it concern you?" he asked, following. "Why do you involve yourself in my affairs?"

"You are arrogant, as well," the old one observed. "Your affairs, as well you know, concern many besides yourself. Anything you do that leads to your discovery, or mine, or both—any mistake you make that compromises the safety of others—is my business. It is particularly important that we keep our presence obscure in so devout a setting as this. You have been here before, but I know the city as it exists today.

"I'm not certain that even I could survive an all-out witch hunt if one were to be launched. We do all need our sleep..."

"Do we?" The words left Montrovant's lips before he could stop them. Something in his companion's tone had seemed a bit too lighthearted.

The old one hesitated, turning his head to look back as he spoke. "What else is there? Feed, sleep—dream—feed again. There is no end, and there is—as the Bible tells us—no new thing under the sun. That includes you, Solomon. You think you are unique and powerful. I am here to tell you that for every ancient, powerful force on this planet, there is another, more ancient, more powerful, and wiser. You would do well to heed this warning, and to use the insight it gives you more prudently."

"Years do not equate to wisdom," Montrovant countered. "They may bring power, or knowledge, but wisdom is an entity unto itself."

"Of course." The old one's smile deepened. "And you have reached the pinnacle of your wisdom—how naive of me not to notice. You, of course, know all truth and could instruct me in the ways of the world."

Montrovant grew silent, but he felt his anger building. "What is it you want?" he spat out at last. "You did not call me into the desert to taunt me."

"I called you into the desert to warn you," the man said, stopping, "though taunting you is not without its entertainment. You were about to make a mistake, a mistake you will no doubt make despite my warnings, but I wanted you at least to make that mistake with both eyes open. You were about to enter the mosque, and I tell you now, powerful as you are—crafty and wise as you may be—you would never have walked back through those doors. You have no idea the power that awaits you within those walls, and you have no knowledge of how to combat it."

Montrovant stopped, staring. "What are you talking about? Is it Santos? Am I right? Do they guard the Grail, then?"

"So many questions, so little patience. Santos is not what he seems. His faith is strong, but you will find little of godliness in his makeup, I'm afraid. He has powers even I do not fully understand, powers that make him a dangerous enemy to one such as yourself. His gods are not the same as your friend de Payen's—they are more ancient, and I know little of their ways.

"I am not certain what secrets he may guard, but I do know this. Though his followers have changed many times over the course of the years, Santos has guarded those catacombs and tunnels since the days when the Nazarene walked these very sands. I don't know how much longer than that he might have been present, but I have seen what I have seen. Father he may be, but to what I would hesitate to guess."

"He is not like you—or I," Montrovant replied, struggling to hide the arrogance he knew was in his tone. "He is not damned, and he is no denizen of the pit of the Wyrm. I have been close enough to sense this. He appears to be nothing more than a man, and yet I know this is not correct either. What is he?"

"You would do well to remember that you resemble a man yourself, by night," the ancient replied. "You may take my warning, or you may ignore it. It is all the same to me. Still," he hesitated, "I would not see you fail in your mission. Santos and his minions have hoarded their 'treasures' for too long, I think. I don't know for certain what it is that they hold, but it is time to return things into the world, to loose powers that can bring about change.

"One thing you will find, Solomon," he added almost wistfully, "is that boredom is your greatest enemy. Never let life lack intrigue, of one sort or another, or you are finished. Change is the one thing eternal, and if that were not the way of it, nothing would be eternal."

"What must I do, then?" Montrovant asked reluctantly. He hated the thought of being indebted to this odd, ancient being. He hated being indebted to *anyone*. Even more he hated not knowing the proper course of action himself.

"You must do as you will, of course," the man laughed, and the sound of that laughter was bittersweet and magical. It caught at the tendrils of Montrovant's emotions, drawing him into its spell. He saw visions—palaces and temples, great stone idols and crowds of soldiers in bright golden armor astride gleaming chariots. Then his vision cleared, and he stood alone once more, cursing the darkness. Santos was not the only one with secrets worth desiring, it seemed.

He will know you, if you enter the temple again, Solomon. He will know your name. Beware.

The voice seeped out of his mind, up through the sand that surrounded him and the breeze that caused his hair to dance about his shoulders. Standing very still, Montrovant concentrated, but he could sense nothing—no one. He was alone.

He didn't know how much of what he'd heard was truth, or how much might have been manufactured for his benefit. The old one was fond of theatrics, that was clear in the sudden appearances and disappearances. One thing was certain, the only truth in his words that could be counted on was that boredom was the enemy. That taken into account, how was Montrovant himself being used to make things interesting and new—and would he survive it?

If the old one had wanted Montrovant dead, he'd have been sleeping the eternal sleep since their first meeting. There was something more, something the other wanted that Montrovant could provide. It bothered him that the old one knew his name. He did not believe that it had been plucked from his mind—he'd have sensed that, even if he couldn't have prevented it. That meant that the knowledge had come through other means. Where might they have met in the past?

The frustration of being controlled so easily exploded into a sudden fury, and he swept back across the sand toward the city. He moved like an avenging spirit, so swift that he might have been mistaken from a mountaintop for the shadow of a soaring owl. He reached out, heedless of what might await him, and he sensed warm blood—a great deal of it.

It was a patrol, one of Baldwin's patrols, a patrol that—in all reality—should have been able to help the caravan that de Payen had saved. There were seven of them, two older knights, three younger knights, and a pair of pages that accompanied them. They'd been on the road, returning to Jerusalem, when de Payen had left the city.

Montrovant fell upon them, beyond rational thought.

Before they were aware they'd been set upon, two of the younger knights were sprawled unconscious on the ground, and Montrovant held a third knight, older, with graying hair and arms that threatened to pop through the metal bands he wore about his biceps—a gnarled old tree of a warrior—aloft in one hand. He threw back his head and howled to the darkness, ripping the man's throat with a single tear of teeth and hunger.

He sensed movement at his back and dropped the man he held, just in time for the blade of the next to cleave the bone and flesh of the one he'd released. The sword buried itself deeply in the old knight's flesh, too deeply to be pulled free before Montrovant leaped over the fallen carcass and ripped at the arm holding the sword. Bone and sinew split with a sickening pop and suddenly the man's face was directly in front of Montrovant's own.

Smiling fiercely, he yanked the man's head back by the hair and ripped a second throat, letting the warmth of the blood soak the front of his tunic and flow down the sides of his chin as he fed. He ignored the others. Their terror was nearly solid in the air surrounding him, so complete that they were no longer to be feared.

They screamed, and still he ignored them. Montrovant sensed that the one remaining knight and the two pages had recovered from their initial shock enough to regain control of their throats, and he knew that the control of limbs and weapons would not be far behind.

He leaped to the young knight's side before he could decide between flight and drawing his weapon. The choice was made for him. Montrovant yanked the sword free of its scabbard easily and swung it so quickly that the boy's head leaped from his shoulders, flying to bounce on the ground at Montrovant's feet before a second scream could rip its way free of his throat.

The two pages had managed to turn their mounts and were galloping toward the city in terror. Montrovant started after them, then hesitated. Who would believe them? There had been a patrol, and they had been set upon and killed—possibly by Turks, possibly by wild animals. If rumors of a dark spirit began to circulate through the city, so be it. Montrovant was tired of cowering in shadows. It wasn't his style to sit back and wait for others to call the shots, and the events of the evening had tried his patience severely.

His anger abated slowly, and his common sense told him the only sane course of action was to track and kill the two pages before they reached Baldwin's castle. He did not. He let them go. Let them fear him…they should fear him. In the end, it would not matter. He would get what he had come for, despite the ancient one, despite 'Father' Santos, despite them all.

He glanced at the two knights still lying at his feet, and he smiled. They too could fuel the fires of rumor. It was unlikely that either of them had gotten a clear look at him before blacking out. It would be interesting to see how their stories corresponded with those of the two pages. He thought, just for a second, of the ancient one's admonition that he continue to make things interesting, and he wondered if something so simple and mundane would qualify in those ageless eyes.

The dawn was approaching, and without a backward glance he took to the air, returning to the graveyard and to rest. When the darkness returned, he would seek Le Duc, and his plans would begin in earnest. Let them *try* and stop him.

They slipped through the shadows behind Montrovant like wisps of cloud. Each kept far enough behind, or to the side, not to draw his attention. Focused as he was, fed and arrogant, he paid no heed to his surroundings.

Darkness shifted and footsteps drew the dust of centuries from the roadway. Deep-set red eyes glowed from crevices and alleyways, locked to Montrovant's retreating form. As he pushed the door wide and entered the tomb, they watched in silence. As he pulled the stone back into place, they held their positions.

There was a soft murmur of sound—voices like the whisper of sand across stone. The shadows gathered around a solitary figure, standing backlit by the failing light of the moon. He wore the white robes of the penitent, and his eyes were filled with an infinite sadness.

NINE

The two new men fit in well. De Payen had been concerned about the stress and complication of adding strangers to his command, but his fears had proven groundless. The two had been accepted readily by his men. It would have been difficult after only a few days' time to tell which were the newcomers and which had come with him on the road from France. They were all pilgrims of one sort or another.

Le Duc kept to himself, spending his time brooding in silence, but he made no complaint about the incredible changes that had taken place in his life. If anything, they seemed to have brought out a new side of his character. He never missed devotion, and his weapons practice was unmatched among de Payen's knights. He was a model of discipline, and Hugues knew that it was an internal control, not due to his own leadership.

Cardin had fit in so easily that it seemed he'd always been there. He'd sought exactly this sort of awakening when he made his pilgrimage, and he was quick to take advantage of the opportunities presented to him. He was studious, dependable, and no slouch with a blade himself. Hugues couldn't have chosen better men had he gone back to France in search of them.

A great step had been taken on the road to the future, and Hugues's mind whirled with the possibilities, and the complications, that step had presented to him.

He had been born to nobility, but he had never been the one destined to rule. His mind and soul had been handed over to God at a young age; his body and the strength God had granted him belonged to the sword. The Bible was full of stories of soldiers of God. De Payen had heard the priests speak of a compassionate, loving Father, a spirit-being of incomprehensible compassion and purity, and he had taken it all in eagerly. It gave him great hope in the face of chaotic times and ungodly rulers. It gave him hope that, though he might never rule his family's lands, or stand by the side of a king, he might make a difference in the world. It gave him the faith that he could be something in his father's eyes.

He'd always done well in his studies, but he hadn't left it at that. He'd studied on his own, devoured every tract he could get his hands on, poring over them laboriously. His father had not been fond of the notion of his boys reading and writing, and the learning had been slow. If it hadn't been for Hugues's prowess with weapons and love of battle, he might have been denied the study altogether.

That reading had brought him to the realization of a deeper, darker reality. His father had been a great man in his time, but he'd not seen the true picture. He had feared God as much as any man, but he'd never truly believed in evil. Hugues had found that evil in the pages of the holiest of books, and he'd made it his sworn enemy.

There was a war in progress. It had been raging since the first moment that time had existed, and it would be won by whichever side was stronger—more vigilant. It would not be won by compassion, but by the sword. Hugues couldn't remember at what age he'd come to this understanding, but it had happened so far in his past that the lesson was ingrained in his mind.

He knew that he wanted to be a part of that fight. He wanted to be a force for God that would help to erase the stain of evil from the earth once and for all, and he believed that his physical gifts had been granted him for just such a purpose. There would be plenty of time for love, and compassion, once the true Kingdom had returned to the earth.

Now destiny stared him in the face, and he meant to grasp it and make it his own. There were other men in Jerusalem who would come to his call, if they thought the opportunity existed. There were those who needed the discipline, the camaraderie his order could provide. There were many roads to the promised land, but there was always room for one more. Even some of Baldwin's own men had begun to look longingly at Hugues and his men when they passed. God was a powerful ally.

Neither Father Bernard nor Montrovant had set these thoughts in his mind, but up until the present moment, it had been they who had directed his actions. The decision to allow new converts to his order had come to him by way of prayer, and by the hand of the two whom he'd saved, the two who'd come to his service of their own free will and without personal agendas. His was a noble cause, and it was not a cause that he could selfishly keep from others. If there was to be a war, he would walk into it leading an army.

That decided, there were plans to be made. He knew that there was only so much he could accomplish in Jerusalem. The forces that Baldwin commanded were limited—that was one of the reasons de Payen and his men had been accepted so readily. The Turks and other warring nobles converged on all sides, and there was still not a clear, safe route for reinforcements to make their way across the desert.

They needed more men, and Hugues was planning for a time when he could take his cause to higher authority—back to Bernard, possibly to the Pope himself. Armies didn't materialize out of thin air, and the righteous often needed to be prodded. Even the Apostles hadn't been perfect in their faith. He would need support, a lot of it, and that meant that the discipline of the order had to be absolute. Bernard was a powerful speaker, and the deeds he and his men had accomplished thus far would speak strongly in his favor, but he had to get back to France to make it happen.

He'd summoned Phillip to his chambers a few moments before, and the young man arrived suddenly, stumbling into the room with a roll of parchment under one arm and his quill, ink, and rasorum gripped tightly in his hands. His eyes shone brightly in curiosity and anticipation. Hugues smiled. Even those who served as pages and servants sensed the presence of the Lord. Hugues could feel it. They moved so quickly to carry out his orders—orders that came from his faith, not from any desire for personal gain. That was his strength. Phillip was a slender lad, but he was growing quickly, and despite his propensity for books and letters, he was beginning to take on some weight. He'd make a knight, one day, and Hugues looked forward to the time when he could tell him so.

"I want you to write a letter for me, Phillip," he began, turning his back on the young man and clasping his hands behind him. "I spent long hours at study, but though I have been granted to read the words of our Lord, the forming of my own words on paper never came easily to me...I envy you that gift."

Spinning, his eyes blazing with the passion that seethed just beneath the surface of his mind, he continued. "I need you to listen to me, and I need you to take what I say and bring my words to the paper. It is vital that they understand the importance of this message. They must see what I mean to do. It is important that they *believe* what I tell them."

Phillip nodded. He felt a lump forming in his throat, and rather than risking words that might sputter out like a snuffed candle, he set his materials out on the desk and waited in respectful silence. De Payen watched as he went about these familiar tasks. It was different this time. There was an energy in the air. Reaching out to that energy, he attempted to pull it about himself as he began to speak.

"Make the letter to Father Bernard," he said, turning away once more to concentrate on his thoughts. "I want it to go further—it must go further—but he is the man to take my message to the Church."

Phillip nodded again, making a note on the paper with a quick flourish.

"To the most reverend Father Bernard," he began. "I have begun the fight for the Holy Land, as you instructed, and it is a glorious feeling. Lives have been saved, and our numbers are growing. Praise the Lord."

There was more. De Payen spoke of his commitment, of the need for a written code that his men could use to pattern their lives. He'd seen the discipline in Bernard's abbey, and he sought that for his men. He spoke of the need for reinforcements. The road to Jerusalem was a long one, and the intrigues and battles waged between the Moslems, the Patriarch, Baldwin, and the other nobles were myriad. The Crusade had begun as a wonderful thing, but the focus had been warped by greed and the desire for personal power. Somewhere along the way the crusaders had forgotten that the goal of occupying the Holy Land was to return it to the followers of the One God.

What Hugues wanted was an army, and he intended to go back, personally, and lead them to the Holy Land. He could train his men to hold the road for his return. With or without his leadership, they could do great things for Baldwin and the city. The only thing in question was, would the Holy Father in Rome understand? Would he be able to see the need—the desperate void that Hugues yearned to fill? Would he mobilize the righteous, or would he send Hugues back to Jerusalem with a pat on the shoulder? The not knowing was the worst of it.

Phillip finished his notes, short symbolic representations that would return Hugues's words to his mind. He had little parchment to waste on memories, but he dared not forget a detail. He cleaned his quill, and placed his hands on the desk as if to rise. His careful, even script filled page after page of the paper he'd brought with him, and his brow was furrowed in thought. De Payen caught his eyes…held them, and the young man took his seat once more.

"You have heard what I have to say," Hugues said slowly. "You know the truth of my words, the immensity of our task… do you think they will listen?"

Phillip did not answer immediately. He pursed his lips, concentrating his thoughts. At last he spoke.

"I believe that you believe, Lord, and I hear your words resonating within my heart. I will strive to bring that emotion to the words I scribe in your letter. I believe that Father Bernard already understands, and I know the incredible power of his voice. If the Holy Father does not listen, it will be because there is something hidden to us…and I believe, since you have asked me as a man, that it is *your* vision that is true. You speak the words that need to be spoken…you will be heard."

Hugues had grown very still as Phillip spoke. His question had been largely rhetorical…he hadn't meant for the younger man to reinforce his faith, and yet it was happening. The boy was only a servant—a slight, wispy lad on the verge of manhood, enmeshed in words and paper, books and philosophy. The hot blood of the warrior did not burn through his veins, though the potential was not completely lost, and the killer instinct had bypassed him completely. None of this mattered in those moments.

There had always been times in Hugues's life when there were forces beyond his understanding at work. This was one. Phillip spoke, but Hugues heard a voice of greater power, a voice of deep resonance and warm, familiar energy. Phillip spoke the truth, and the sudden release of tension was a wonder worthy of a three-day fast. Never more than in that moment had the words "The truth shall set you free" meant more to him.

"Go," he said at last. "Write the letter, then come to me and read what you have written. I will send it ahead of me, and I will follow our words to the Holy Father himself. I will leave this place in the hands of Baldwin, and of my knights, but I will come back at the head of the greatest army of God that has ever existed."

Phillip nodded. The voice that had carried him through the previous moments had departed, leaving a frightened, if very devout, boy in its wake. He spun on his heel, scurrying from the room in a flutter of cloth and parchment. De Payen watched until the boy was out of sight, then turned to the window.

So many responsibilities. So many choices. He didn't know if he'd done the right thing, but it felt as though he had, and Hugues had always trusted his heart. He dropped to his knees, his chin coming to rest against his chest, and he let the light that burned within his heart pry the thoughts from his mind. There would be plenty of time for thought in the days to come—for the moment, he belonged to the Lord.

Montrovant wasn't worried about de Payen this night. He thought of dropping in, just to see what thoughts might be going through the man's mind, but the call of other matters was too pressing. He had not come to Jerusalem to look after a budding military order, no matter how responsible he might be for its existence. Hugues would do fine, and if Montrovant needed him, it would be a simple enough matter to appear and make his wishes known.

In fact, the more closely he associated himself with the knights of the temple, the greater the chance that questions would begin to arise. Montrovant was adept at concealing his nature, but over a period of time, even the wisest of his kind would slip. It was best that he keep to himself and let de Payen go his own way. He had all the authority to come and go that he needed, and the knights would make a good screen for his activities.

For a fleeting moment it occurred to him that he might be underestimating de Payen. He was taking a great deal for granted, including the total obedience of the huge knight and his men. The moment passed swiftly. De Payen was nothing to him, and if he distracted himself with such trivialities, he would never reach his goal. None of them could stand before him. None of them was worthy of anything but his contempt.

Montrovant's last meeting with the ancient one in the desert, though he knew it should have warned him away, had merely convinced him that his suspicions were correct. What he sought was being held beneath the mosque—which he still couldn't see as anything but the temple that had stood before, grand and impressive. That temple had been named for Montrovant's own namesake, and this fact made it even more personal, though it shouldn't have mattered. It made the name Baldwin had bequeathed to de Payen's order all the more amusing and appropriate. *The Poor Knights of the Temple of Solomon.*

He did not hesitate as he reached the shadowed wall of the mosque, but began to climb, making his way to the spot he now knew to be Le Duc's quarters. The window was several stories above the street level, but it took Montrovant only seconds to make the ascent. He slid across the surface of the stone like a huge spider.

This night he was not worried about encounters with guards, or detection by Santos. He wanted to get in, see what he could see, and get out before anyone was the wiser, but if he were caught in the act, well, that would be too bad for whoever caught him. None walked the streets in the immediate vicinity,

he'd combed the shadows with his mind before beginning his
ascent, and the entire climb took only short seconds.

He hesitated at Le Duc's window. He sensed something
at his back...a presence besides himself...several presences.
He looked quickly over his shoulder, but he saw nothing. He
returned his concentration to the window and the mosque
beyond. There would be no intrusions this time. Even if the
ancient one called him, he intended to go in. There were others
in the city who might be interested enough to watch and see
what he might do, but he did not fear them. Let them come for
him, if they dared.

He felt Le Duc's presence before he saw him, and he heard
the even breathing that told him the man was asleep. Perfect.
He would slip in, take a bit more of what was his due—then he
would wake the man and they would make their way into the
tunnels beneath the temple. Montrovant's thirst was growing,
itching at the edges of his control, and it would be good to feed—
however little he was able to take. It would sharpen his senses.

Le Duc stirred slightly as Montrovant approached, but he
did not wake. Montrovant placed a strong hand behind the
man's head and drew Le Duc's throat to his lips. He felt the
man stiffen, saw the eyes fly open wide, but it was too late even
to mutter a muffled protest. Montrovant had locked on, and
his mind was in control. Though he trembled and quivered in
Montrovant's strong arms, Le Duc made no sound.

Forcing himself to release more quickly than he would
have liked, Montrovant lowered his servant back to the cot and
stood over him, watching. Le Duc was pale, his eyes had closed,
and his breathing was shallow, but still regular. Their bond of
blood was so close that Montrovant could still feel the pulse of
Le Duc's blood as it made its way to and from the heart. The
salty, coppery taste lingered on his tongue, and he savored the
moment. If the ancient one were correct, it might be his last
meal.

Montrovant smiled, suddenly, and reached out to grab Le
Duc by the shoulder, drawing him to a sitting position and
holding him there. "Jeanne," he said softly. "Arise. We have
work to do this night."

Le Duc's eyes opened, but they were glazed, as if he were looking straight at—and through—Montrovant's face. No comprehension. Then the expression altered subtly, and Le Duc's shifty, nervous features began their normal dance, avoiding direct contact with Montrovant's gaze and seeking to orient his mind to its present circumstances.

"What is it that you want?" the man asked.

"We are going on a little adventure, Jeanne," Montrovant explained. "There are tunnels and vaults beneath this temple, and there are things hidden there that I would like to find. You are going to come with me. I will have to concentrate on my search, and I will need someone to watch my back and to keep a lookout for Father Santos and his friends."

Le Duc eyed him curiously, and he realized that the man was probably not even aware of Father Santos's existence. It didn't matter. The less he knew, the less he suspected, the better, even though Montrovant could control him easily. The last thing he needed was a recalcitrant slave. He would find out about Santos and his minions soon enough if they encountered them in those dark tunnels.

"Come," Montrovant said, holding out his hand to help Le Duc to rise. "I don't have much time before I must leave you."

Le Duc nodded, rising quickly and slipping into his boots and a robe. Montrovant noted with approval that the man tucked his sword beneath that robe before turning and signaling that he was ready to depart. There was no telling what they might encounter on the lower levels, and even the weak sword arm of a human might make the difference in a tight situation. It would make him last longer, should he need to be sacrificed for the seconds necessary to escape.

Montrovant sent Le Duc into the passageway ahead of him. Though there was a strict curfew, Le Duc would still command less attention, should he be spotted, than Montrovant himself. De Payen required a good night's rest of each and every knight under his control. It was their "sacred responsibility" to be strong and ready to fight at a moment's notice. For once, rather than chuckling under his breath at the notion, Montrovant was pleased. It meant that most of the inhabitants of the mosque would be sleeping, or deep in meditation and prayer. They were unlikely to hear him moving about, once he got beyond the main floor.

Le Duc moved unerringly through the darkness, and Montrovant followed. Something was happening, something he had no explanation for. He could sense it, a menacing, powerful emanation that rose through the floor and nibbled at the corners of his mind. He felt a deep, rhythmic pounding seeping through the stone beneath his feet, and he had the odd sensation that it was a heartbeat—the heartbeat of the temple.

Stopping, Montrovant put his hand out to steady himself against the wall. His thoughts had wandered, and the sudden notion that he was being duped, that he might be walking into a trap, hit him like a sledgehammer. What was that damnable *pounding*? The ancient had mentioned nothing of the nature of the danger he would face in those tunnels—was he a fool to disregard the warning?

"What is it?" Le Duc whispered softly, turning to watch Montrovant curiously. There was fear in the man's eyes, but behind it Montrovant saw the cold calculation of a snake. Le Duc was seeking weakness in his new master, a means of bettering his own position. This one would have to be watched closely.

"It is nothing," Montrovant replied. "Quickly, we must get below."

Le Duc watched him for a second longer, then nodded, turning back toward the stairs that led to the labyrinthine tunnels below. Montrovant saw him tense, just for a second, and knew that the pounding had reached Le Duc's lesser sensory perception. It had grown from a tingling vibration to a steady throbbing beat as they descended through the temple. If it grew much louder, Montrovant thought, it would wake the entire temple.

They continued downward, plastering themselves against the stone walls to either side of the stairs. There was no indication of life below, other than the sound, and the closer they came to it, the harder it grew for Montrovant to concentrate. Shadows leapt about the periphery of his vision to mock him, and his thoughts seemed intent on losing coherency, despite his efforts at control.

Le Duc seemed not to feel the effects of the sound as strongly, but it was clear that the man was nearly mesmerized by the power of it all the same. He was not used to assaults of an other-than-human nature, and his defenses were not strong. A sickly, greenish glow seeped up from below. Though there was a clinging malevolence alive in that luminescence, it was bright and powerful.

Montrovant stopped again. The sounds had changed, or his perception of them had deepened. It was not a pounding, but a series of guttural words spoken with unbelievable force. He was drawn into the beat, dragged through the chant as he fought vainly to understand the meaning of those words. There were names, some of them angelic, others he'd never heard, but each drew images instantly from his memory—images so vivid that he felt his limbs growing weak.

Pressing himself tightly into the stone, he concentrated his will. This would not happen. He would not be led about like a leashed animal. He fought free of the cloying, grasping tendrils of the sound, grasped Le Duc suddenly by the wrist and spun the man to face him. He dropped his lips to the man's throat quickly. His fangs sank through Le Duc's flesh for the second time that night, and he and he drew forth just enough to sustain him—just enough to break free of the hold of the strange chanting from below.

There was a disturbance in the sound, and Montrovant knew they had sensed his presence. Taking Le Duc by one arm, he turned and began to drag the man bodily up the stairs. His sudden attack, and the loss of yet more blood, had sapped Le Duc's strength.

Montrovant cursed the added delay, but he still needed someone on the inside, and he certainly couldn't leave Le Duc for Santos to find. The man knew too much already. It was all or nothing, escape or destruction.

Taking the stairs at a dead run, Le Duc slung over his shoulder like a sack of grain, Montrovant made it to the upper floor in three long, leaping bounds. He slipped quickly into the passageway that led to Le Duc's chamber, and moved away from the stairs. There was no sound behind them, but he could sense the malevolent energy that permeated the lower levels seeping upward slowly. He knew there was a dark intelligence behind that energy, and he knew it was seeking him.

He paused, drawing back into a shadowed alcove and placing a hand over Le Duc's mouth to silence any sound. Even with the threat that rose from below, he couldn't risk being spotted by de Payen or one of his men. If that were to happen, even Le Duc would be of no use to him. He waited what seemed an eternity, but no door opened, and no footsteps clattered in the passageway.

Montrovant melted from the shadows and made his way quickly to Le Duc's door, opening it with his free hand and dragging the man inside. He dropped his burden roughly across the hard cot that lined the wall and turned back toward the door, concentrating.

The essence of whatever had followed them was gone. The stone of the temple was as silent as a tomb. There was no vibration, no sickly light. Nothing.

"What is it, Lord?" Le Duc croaked from where he lay. "What happened?"

Turning back to his servant, Montrovant frowned. "I'm not certain," he said at last. "One thing I know; they expected me."

"Who are they?" Le Duc's strength was returning, and the gleam of curiosity was back in his eye. Montrovant sensed that the man was seeking a weakness, even after what had happened, an advantage that might be gained. He marvelled at the smaller man's resiliency and courage.

"I wish that I knew," he answered. "I need to know what they are doing, what they are guarding. There is not much time."

"I will go to them," Le Duc said simply. "They sensed you, but I do not believe that they sensed me."

Montrovant's frown deepened. He concentrated on remembering. Was it possible that Le Duc was correct? If so, there might still be hope. He knew that what they'd experienced had been aimed at him specifically, but he couldn't remember anything that would have indicated a knowledge of Le Duc's presence.

"Be careful, Jeanne." Montrovant said at last. "Find out what you can, but take no risks. They can use you to find me—and that would be a mistake. It would be a mistake for them, and for you...do you understand?"

Le Duc didn't speak, but he nodded almost imperceptibly.

"You must also watch de Payen," Montrovant continued. "He will not want you associating with Father Santos, and he will not like the idea that you do things on your own. Discipline is very important to him. Your presence here is too important to me to be risked by carelessness. There is time for caution. Take that time and use it to your advantage."

"You will find," Le Duc said softly, "that I am not a careless man, my Lord."

Montrovant stared at him for a moment longer, trying to read the emotion behind the words. He knew he could have invaded Le Duc's thoughts and forced the issue, but something held him back. He liked this one's spirit.

"I will see you soon, then," he replied, moving to the window.

Without a further word, he launched himself into the night. He felt Le Duc's eyes on his back, watching as he disappeared. The sensation was like the prickling of sharp ice daggers between his shoulders.

Before he reached the ground, he sensed the others, those who'd watched him as he entered the mosque. By the time they registered in his mind, it was too late to avoid them. Shadows drowned the moonlight, and something powerful and cold grasped his mind. He tried to fight, tried to cry out for help, but he could not. Darkness swallowed him, and the night returned to its silence as he spiralled down and away...dropping from consciousness.

TEN

Montrovant awoke to a rustling sound, and the first impression that came to his mind was that of a huge swarm of bats. It was dark, and the comforting sensation of thick walls of stone surrounded him. Wherever he was, he was at least safe from the sunlight. He lay still a moment longer, orienting himself. He didn't want whoever had taken him to know he was aware until *he* had chosen the moment. He nearly leaped to his feet in shock when the ancient one spoke.

"You do not listen well, Solomon."

Rising to a sitting position, Montrovant looked about himself quickly. They sat in the center of a small cavern hollowed from the center of a mountain, or a hillside. Montrovant could feel the weight of the stone above them. He and the old one were not alone. There were others surrounding them, a large circle of glowing eyes and yellowed teeth. Nosferatu. He knew that they couldn't be of the ancient's clan, but it was obvious that some arrangement had been agreed upon.

For the moment he sensed no danger in his position, despite the method of his arrival. Montrovant turned his gaze back to meet the eyes of the old one, dismissing the others for the moment.

"I have returned to Jerusalem for a reason, as well you know," he retorted. "I have seen things that lead me to believe that I may succeed where others have failed. You claim to help, but your help comes in riddles and warnings. With such help, I had no choice in my actions—my knowledge of Santos and his powers is limited."

"There are always choices," the old one laughed. His eyes

glittered brightly in the darkness, illuminated by some inner light. "The problem is not that there are no choices, but that you refuse to see any choice that does not lead you down the road you have already decided upon. You have chosen the outcome of it all, as well, and there is no way you can be certain you have not chosen foolishly.

"You are so intent on this *grail* you seek that you are blinded to the world around you. There are signs of most dangers waiting for those who know how to look. This quest has robbed you of your sense, and it will be your undoing if you continue as you have begun. Last night was nearly your last upon the earth."

"Who is he?" Montrovant asked, changing tacks. He decided against asking how the old one would know what he'd done the night before. It was enough to realize that he did.

"Santos," he asked, "who—what—is he really? I have never felt a power like that from any who were not damned as I. There was a force behind those voices, behind their chant. It shook the very stone of the temple itself, and yet it seemed to speak only to me."

"Santos is the tool of an ancient evil," the old one said softly. "I felt the touch of his power myself, long ago. He is not one to trifle with, and if anything he is even more single-minded in his purpose than yourself. Of course, that makes it his greatest weakness. His is not the power of the night, but of words and form. He also does not have me to point out his mistakes."

"He is a guardian," Montrovant said quickly. "I have sensed this. But does he guard what I think he does?"

"He is a guardian, yes, but you do not have a complete picture of what that entails. I'm not certain that you are ready for so much. Santos truly believes in what he does as the right course. He was created for this purpose, and he is quite adept at fulfilling the responsibilities of his post."

"I am ready for anything you might be able to share with me, old one," Montrovant grated. "Who are you?" he added. "You speak of these others as though you've known them a very long time—you have mentioned my sire, Euginio, by his true name—and yet you give no name to yourself.

"I dislike dealing with those who hide their nature. How shall I call you, and what is your stake in all of this?"

"I have no stake in anything these days beyond entertainment," was the quick answer. "I have no purpose other than to fill my days with reasons to continue on into further days. You will understand that, should you last the lifetimes that I have. Boredom and entropy are the greatest enemies our kind face. I consider myself somewhat of an expert in entertainment."

He hesitated for a moment, then added, "I hope I am around to discuss this with you in a couple of hundred years. One such as you will no doubt have some truly interesting tales to tell by then. That is one of the reasons I bother to explain myself."

"Your name," Montrovant insisted.

"I do not give my true name," the ancient one replied, growing suddenly serious, "and it would be a good practice for you to learn to keep yours a deeper secret, as well. It is the power of your name that was almost your undoing in the temple, and Santos is not the only power in the world who can make use of it.

"All language emanates from a single source, and at the base of things are their true names. Much like your essence, your true name is an intimate part of your makeup. There is a great strength in the knowledge of these names and the ancient tongue that spawned them. Santos, as he is now called, knows the use of this power. He may be the most adept at it still walking the earth."

"You know my name, and you have not used it to control me," Montrovant countered.

"I do not need your name, Solomon, as well you know. Were Euginio here, it would be the same with him. He is old, I am older. You are like a child to me in many aspects. We have our own ways, you and I, but they are not the ways of the mystic."

Montrovant grew silent, waiting. He knew there was more to hear, but he didn't know the proper questions to elicit a useful response. The ancient one was more irritating than a mortal.

"Some call me Kli Kodesh," the old one said at last, and the name set Montrovant's mind awhirl. He had heard that name spoken in fear, contempt, and wonder since the earliest days of his embrace. Euginio had told him tales of Kli Kodesh long before the monastery had claimed him—before Montrovant had set off into the world on his own.

"Kli Kodesh," he breathed. "I should have known. If it were anyone, it would be you who found me here. I'd thought you long gone from the earth, from the way Euginio spoke."

"You have heard the name?" The grin on Kli Kodesh's face was mischievous. "I thought Gino might remember me. He spoke of you, last time I saw him, and I have looked forward ever since to the time we would meet."

"He spoke of you, as well," Montrovant replied, wondering at the comfortable intimacy with which this ancient creature spoke the name of his sire. Measuring his thoughts, Montrovant continued. "He named you a lunatic of great power. He said your mind was filled with visions of fantasy worlds and beings that never existed. He told me that you spoke with Christ. He also told me he believed you must have fallen to dust by now from sheer madness."

Kli Kodesh's expression grew distant, suddenly, and a wistful smile replaced his grin. "Yes," he said at last. "Those things would be an apt description, I suppose, given that they spring from incomplete tales and whispered legends. All except the dust, of course. I assure you, there are a few amusing years left in this old frame."

"Did you?" Montrovant asked bluntly, not wishing to fall into a discussion of times and events he cared nothing about.

"Did I what?" Kli Kodesh turned to stare at him, shocked back to the moment by Montrovant's question.

"Speak with the Christ," Montrovant said almost impatiently. For one so old, the ancient seemed hardly aware of his surroundings. In a human, this would be expected from an elder; but among the damned, age brought power.

"Of course. Did your sire not say it was so? I not only spoke with him, I traveled with him, shared bread and prayer with him, and loved him. Not that any of it is business of yours. You forget yourself, Solomon, but I will forgive you. Those were interesting times indeed. One day when your 'quest' does not call you so strongly, and we have a few years to sit around and catch up on things, I'll tell you about him."

Montrovant sat back, stunned. He'd known Kli Kodesh was ancient, but it had never occurred to him just *how* ancient. He'd thought the stories merely the trappings of a very powerful madman, but in the ancient's presence, he had difficulty in picturing it that way.

There was something hidden about Kli Kodesh, something odd, but it was not the taint of madness. Whatever else might be true of what he'd heard, it would seem that the madness was exaggerated. While this was true, the age had been understated, and the power. Montrovant found himself liking this ancient buffoon of a vampire a bit more than he'd counted on. There was much to be said for his opinions on entertainment, and it occurred to Montrovant that Euginio would have done well to listen to those words a bit more carefully himself.

"You sought the grail," Montrovant broke in, half in question, half accusingly. "The tales of your quest were the inspiration that drew me back here."

"I have done a great many foolish things," Kli Kodesh replied. "That is one of them. I sought a power that I have since come to realize lies within my own mind. There was no need of the symbol, a simple cup, to bring it to life. I felt that a piece of something that had been important to me in my daylight life might bring me all that I sought in this second life. What I found was that my time had been spent seeking children's tales. I decided not to spend my second chance at eternity so readily."

"You speak in riddles," Montrovant said. "Did you find the grail? If not, how could you have come to these conclusions, and what did you do with it?"

"I found what I sought."

"Father Santos guards something of great power and importance beneath that temple," Montrovant said angrily. "If it isn't the Grail, if there *is* no grail, then what is in those caverns?"

"I do not know," Kli Kodesh answered simply. "I attempted to enter those caverns, much as you yourself, and I met a similar result. I was too powerful for him to control, but I could not gain entrance. I decided that the continuation of my existence was more important to me than the answers I might find, once inside. Now I find that there may be some entertainment to be had in renewing that quest."

"You quit." Montrovant knew that the venom in his voice was a mistake, that the other could end his existence as surely and easily as he himself might snuff a candle-flame, but he couldn't help himself. He was disgusted that any could come so close to such power, then cast it aside in fear.

"I did."

"I am not prone to quitting," Montrovant went on. "I have a goal, a purpose, that drives me from sunset to sunset. What drives you, old one? What is there left, if you've given up your dreams?"

Kli Kodesh laughed then, and the sound chilled Montrovant through to the bone. Rising and dancing suddenly in a tight circle, Kli Kodesh grinned down at him. That grin was more skull than face, and the eyes were so distant and empty that stars seemed to whirl in the depths of his skull. Montrovant jerked his gaze from that trap.

"So young, so certain of yourself," Kli Kodesh cackled. The sudden unpredictability of his behavior set Montrovant's senses on edge. Perhaps Euginio hadn't been so far from the mark.

"You believe a symbol of the Christ can bring you power, and yet you miss the point entirely. Do you really suppose that Jesus was the most powerful entity of his day? Do you not understand that his knowledge came from others, that others— truly ancient powers—walked the earth long before his birth? Did they leave their magic in a cup for you to drink? Did they depart at all, or was it the Christ who fled?

"I walked with him, Solomon, and I learned from him. His power was great, and his sacrifice was a true one. You may believe in his Godhood if you like, or not—it makes no difference to me—but his power did not come from relics, or from prayer. It came from within his own mind—his essence. You seek that power, and you claim a desire to sacrifice for your sire—for your clan. You sacrifice nothing. You don't come at it with sincerity, but with greed. It is your own gain you seek, and that is why you will find nothing.

"That is the secret that I lost, then found again, all during my time on the road. I searched for the Grail, and I saw that cup when it was first handed to him, saw the wine spilled into its depths and heard the words you set such store in. 'Drink, this is my blood,' a very close quote, despite the inaccuracy of most of the Gospels. Many things happened on that road, Solomon. Miracles took place that will never be repeated, but they were generated by a man, not a relic.

"Did you think he was being symbolic and deep? He spoke to *me*, Solomon. He offered, and I received. 'Drink, this is my blood,' he said, and I did. I walked that road with him; but when his father was young, I was already old. You would not believe the savor of that draught, Solomon. You could not comprehend what it brought to my mind."

Montrovant rose, backing toward the wall, but in that instant he became aware, once more, of the others. He heard hissing, sibilant voices, and the feather-touch of gibbering, insane thoughts tickled at the barriers surrounding his mind. They were servants, entwined so deeply in Kli Kodesh's madness that they had created a pocket of surreality he found it difficult to resist. It was like a vortex, drawing him in. He could sense that they were not mad, but in that instant, reality had warped.

"I see that Euginio was not so far from the truth in his tales of you," Montrovant said, expecting the words to be his last. "Is this the end, then? Did you only bring me here to entertain you for a few moments before you cast me to your ghouls? Not much of interest in such trivial games in the face of eternity."

Kli Kodesh's features shifted magically back to the serene, contemplative expression Montrovant had first witnessed, and the ancient one took a step forward, holding out his hand. The transformation was so swift, and so false in its semblance of normality, that it caused Montrovant to shudder anew.

"I am sorry. I sometimes forget...things. I brought you here to explain myself, and I'm afraid that I may have confused you further. I have that effect on others."

"There is no confusion here, except that within your own mind, Kli Kodesh. You spout madness. You wish me to believe, now, that you drank the very blood of the Christ? How would that be possible? How could you not have been transformed?"

"I have been," was the simple answer. "I walk by the light of day—my thirst is sated. I tell you this, though I know you will not believe. I have not fed on the blood of a human being since the Christ walked the earth, and yet I endure. There is no hunger, only the eternal wait for His return. That, and my new quest—the quest for that which can keep me sane. Entertainment. For that, I thank you; and for that you have kept your life, such as it is."

"If you are as old as that, as powerful," Montrovant took a tentative step forward, "then tell me Santos's secret. You must know how to reach those vaults."

"Did I not tell you that there were powers more ancient, more powerful, than the Christ, whose blood you seek? Santos was created in a time before any you have known of were born, died, or walked on into the shadows. I am ancient, but I was a child when Santos came to be. He was created by an ancient whose name I've learned was Hermes. Not the first to bear that name, certainly, and it is undoubtedly not a true name, but it gives you a point to concentrate on. Egypt."

"Egypt?" Montrovant scowled. "How does knowing Santos is an Egyptian help me?"

Kli Kodesh appeared to be growing impatient, and his eyes were dancing again, in agitation. "You must *listen* Solomon. I will provide you the keys, but the locks are yours to fathom. You must find his name. The power to defeat him, the power to enter those vaults, lies in the simple word that was affixed to him at birth."

"You know this name?" Montrovant asked excitedly.

"It is possible, but not relevant," Kli Kodesh grinned. "The entertainment lies in your own quest, not in any help I might provide. You must seek your own answers. Be glad that I have decided that I will not hinder you."

Montrovant grew silent. He could not force an answer from Kli Kodesh, and he was less than certain that the old one's apparent stability would hold. "Am I free to go, then?" he asked softly.

"You may if you wish," Kli Kodesh answered almost dismissively. "You will find it a bit uncomfortable, though, I believe."

"Uncomfortable?"

"It is morning, Solomon," Kli Kodesh said softly. "I have been holding that knowledge from you, giving you the energy to continue our conversation. I knew that you would not take my words for their face value, and so I have provided a bit of proof. You see that I am not affected by the hour. This place is safe—you are welcome to sleep here, beneath the mountain. We will watch over you until the sun falls."

Montrovant sensed that Kli Kodesh spoke the truth. The lethargy hit him with sudden force, nearly bringing him to his knees. He felt the draw of the earth, and though he fought to remain alert, the torpor seized his limbs, and he fell back softly. He managed to keep his eyes open long enough to see Kli Kodesh standing above him, watching, but he could not force himself to move. More of Kli Kodesh's power?

The others danced about madly in the shadows, flickering across the edges of his vision like a flock of enormous bats. Kli Kodesh was powerful indeed if he could hold the lot of them from the sleep the day should have brought. Or perhaps he'd fed them from his own blood. Perhaps they shared his madness.

"Sleep well, Solomon," Kli Kodesh's words seeped through his thoughts. "Rest. You will need your strength for that which is to come. Seek the books in the temple—you will find that which you seek within the halls of Baldwin."

Blackness rose to consume him, and the room spun away, leaving him isolated and alone.

That was how he found himself when he awoke. He made his way through a side tunnel from the room, sensing the upward slope of the tunnel, and when he came to the surface of the desert, he could see the brilliant twinkling of stars in the sky.

Kli Kodesh and his Nosferatu minions were nowhere to be seen. There was the faintest hint of their presence lingering in the stone, but Montrovant stood alone, thinking.

Shaking his head, he softly cursed the night. First he'd come up against powers he couldn't understand or comprehend; now he was forced to combat those forces with the words of a madman for a guide. Perhaps Euginio was right. Perhaps he was a fool.

With a sudden leap, he took to the sky, the transformation grindingly painful and comfortably familiar all at once. He needed to return to the city, to feed, and to plan. He blended with the inky darkness, a shadow against the moon. Below, standing on a mound of stone and sand, Kli Kodesh watched, and he smiled. The entertainment had only just begun.

ELEVEN

Le Duc had not managed a moment of sleep after Montrovant's dramatic exit from his balcony. His mind was in a turmoil, fear battling with greed, desire battling with the first blossoming of loyalty that had ever entered his mind. Or was loyalty even a factor? It seemed he would be controlled whether it was his desire or not. It could hardly be considered a choice.

He was no fool. Montrovant was the most powerful being he'd ever encountered. Despite the cold thrill of fear that screeched through him as his imagination toyed with his future, that power drew him to the man. Jeanne had always had something of a death-wish; who was he to complain when that wish came true? If such a one wanted to throw in his lot with Jeanne Le Duc, then that was a very good thing indeed.

There had been precious few alliances worth the time or effort during the span of his years. He disliked the notion of being little more than a servant, but it appeared that there might be more in store for his future, and he put great stock in planning for the years to come.

It was the control that troubled him. He had none, not over his life, nor the situation at hand. That was a factor that would have to change, were this odd partnership to continue. He could follow a leader as well as any other, but slavery was out of the question. He would have to let Montrovant know how he felt, but the question was, how?

The only thing he might possibly construe as a weakness in Montrovant was the reaction he'd witnessed on the stairs leading to the lower levels of the temple. Something down there was powerful enough to scare even the dark one; but what could it be, and could it be used to Le Duc's advantage? If it had been enough to set Montrovant to flight, what would it do to one such as Le Duc? There was only one certain way to find the answer to that, and that was to do as he'd been instructed.

He would have to make his way to those lower levels, preferably by day, and he would have to find what it was that Montrovant sought. Beyond that his hopes lay in the possibility that he would be able to discover more than Montrovant believed he would. He had not been told where to stop, and that left the margin for a bit of spying of his own.

Whatever was down there, it had not been paying much attention to Jeanne Le Duc when he'd last dropped in, and that would prove a mistake, if it were to be repeated upon his return. He might not have any strange abilities, or be able to leap from temple windows into the night sky without falling to his death, but he had a sharp wit and a sharper blade that it would be best not to ignore, even minus a few flagons of his own blood.

That was another issue to be taken up with his new lord. As a child, he'd been told the legends of the Vampyr. He'd heard tales of dark Lilith swooping from the night sky to carry off children, and of the dead rising to feast on the blood of the living. He'd thought them just that—legends. In the days of his youth he'd not been truly frightened by the stories because he'd been able to distinguish the lack of that fear in the adults telling the tales. None of them, he now concluded, had met one such as Montrovant. The boundaries of his world would have to be redefined, it seemed. Legends would need to be pushed a bit further into the void and he would have to come to grips with things that had previously lain beyond that barrier. He would have to find a way that his mind could cope with and reconcile this new knowledge.

Rising early, Le Duc went about his morning rituals, took his breakfast with the others after prayer, and managed, with a bit of quick thinking, to get himself assigned to work in the stable for the day. None of the others liked that detail—Le Duc didn't blame them. The stables were beneath the temple, dark and dank. Cleaning was no easy task, since everything that was removed from the stalls would have to be hauled to the surface in small carts. Stable detail was often handed out as penance.

Most of de Payen's knights had come from royal families. None of these men had been accustomed to caring for their own animals, or cleaning after themselves. De Payen's discipline was a harsh lesson for such as these. Though Le Duc came from nobility, he'd been the bastard child of a minor noble. He'd seen his share of manual labor as a boy, and the skill of his sword arm was the only thing that had won him his freedom. He'd signed on with his uncle's army as a lad of sixteen and never looked back.

His plan was simple. It was only a short distance from the stables to the stairs he and Montrovant had descended so disastrously the night before, and since only a small number of men would be on the detail with him, and none of them in a mood to pay much attention to their surroundings, he thought he'd be able to find a moment to do a bit of preliminary exploring. At the very least, he hoped to get a glimpse of those who lived in the tunnels below.

He'd heard stories, rumors that were whispered between weapons practice and meals. De Payen was not the only master in the mosque, and apparently the huge knight was not pleased by that fact. Another factor to be used in his favor, or another obstacle to overcome? Only time would tell. Once he had more information on what was going on beneath their feet, he might have more answers.

He moved slowly through the halls and down to the stables with his two companions, trying not to appear too eager for what was to come. Pierre Cardin joined him, as did two of the servants, and he wished it had been anyone but Cardin. The man had never trusted him, and with more planned than just stable cleaning, Cardin would be the worst possible choice of those who might witness his actions.

Le Duc was trying to make sense of de Payen's insistence that his knights perform their own menial labor. He knew it had something to do with discipline, or de Payen's version of it. Their leader told him that, in battle, the only thing more important to a knight than his weapon was his mount—that it was important to be as familiar with the animals as possible.

Familiarity with the animals was one thing, but familiarity with their dung a completely different matter.

Le Duc had always believed in the method of riding the animal until it was ready to drop, then taking another. It was a habit he'd paid dearly for during his short stint in his father's guard. Horses were not cheaply come by. For the moment, he did not complain. The excuse to go below was exactly what he'd needed, and he grabbed the gear that was provided and went about his work quickly and efficiently, if not enthusiastically. He would need to be done with the section assigned to him well ahead of the others if he was to have the time to look around. It was one time in which his upbringing served him well. He had a lot more experience in stables than most of the others.

He moved steadily from stall to stall, hauling in grain and water and cleaning out the manure. The process was a slow one. The stench began to get to him after only a short time, and he realized that the lack of sleep and the loss of blood had weakened him further than he'd imagined. He wondered what Montrovant got from what he'd stolen. He rubbed at the raw spot on his throat and stopped to catch his breath.

Luckily, neither Cardin nor the servants seemed in any great hurry to get back to the upper levels. Cardin, Le Duc knew, was a lover of animals. He probably found something to enjoy in this dirty, monotonous task. He wished he could be so lucky. Jeanne found nothing but frustration. The animals tended to shy away from him, being uncooperative and surly. He cuffed more than one, and once he caught Cardin scowling at him as though he might say something. Le Duc met the man's gaze steadily and waited, almost hoping something would be said. Anything would be better than hauling off horse droppings. He knew that any fighting between knights of the order would result in punishment—likely another tour of the stables—but at that moment the distraction would have been well worth the trouble.

Cardin turned away without speaking, and Le Duc went back to work with a vengeance. He turned his anger to the task at hand, and he found that his strength was returning as he found the rhythm of the work. It was well ahead of his allotted time when he rested the handle of his cart on the ground for the final time and set aside his shovel.

He was sweating profusely, and the grime matted his hair and clung wetly to his boots. He wiped his eyes with the sleeve of his shirt, feeling the burn of the salt as he ground it deeper into his skin with the soaked material. There was light, but it was dim, and the perspiration had cloaked each torch with rainbows, blurring Le Duc's sight.

He slipped away to the right, steering clear of Cardin's area, and found himself facing a large tunnel that led inward. Considering the slope, and the angle of the passageway in relation to the stable entrance, it had to be the same that had lain at the bottom of the stairs he'd climbed the night before. The answers he needed waited ahead of him in the darkness, and with a last look over his shoulder to be certain he wasn't noticed, he slid into the shadows. If any asked, he could say he'd gone in search of something to drink or had had to relieve himself.

Cardin and the others would be too tired to question him, and who else would know? Such labor as he'd just completed was a torture to them all. They'd readily forgive any slip of discipline associated with it, even if de Payen would not.

He passed several branching tunnels as he moved toward the center of the lower levels, some with doors, others wide open. There were small alcoves carved into the stone of the tunnels, and sconces holding lit torches lined the walls. It would make a great place for an ambush, he thought to himself, and that thought doubled his caution as he made his way further in. There wasn't much time, and so far he'd seen nothing worth a second glance.

Suddenly the echo of footsteps rang through the silence, and Le Duc ducked into one of the small alcoves, secreting himself just out of sight and waiting. He could hear voices, one sibilant and silky, the other light—almost airy. He couldn't make out the words, but the sounds were growing closer. Heart pounding, he drew himself more fully into the shadows, pressing firmly against the cold stone at his back.

A sense of dread had dropped over him like a cloak the

second the silky tones of the first voice had reached his ears, and he felt himself trembling against the stone, praying to a God he'd long set by the wayside on any but a cursory level. Even as they drew near, he could make out none of what they were saying. They were speaking in a short, guttural language that he did not understand. He couldn't ever remember hearing anything quite so foul spewing from the mouth of a man, and the unfamiliar darkness of their language blended itself with his inability to see who or what they might be, compounding his fear.

Their steps came level with the alcove where Le Duc cowered, then continued on beyond it. He was preparing to draw a breath in relief when the steps suddenly stopped and the voices grew quiet. A soft, tingling sensation transited his spine, and he felt as though something were poking at his mind. He concentrated, blanking his thoughts, becoming as much one with the wall behind him as he could manage. He felt the hammering of his heart like the tolling of a bell, and even as he fought to control his breathing it gasped from his throat like hot air from a bellows. He was certain it would be heard, but there was nothing to do but to hold the next and pray that he was wrong.

Eternities passed as he waited, and images floated through his mind, childhood fears, nightmares coming around for a second visit. He gripped the stone tightly, clawing so deeply into the cracks and crevices that met his grip that he felt the flesh separating from his nails...still he gripped tighter. The shadows swirled about him, the world dropped away and he saw endless spirals of darkness descending through the floor of the tunnel, winding away into surreal realms of madness that he could not quite comprehend.

Le Duc fought. He felt the grip on his mind, and he rebelled against it. Each image he replaced with one of his own. Each new horror that was dredged from his subconscious he met head on with a memory of daylight. He felt his sanity slipping, and that was the one thing he would never release. They might take his body, and whatever demons toyed with him might seek his soul, but his mind was his own. With a sudden insight, he smacked his head backward, cracking it on the stone wall and sending a blinding white rush of pain blossoming through his failing consciousness.

The sensations that had haunted him departed as suddenly as they had invaded, and Le Duc collapsed to his knees in the shadows. He brought one hand up to the quickly growing knot the wall had provided him, and he choked back the bile that threatened to spew from his throat. There would be plenty of time for sickness once he'd found his way back out of the tunnels.

There were no sounds in the passageway, and he sensed that he was alone, but he remained kneeling in the shadows for several moments longer, re-ordering his thoughts and drawing the shreds of his self-confidence about himself like a shroud. Such darkness. Such a challenge to his senses and his self-control.

It was personal now. Irrational as the thought was, he knew that whoever had done that to him, whoever had entered his mind and toyed with things that Jeanne Le Duc held dear, that person, or thing, would pay for its infraction. He didn't know how, but that was a matter for planning and deep thought. He stuck his head slowly out of the alcove, and seeing that he was indeed alone, he began to make his way back toward the stables.

This time he paused at each of the entrances along the way, checking the alcoves carefully and pulling open any unlocked doors to peer inside at whatever contents they might conceal. In one he found what seemed to be the answer to his dilemma. There were hooks along one wall of the room, a small table in the center, and on the hooks hung dark robes. The color was difficult to make out in the flickering light of the torches in the hall, but they seemed to be of a deep, dark brown—rippling with hidden swirls of color and glittering strangely.

He checked the hall in both directions, then slipped inside, grabbing the first of the robes he reached and tucking it beneath his own cloak. He would have to hide it better, once he got out of the tunnel. There was no way he could explain its presence to the others as they ascended to their quarters.

He exited the room, closing the door softly behind him,

and headed quickly and silently back the way he'd come. His thoughts were scattered, and his head was light—he wondered if he might be feverish. The combination of the lack of sleep, the morning's labor, and the confrontation in the tunnels had drained him more fully than he'd believed possible, yet his anger goaded him onward.

He would have to complete his day—weapons practice, confession, devotion, and the evening meal—all without drawing undue attention to himself. He reached the end of the tunnel, where he'd left his cart and shovel, and looked about carefully. He could see Cardin just finishing up his own wing, and, moving slowly and taking care to conceal the robe tucked under his arm, he made his way toward where the other man was bundling out a last load of manure.

Cardin was dripping with perspiration and not moving too quickly himself. No words passed between them, and that suited Le Duc just fine. He had never cared for Cardin, and he knew the feeling to be mutual. Their induction into the order had not changed this. They came from two different worlds, and no amount of 'camaraderie' would change that. They might fight side by side, but they would never be brothers.

They met the two servants on their way out and upward, and the small group exited the stables. The fresh air quickly brought new life to Le Duc's tired limbs. He hadn't been aware, until that moment, just how much he'd hated the stench of the horses, or how the labor had been dragging at his mind. He took in great gulps of air, and the sunlight that filtered through the temple windows energized his steps.

They separated, and he and Cardin made their way to their chambers. They had less than half an hour to get cleaned up and ready for weapons practice. It would be an intense two hours, and neither of them was prepared, after a morning's work like they'd shared, to face de Payen's wrath for tardiness. They needed all their energy for the practice itself.

Miraculously, Cardin either did not see the extra bulk that Le Duc had added to his clothing, or just did not have the energy to care about it. Jeanne made it to his chamber and inside, packing the robe carefully beneath the stiff mattress on his cot. With careful arrangement, he was able to obscure the extra bulk without causing the bunk to appear untidy.

He wasn't certain how he was going to use the robe to his advantage, but his instincts told him it was his key to the lower levels, and he wasn't about to give up any advantage that fate stuck in his path. He was beginning to wonder if there were not truly a God in Heaven, and if he himself were not more blessed than he'd believed. That would be an interesting thought if he was ever afforded the opportunity to give it serious thought.

He hurried to clean himself and buckled on his sword. Though weak, he felt refreshed enough to face most of the knights in one-on-one practice. Maybe even strong enough to hand out a lesson or two. He'd already garnered somewhat of a reputation for his quickness and agility in battle and the vicious concentration he applied to his swordplay.

As he joined the others in a preliminary prayer, then faced off with his first opponent, his mind drifted back to his cot, and to the tunnels beneath his feet. The night would bring some answers, one way or the other. As he moved skillfully across the practice field, pressing his opponent back toward the wall with a lightning-fast flurry of flashing steel, plans began to form. Smiling, he slipped past the other man's guard and jabbed his blade lightly against the chain-mail he wore for protection. The blade came to rest directly over the man's heart.

Far below, two figures made their way silently back down the passageway and into the catacombs beyond. Father Santos did not speak this time—all the words, all the preparations had been made. None of his followers would have anything useful to add. It was time to take matters more firmly into his own hands.

He watched the shadows carefully, spreading his senses out to encompass each bit of stone lining the corridor and every hidden alcove. Someone had been there that morning, and he'd almost had them—had almost broken their mind. The net had been falling into place when something had slammed into his thoughts like a hammer blow. There was no presence lurking as he passed back toward the vaults, but he couldn't erase the thought of that instant of pain, and the power behind it, from his mind. How could any being powerful enough to cause him such pain have slipped in past his guard, and why couldn't he sense them now?

He should have been more careful. He should have spread his guards further into the accesses of the tunnels, de Payen be damned, but he'd been arrogant. His control was as absolute as it had ever been, and there had seemed no need for over-zealous caution. Now, on the heels of his failure to lure the dark one into his clutches, another had come into his realm, alone, and had escaped unnoticed. He couldn't even say for certain what he faced, since the pain that had exploded through his mind had rendered him without any but mortal sight for a period of hours. It hadn't felt like another of the undead, but there was no way to be certain. And if not the damned, then who?

He'd not sent others to search the tunnels. None among them could face such a power as he'd felt alone, and there was, as yet, no indication that the intruder had posed any kind of actual threat. No sense sacrificing his followers until he knew that the sacrifice would do him good. Besides, curiosity was not an unknown factor among immortals. Whoever or whatever it might have been, his visitor might have had no more than passing interest in Santos, or the tunnels. Still, it wouldn't hurt to consult the oracle, or to draw in some further support, just in case.

He needed to take out the dark one first and foremost, but he couldn't afford to let this new threat roam his domain freely. The objects in his charge were too important, and the draw of that responsibility on his being was absolute. He had been created for a purpose. That purpose was the ultimate end-all of his existence, and he could not fail it and survive.

A quick wave of nostalgia passed through the dusty corridors of his mind. Other temples—dry and well-preserved walls, gold and jewels...more familiar gods. This place was not his home, and he yearned for the sands and sun of his people. It had been too long, far too long, since he'd walked among them. Since there had been any he knew to walk among.

He turned to the robed figure walking at his side and

grunted a command softly. Without acknowledgment, his companion turned off and made his way quickly down a side passage. Emir would spread the word, and the preparations would be made. Santos would find some answers this night, and he would put an end to these new threats troubling his little shadow-realm once and for all. All he needed were names, and he knew well enough how to come by them.

Pressing his hand into a section of stone, he stood silently as a panel opened inward in the tunnel wall. There was no sound, but the massive block of stone slid easily inward, and he slipped by it, pressing it closed behind him and leaving the wall as seamless and bare as he'd found it. Some of the secrets of home had made their way to this place. He'd seen to that.

Beyond lay the vaults, and he made his way past these as well. He would need to rest and to clear his mind if he were to reach his goals that night. What he'd planned was no small feat, even for one such as himself, and there were preparations to be made. He passed into the shadows behind a long, embroidered tapestry that hung from the ceiling of the cavern and reached nearly to the floor. It cut off the main chamber of the room from the smaller alcove beyond. The fabric fell heavily back into place as he passed.

In one corner of the shadowed cavern, on an altar of wood brought from lands far away and crafted carefully—carved with intricate symbols and draped with a cloth of the same oddly iridescent brown of Santos's followers' robes—the deep red glow of a pair of eyes flashed for just a second, then vanished.

TWELVE

Montrovant made his way slowly toward the temple, but he did not intend to visit Le Duc this night. The direct approach had failed, and it was time to bring some of the planning he'd done before returning to the Holy Land to bear. He wasn't without his assets, and Le Duc was only one of them. This was important because the man was, after all, only human, and there were limits beyond which he could not be physically pushed. There were many useful days and nights remaining to Le Duc, and Montrovant wanted him as healthy and alert as possible.

It was also important that de Payen not know where Le Duc's loyalties truly lay. The inside information Le Duc could supply would prove useful eventually, and there was no need to burn him out so quickly. Montrovant had no desire or intention of continuing as de Payen's personal angel. The order would grow, or fade into oblivion, on its own. Besides, there were other concerns that required more delicate handling. As his perspective on the situation grew clearer, the methods Montrovant chose for dealing with these concerns became, as a consequence, more complex.

Santos had proven more powerful than he could have imagined, and it seemed that to repeat his attempted entry to the lower levels of the temple might prove both foolhardy and fatal. This in mind, alternative plans had begun to form in the back of his mind, plans that did not involve such direct risk, but that would bring him as surely, and possibly more swiftly, to the ends he sought. Intrigue was an old game to him.

Father Santos had the superior power on his side, but he

shared one thing with Montrovant that was unavoidable. No one knew the truth of his existence. He desired—no, needed—secrecy. He could not let those in the upper levels of the temple know what was going on below. If it came to light that anything other than a religious commune resided in those tunnels, de Payen would never stand for it. Hugues might not be truly a power in Jerusalem, but he was well on his way. One thing that none could deny was his righteousness, and it would be that purity of spirit that would force Daimbert's hand. It would mean that, if de Payen wouldn't stand for Santos's presence, the Church would not be allowed to stand for it either.

The Patriarch might be inclined to side with Father Santos, and not to act against orders from Rome, but it would not matter. He was the religious focal point for the Christians of the city. If he made a decision, they would go with it, and if something came to light that was unholy, it would be his duty to stand against it. So much, in such a case, for secrecy. No matter the word from Rome; if the citizens and royalty of Jerusalem believed Daimbert was consorting with or approving of something evil, they would not hesitate to strip him of his power.

Montrovant made his way directly to the mosque. He didn't slip through the shadows, or skirt the main streets, but walked straight through the front door. He called out to the first servant to meet him and sent him scurrying to de Payen's chambers. He was through with midnight balcony escapades and shadowed entrances. None of this would exist were it not for him, and it was time to call in a few cards from those he'd bequeathed it to. The time had arrived for more direct control of the matter at hand, and he didn't intend to allow the edge to Santos in this. If one of them could walk freely in the city and the temple, there was no reason that they both could not. Santos would not be the one to step forward, risking his own position. It would be a stalemate.

The servant returned almost immediately, trembling with excitement, and he led the way down the corridor and up the stairs to de Payen's quarters. Montrovant snatched bits of thought from the young man's mind. It seemed that visitors for de Payen were rare enough—a visit in the middle of the night was beyond belief. The miracle was not that Montrovant had come at such an hour, but that de Payen was not only willing, but *eager* to see him.

Hugues was a private man. It had been so in his keep in France, and it was the same here. He believed in simplicity and devotion to his Lord. This didn't leave a lot of time for social occasions.

Montrovant could barely conceal his smile. Rumors would fly, now, and he would be their focus. Rather than worrying about being spotted skulking about in the shadows, he would walk among them openly. It felt right, somehow, to be back in the forefront of action. Shadows might be his home, but they did not suit him as well as the center stage.

He walked into de Payen's chambers without waiting for the servant to perform the introduction. It would be more fodder for the upcoming rumors, and it helped to solidify their impression of his position with their leader. He saw that Hugues had barely contained the urge to drop to his knees at his entrance, and he was fairly certain that the servant had seen it, as well.

"That will be all, Phillip," de Payen said quickly, and the young man reluctantly withdrew to the hall beyond, closing the door behind himself.

De Payen met Montrovant's eyes, his expression communicating his questions before the words could make it to his lips. It had been a long time since they'd last spoken, and much had happened.

Montrovant held up a hand to keep him silent, wanting to establish the mood and direction of the conversation himself before de Payen took it off on a tangent. There would be plenty of time to answer questions and set Hugues at ease once he'd finished with his own business.

"I have come with a warning," he said quickly. "You have done well, Hugues de Payen, but evil walks the very halls you have chosen for your own. You have accomplished more than you could have hoped, but the road ahead will be the hardest of your life."

De Payen stared at Montrovant in bewilderment. He'd

expected many things upon seeing his patron, but this had not been one of them.

"But—we devote ourselves to prayer daily, and only the pure ethics of work and the sword consume our time. When we are not on the road, we are here, working toward the end of increasing our worth in the eyes of our Lord. I have done nothing but that which I was tasked to do, yet you say evil has fallen upon us? Who among us contains this evil? I will strike it free myself."

"It is none of your knights, Hugues," Montrovant assured him. "It is another evil, a deeper evil. It has been here all along, awaiting one such as yourself to see through the veils of secrecy that keep it hidden. You know of the priest who inhabits the lower levels. You have seen him yourself. Did you not feel it seeping from him like the very stench of hell?"

"Father Santos?" De Payen's eyes narrowed as the words passed his lips. "But...he is a priest! I have seen him at prayer."

"You have seen him going through the motions of prayer," Montrovant corrected, "but you have seen no devotion to your Lord pass his lips. If you could hear the words he actually speaks, you would understand as fully as I what he is. He is an abomination and his presence here negates the good you are doing. It is a danger to you, and to your men—your souls are at risk, Hugues."

"But what can we do?" De Payen's eyes were wild. "He has the support of the Patriarch, and that of Baldwin himself. I cannot disobey their orders. I have been told that the chambers beneath the mosque are to be left to him for whatever purpose he sees fit."

"You would rather disobey the Commandments?" Montrovant asked, pausing to let the words sink in.

De Payen jerked as if he'd been slapped. His eyes blazed, and for an exquisitely extended moment, Montrovant believed he would snap. Montrovant held the reins in this relationship— sinner and saint, dark angel and mortal man, but even in this role, there were boundaries. He was stepping casually across the raw nerves of de Payen's faith, his insecurities and self-recriminations. He had questioned, in a few short words, the very essence of Hugues's makeup. The question was, would that makeup hold.

"I..." de Payen paused, sucked in a great heaving gulp of air, then took a step forward, ignoring the icy depths of Montrovant's gaze. "I obey my God in all things."

There was much more behind his words than simple outrage. There was a depth of faith beyond anything Montrovant had encountered in all the days of his life. Bernard believed, in his own way, but this man lived for God. He might be a warrior, his body and soul trained to end the lives of others for a cause, but that cause meant more to him than his own life—perhaps more than his soul.

"I do not blame you for what has happened here, Hugues," Montrovant continued, ignoring the man's outburst. "There is no way that you could have known, and that is why I am here. I do not doubt your faith. I have come to fulfill it. You have asked to be the strong arm of God, and this is the first true test of the strength of that arm."

De Payen's expression shifted miraculously from self-reprisal to wonder, then to a stone-set of pure purpose. "Tell me what I must do. I will gather my men, and we will take them by night...before they know what has hit them. If Daimbert wishes to punish us in the morning, then we will go with a clear heart. God will forgive us."

"He already has, Hugues," Montrovant said with a wide grin, "but midnight invasions will not serve your purpose. The evil you will face is no simple lack of faith, or sin performed in shadowed corners while the faithful's eyes are turned away. Santos is a minion of Satan himself, and his power is nothing to be taken lightly. You must defeat him at his own game. I will give you guidance."

De Payen hesitated. Subterfuge was not his way. He was made for direct confrontation, and that solution had answered every conflict to face him since a very young age. He gave Montrovant's words careful thought, but finally he nodded. He was willing to listen, but the expression he wore painted anything but a portrait of certainty.

"Do not worry, Hugues. There will be a time for action, and

that time will not be far in the future. First we must trap him in the light of God and expose him for what he is. Once his evil is common knowledge, the time for cleansing will be upon us. With the Church behind you there will be none to hold you back. You will be glorified for that which is to come, glorified in the eyes of man and God alike."

Montrovant nearly gagged as the sanctimonious drivel dribbled from his lips, but it had the proper effect on de Payen. Over-dramatization was the key in such an instance, and Montrovant played his part to the hilt. Each and every action had to appear of earth-shattering consequence to maintain the deception. Montrovant could almost imagine the glow of a halo surrounding his own brow as he spoke.

"Tell me what we must do, Lord. I have distrusted Father Santos since I first laid eyes on him. Now that you have exposed him to me, I can feel the dark touch of his presence through the very stone of the temple. I will not be able to sleep, nor to eat, until he has been brought down."

"You must keep up your strength," Montrovant chided softly. "I have heard you say the same to your men. It is your sacred duty to be at full strength when you are called, and how can one ever know when that moment might fall upon them? More than ever, you must be ready—you must keep your thoughts pure and focused."

"Tell me," de Payen replied.

"You must go to the lower levels," de Payen replied, "and find the answers for yourself. There are things taking place in those caverns, rites so unspeakable that they defy description in any terms I can freely use. You must go there secretly, and you must see for yourself. Once you have found the proof you need, it will be a simple enough matter to take that information to Daimbert. You are known as a man of truth among the Patriarch's men. If you say you have witnessed a thing, they will have to believe. Once exposed, Father Santos will find that even the misguided protection of Rome will fail. The flames are licking at his ankles, even now, and he does not realize it."

"I don't understand." De Payen's eyes dropped for a moment as he tried to reason something in his mind. "If Rome protects him, how can it be that he is evil? Is the Church not the support of the Lord on the Earth? There are mysteries, even within the Church, that I have no understanding of."

"Even the Pope began life as a man," Montrovant answered carefully. A slip here could set things sliding in directions in which he was not prepared to take them. "There are things in Rome older than the Holy Father, and there are things here in the Holy Land older still. Santos is one such, and the threads of his power are far-reaching. Do not let the deception he has so carefully set in place blind you to the truth, Hugues. Go and see for yourself."

"You are saying that the Holy Father does not know he supports this evil," de Payen replied, still trying to sort it out in his mind. He was obviously reluctant to oppose Rome, even if Rome were wrong.

Montrovant chose not to reply. This was the crucial moment. He sensed that de Payen was on the brink of either accepting or rejecting all he had said, and he resisted the urge to send a tendril of his own thought out to sway the decision in his favor. It was more interesting to see how it would play out without his interference. He could always reverse things later—it was never truly a matter of control.

De Payen spun suddenly toward the wall, slamming the palm of his hand down onto the top of the table so forcefully that the wood bowed and nearly broke. It was an impressive display of strength.

"I am a fool!" he cried, spinning back to face Montrovant. "How could I not have known? How could I let that filth remain beneath my very feet and not have seen the connections? They live below, as does Satan. Santos—I will not call him Father again—has the very stink of hell about him. I knew it, but I let it pass. I forget, at times, that this is a war. I forget that we have been warned that the enemy will cloak himself in pleasing forms and walk among us. I remember that there is a God, but I forget too often that there is a Devil."

"You cannot blame yourself, Hugues. You followed the orders of the Church."

"There are higher authorities," Hugues muttered, his hands

now clasped behind his back as he paced about the room. "This is not the first age in which the Holy Father needed the aid of those around him to carry out God's will. I was so eager to please, so eager to follow orders, that I didn't see what stared me right in the face. My orders are, first and foremost, from God himself. I can read the Bible, and I know the histories as well as any. I should have known."

"It is enough that you see now," Montrovant said soothingly. "There is time to wipe this smear from the Holy Land—time to set things right. Perhaps Rome will never know the service you perform, but you will know. God will know. Is that not enough? Is that not all that matters?"

De Payen stopped his pacing. "You will know, as well," he said, "and again, I thank you. You appear to me when I need you most."

"I will not leave you this time, Hugues," Montrovant asserted. "I will make myself known in the city, for the time of your great triumph is at hand. We will see this through together and laugh about it over a flagon of wine when it is ended."

"I have decided to make a journey back to France, and then to Rome," de Payen said suddenly, deciding that the moment was right to reveal his plans. "I need to speak with Bernard, to build a true army of God, and to return with that army to continue my work. What we have done here is only a beginning, and even in this remote place others flock to our banner."

It was Montrovant's turn to be surprised, if only for a moment. He did not let his reaction show, but he waited, wondering where de Payen's words would lead him. When he'd spawned the idea of the Poor Knights, it had been nothing more than a vehicle toward his own end. It seemed that he might have chosen better than he'd known in de Payen. *Perhaps*, he grinned inwardly, *I've made history*. Kli Kodesh would be pleased by the entertainment.

De Payen went on, explaining his plans, the oath that he would have the knights swear to, and the code by which they would live. Montrovant listened, but his thoughts slipped away, downward, toward the depths of the temple. Somewhere below him lay the object of his desire. Before the grandiose plans of de

Payen could be allowed to bear fruit, Montrovant would have his own reward.

Montrovant's mind suddenly snapped to attention, and as he stiffened, de Payen stopped his discourse in mid-sentence. "What is it, Lord?" he asked quickly. "Is something wrong?"

"There is a disturbance below," Montrovant said softly. "Santos is performing his evil ceremonies even now. Can't you feel it, Hugues? It seeps through stone and darkness like a tide of blood. He is mocking you, and he is mocking God."

Hugues stood very still and his eyes grew cold and distant. Montrovant saw a shudder run through de Payen's frame, and for that instant he knew that somehow the man *did* feel what he felt. Whatever lies Montrovant might be weaving to his own end, naming Santos evil was not one of them. A darker force Montrovant had never encountered, nor more powerful.

As Montrovant concentrated, he began to unravel the veil that cloaked the power being set into motion. He felt a sudden tug at his mind, a sibilant mental whispering that drew at his being like a vortex, attempting to draw him into its spell. At first it was only a sensation, but then words slipped free of the energy. He began to sift those words, putting structure to phrases.

Your name, dark one, your name. You are called Montrovant, but this is not your name. Give me your name.

He fought free of the shadowy hold and made his way quickly to the door. He'd stayed too long, and Santos was making a second attempt to control him.

"I must go, Hugues," he said hurriedly. "This is not truly my fight. Take caution with Santos: he is not a man as you are, and there are things you do not yet understand about your own destiny."

"I will be careful," Hugues said gruffly, "but I will not hesitate. I will go this very night and I will witness this evil with my own eyes. When I have seen what the enemy has brought upon us, I will find a way to bring it to an end."

Montrovant nodded, then turned and disappeared down the corridor. He needed to get free of the mosque and put as much space as possible between Santos and himself. Kli Kodesh had said that the power of his true name would give the victory to his enemy, and Montrovant had no desire to test the veracity of the warning. It was bad enough that the ancient himself bandied it about so freely.

Le Duc was not aware that any others were moving about the levels of the knights' quarters. He knew the hour of the curfew was past, and he also knew the route and schedule of the guards. It was as rhythmic as the works of a German clock, a fault he'd meant to mention to de Payen on more than one occasion, but was now glad he'd kept to himself. The huge knight was proud of his security precautions, but he understood little of strategy.

That worked to Le Duc's advantage. As long as he was cautious, he knew that during certain hours he'd have only Santos and his followers to worry over. De Payen and the others would remain asleep and out of his hair, or would be devoting themselves to prayer. Even if he were spotted, it was likely that his punishment would be held over until the following day.

He'd removed the robe from beneath his mattress. There had been no real reason to hide it, but somehow he'd felt the need for secrecy. None of the others paid him any mind, let alone social calls, and he was responsible for all upkeep of his cubicle. There was little chance, short of a routine inspection, of any other entering his quarters.

He held the robe at arm's length, staring at it. The cloth felt oily to the touch, and he tucked it back under his own clothing reluctantly. It gave him an unclean sensation to have it so near his skin, but he had no other means of access to the lower levels. He only hoped that the original owner hadn't missed it yet.

He was still weary, but he'd slept from the moment evening devotion had ceased, and he felt that he had the strength to carry on. There was no time to be wasted, and he was fairly certain he couldn't have slept any longer. Too much was riding on the outcome of what he was about to attempt to allow his mind to shut down for long.

He opened his door carefully, inching his way slowly into the passage and listening for the tell-tale squeak of hinges, or the groaning of the wooden frame, that might give him away as he pulled the door closed behind him. Moments later he found reason to praise the Moslems who'd crafted the mosque, because he made it as far as the hall in silence.

Without a backward glance he sprinted quietly down the hall to the stairs. He had no memory of having come back up those stairs on the previous night, but he knew that he had. He owed Montrovant for that one, and he meant to pay that debt, even if he planned to skim something off the top for himself. Jeanne Le Duc was not the most moral of men, but he did have his honor.

He heard no sounds from below. All remained quiet in the wing that housed the knights, and Le Duc made his way down the stairs toward the lower levels, taking a deep breath to steady his nerves. He did not fear what was to come, but he'd have been a fool not to admit the danger. Whatever they'd faced the previous night was old and dark, darker than anything Le Duc could imagine, and that would make it dark indeed. He had no intention of barreling down the stairs again and making a target of himself. Particularly when that which awaited him was capable of frightening one such as Montrovant.

Instead of taking the main stairs, as they'd done the night before, he made his way to the stables. His adventure earlier that day had convinced him that this was the safer route. There would be none to witness his passing but the horses, and they were as trustworthy a group of companions as he might ask for under the circumstances.

Once he was out of sight of the main level of the temple, he stopped and pulled the robes over his own clothing, pulling the hood up and drawing it tightly about the contours of his face. He meant to blend in with those below, and it wouldn't do to have someone spot him before he'd even entered their realm. For the first time in his life he was glad for his slight stature. A larger man, like de Payen or Montrovant, would have stood out in any crowd.

He encountered no one, and he'd made his way past the point in the passageway beyond the stables where he'd found the robe before he met any indication of life.

The first thing he noticed was the glow. It was not the light of torches, or even candles, but a more subtle illumination. He couldn't pinpoint the source, but it filled the passageway, dripping from the darkness to run down the walls in flaming rivulets. The light grew brighter the deeper he went, and soon he began to hear the sounds again.

It did not seem exactly the same as he remembered it from the previous night, but his memories of that time were strangely blurred, and he could not be certain that it was not the same. He could feel the power of the chant flowing through the stone beneath his feet. His hair tingled as the air around him vibrated in cadence. Something was going on, something powerful, but for the moment that power seemed unaware of his presence.

That was the difference, he decided. He did not feel as though he were the focus of the power. He sensed it, but it did not yet sense him. Another advantage. Perhaps the odd material of the robes warded him against the probing darkness. More likely, it was the fact that Montrovant did not walk at his side. It did not matter why, only that it was so. He quickened his steps, trying to keep beat with the hammering of his heart. It lessened the impression that it could be heard for miles around.

Ahead, he saw a patch of deeper darkness to the left, and he realized he was approaching the stairs to the upper level. He'd not made it to the bottom of those stairs before, but here he was, on his way into the very interior of Santos's realm, and none seemed the wiser. If he'd not been half-paralyzed with nervous fear, he'd have smiled.

It was then that he heard footsteps, and he slammed himself against the wall. Shocked by the violence of his own reaction, he caught his breath and silently cursed himself for a fool. If one of Santos's men saw him react in such a manner, he would be dead. He had to blend in with the others, and that meant that he would have to steel his nerves against the growing dread that seeped through his bones and ate at his concentration. It was the chanting, he knew. Something in the words was stealing his control.

The knowledge was strength, it seemed. As soon as he recognized the enemy he faced, it ceased to worry him, and he pulled away from the wall, continuing down the passage slowly. The chant still had its power, but an enemy known was an enemy he could face.

Ahead, he saw a furtive, shadowy movement off to his left, and he slowed a bit more, trying to focus his sight through the dim light. It did not appear that the form he'd seen had been wearing robes. Another visitor? Speeding his steps, he remained as silent as possible and crept along the wall.

The figure ahead of him was moving even more slowly, and as Le Duc drew near, he realized with shock that it was de Payen. He couldn't decide whether to make himself known and risk exposure of them both, or continue as if he'd noticed nothing and not take the chance of drawing unwanted attention to either of them. As he continued to follow, his heart pounding, the choice was taken from him.

The pitch of the chanting shifted suddenly, and de Payen stiffened. At first the knight stood firm, pulling deeper into the shadows, but Le Duc felt the energy suddenly pouring from some source ahead, and de Payen broke and ran for the stairs. Neither man could see anything, but the sensation of impending danger was so intense in the air, the dread that dropped over them like a cloak so complete and overpowering, that it nearly drove Le Duc, who had opted not to retreat, to his knees.

The most he could do in his own defense was to press into the stone wall and hang on. The energy was not focused on him this time, and as he felt the power rushing past, he closed his eyes and began to recite psalms, any verse that came to mind, soundlessly, over and over. It was ironic that de Payen's influence should come to his aid at that particular moment. He'd never been one for scripture before he'd come to the mosque.

As de Payen's steps and cries of anger and outrage retreated up the stairs, others—countless others, followed in his tracks. Remaining where he stood, Le Duc ignored them. He kept his concentration centered on his goal. He had not been discovered, and he knew—somehow—that the only hope of maintaining that status was to blank his mind from those who pursued de Payen.

Wishing the knight godspeed, he sank into his own mind. Darkness greeted him with open arms, and the tempest thundered past.

THIRTEEN

De Payen had never run from a fight in all the years of his life. He'd faced each and every challenge the Lord had set before him stoically. It was a new experience when fear invaded. For that single moment in time his mind lost control of his limbs. He floundered up the stairs, missing as many as he found and banging himself roughly against the walls on either side. Twice he fell to his knees, but he forced himself back to his feet and drove onward. He ignored the dull, throbbing pain that pulsed through his knee when he fell the second time.

He would never have run if all that were at stake was his body, or his mind. It was a much deeper terror that gripped him; he felt the fingers of darkness reaching for his soul. It was an awakening. In that moment, more clearly than in any other, he knew the reality of his faith. He experienced the helpless frailty of his belief, and clung fiercely to the thin, barely cohesive threads that bound him to a God so far removed He could not be reached directly, even at a times such as this.

He could pray, and he could cower in the corner, waiting to see if he would be delivered, but somehow he knew this would never save him. His God was benevolent and forgiving, but He did not coddle His followers. He asked for faith, complete and unwavering, and it was up to Hugues, or any other who sought salvation, to provide that faith without question, and without physical support.

The problem was that the evil on his heels was real. As real as Montrovant had been, a short hour earlier, standing before him. As real as the stone beneath his feet and the air he breathed. His faith was real, as well, but he could not reach out and grab it to pull himself free of the dark morass that seeped up from below, groping for his legs and confusing his mind. It was trying to draw him back to the depths of the caverns stretching away beneath him.

He thought about calling out to his men. They would come, if they recognized his voice. They would come, but what could they do? Either he would make it back to the safety of his quarters, and he would survive, or the evil would force him to take a stand, and he would find a way to fight. Nothing the others could do would stand against an enemy such as this, should Hugues fall. It was better to test his strength alone and risk no other soul than his own.

Montrovant had been right about Santos, right about the darkness in the tunnels below. More than any moment since they'd met, he wished he had the tall, gaunt man at his side. That presence would have given him a confidence he could find nowhere in his own makeup at the moment. Finding the breath to curse, finally, he scrambled the last few yards up the stairs.

Below, the sounds had shifted subtly. He heard whispered renditions of his name caroming about in his mind. The sound seemed to be seeping through the stone. He felt the breeze that wafted past his ears picking at his mind with icy, numbing fingers. Someone—something—was trying to gain entrance to his thoughts. He surged upward, barreling into the main passageway of the temple and staggering to the next set of stairs—the stairs that led to his quarters—his bible. Sanctuary.

He fixed his mind on that thought, that word. Sanctuary. He had heard it used by bards and kings, priests and bandits. He had heard it, and yet he had never understood it. It had always seemed a cowardly concept to him, hiding behind the vestments of the Church, rather than facing up to one's enemies. Now he saw that it wasn't the same as merely hiding. Sanctuary was a state of mind, a protection against attacks on levels beyond sight and sound.

He didn't understand how he knew, but his heart told him that the one place most sacred to him would be safe. He spent hours communing with the Lord in his chambers. The stone of the floor bore the indentations of his knees. Santos might seek him there, but he could not enter and take his soul. He found that his movements came more easily as he made his way upward, and he felt the tendrils of thought that had snaked up from the darkness to grope after him release with a snap. As their influence sank down and away, he breathed a bit more easily. He barreled through the last section of hallway, flying by so quickly that the sound of his footsteps awoke several of his sleeping men. None entered the hall, but he heard them stirring. A few opened their doors tentatively, peering out through the cracks. They knew only too well Hugues's strict views on curfew. They knew there would be a punishment for breaking that curfew, and it would not have been the first time Hugues had tested their obedience.

"Go back to your rooms!" Hugues gasped, slamming the door to his own quarters wide and diving through. "There is a darkness among us. Do not open your doors unless I call to you, and ready yourselves for battle!"

He managed to kick his door shut behind him as the last of his words echoed down the passage. He heard other doors slamming quickly, as well. Moving to the window, he fell immediately to his knees. He prayed for forgiveness of his fear. He prayed for strength. He prayed for a renewal of faith, and he prayed his thanks for the lessons and challenges laid before him.

He was a man of action. A sword, a horse, battle—these were things he could understand. Strange chants and beings who could invade your thoughts—demons from the depths of Hell itself, he would need to reevaluate his reality to work them in. He only knew of one way to fight a spiritual enemy. He knew one weapon against sin, and that weapon was prayer. He fell to that prayer with a vengeance, certain that some failing of his own had caused the weakness that had driven him to flight. If his words were to be his sword this night, he would make them sharp and clear.

As he prayed, he planned as well. He would go to Daimbert, were he to live through the night, and whatever was going on beneath his temple would stop. He would gather the strength of the Church at his side, and he would lead them back into the battle he'd fled moments before. He had retreated for the first time in his long life, and the sensations this weakness had brought with it ate at his mind and heart like an acid.

Already his fear was being replaced by righteous anger. He would have revenge, and it would be swift and certain. Nothing less could redeem him, not in the eyes of God, and not in his own mind.

He listened carefully with the part of his mind that still echoed with the power of his enemy's words. He listened for those words to be repeated, for the clawing sensation that had told him something sought his name, his being, his very soul. There was no sound. The mosque had grown as silent as a tomb, save for the sounds of his men. The clatter of weapons and the scraping of feet carried clearly through the stone walls.

The sounds reminded Hugues of the responsibility he had to those men. He had given his strong arm and his heart to the Church; it was time that the Church backed him up in return. He didn't know what he would be able to show Daimbert in the tunnels below, but he knew that it would have to suffice. Nothing so evil could be hidden away, not by the light of day.

He would set things to rights, and then he would make his journey to Bernard, and to the Holy Father in Rome; but he would not set foot out of Jerusalem until this was ended. None could ever challenge him in such a way and live to tell the tale.

His prayers continued uninterrupted, and he drifted into a trance where shadows chased him across vistas of time and deserts of his imagination. He did not open his eyes.

Le Duc returned slowly to his senses. He stood as he had before, alone and pressed back into the shadows of the passageway. The sound of the chanting had faded into the rustle of a different sound, the shuffling steps of others moving past, and then away from him. The situation popped clearly into focus in an instant, and he took a firm grip on his nerves. With an effort, he staggered to his feet.

He'd almost missed his chance entirely. The robed monks were returning from their pursuit of de Payen, whatever the outcome of that might have been, and now was the moment to seize his opportunity to join in with them. If he could melt carefully from the shadows, he could blend into the crowd and follow them into whatever dark place they were returning to. Questionable as the sanity behind that act might be, he intended to carry it through. He realized that it would very likely be the last act of bravery accounted to the history of his lifetime. It was still the lesser of two evils in his mind. He knew, somehow, that failure in the eyes of Montrovant would not be less unpleasant than whatever these dark monks could contrive.

Straightening his shoulders and dipping his chin so that he watched the ground before him as he moved, he stepped to the center of the passageway and began to move forward. There was a long line advancing ahead of him, and he hurried slightly, falling in at the rear and matching the shuffling gait of those ahead of him. There was a hair-raising moment of uncertainty when the monk just ahead of him turned—looking back to see who followed. Jeanne nodded almost imperceptibly, concentrating every fiber of his being on placing one foot evenly in front of the other. The man was apparently satisfied and turned his gaze back to the front. Heaving a silent breath of thanks to whatever God might be listening, Jeanne continued to follow.

They moved down the corridor, which was no longer lit as brightly by the torches lining the walls. There were just as many torches, and they burned as well, dancing in the shadows to the music of a slight breeze from somewhere above, but they didn't cut the gloom as at this end of the tunnels. Something ate at the light, licking the edges away and pushing the shadows farther and farther toward the center of each flame. Le Duc shivered, scanning the shadows furtively. The air felt much cooler than it had moments before, the damp cold chill of a fresh grave in the morning. Le Duc had dug his share of those in times of war, but the scent was so out of place in the tunnel that it nearly nauseated him.

He craned his neck at every opportunity, peering around the monk's shoulders, but there appeared to be nothing to see, beyond the long column of robed figures he followed. Ahead, he heard the beginnings of the chant growing again. The line ahead of him seemed to be disappearing, and at last he saw what had caused the illusion. A large doorway loomed to his left.

He hesitated, just at the doorway, then stepped inside. The action had an air of finality about it that he didn't care for, but it was too late to turn away. If they found him now, he would be a dead man. He preferred to be a dead man who understood why he'd died.

The lighting inside the large chamber was not much better, but Le Duc's eyes were beginning to adjust to his surroundings. He could see rank upon rank of the robed monks, gathered in tight semicircles around an altar that was positioned in one corner of the room. It was eerily reminiscent of worshipers gathered in a Christian temple, but he shook the image from his mind.

To the right of the altar, and raised slightly, there was a second platform. One lone figure stood upon that raised surface, and though he'd only seen the priest from a distance, he knew who faced the crowd. Santos.

The man's head was bowed, as if in prayer, and he wore the collar and vestments of a priest, though the chanting that Le Duc heard was not the mass. Something about the words was off-kilter, and the chill he'd noticed in the air had deepened considerably.

He couldn't make out the substance behind the words, only a monotonous, rhythmic cadence that seemed made up more of different sounds than of words. The pattern of the vibration that arose from the chant echoed through the room. Visions coalesced in his mind, dragged from his subconscious mind by that sound, and he fought to keep himself centered. Now was not the time to be losing himself in a new religious experience; he needed to figure out what was going on, then he needed to find his way back out of that room and back to his quarters without being discovered or killed.

It was like some fanciful tale of heroism and dark magic told at fireside by a bard with too much wine beneath his belt. The incessant pounding of the sound on his eardrums and the eeriness of his surroundings were combining to confuse him beyond coherent thought. He wanted to move forward, to join the ranks nearest to the altar. He swayed in time with the chant, as did the others surrounding him, and lost himself in the sound. He felt his lips move, knew that his own voice had joined with that of the others, but the sounds he emitted did not originate in his own mind. They were dragged outward by something far more powerful than he, something that hungered for his attention, his devotion. It was a drunken celebration of something so dark and alien to his mind that comprehension was never an option. He was an instrument, played by Santos's hand. Those surrounding him were the same. It was not a group chanting, but a single entity using multiple voices to achieve a single end.

He moved a couple of steps forward, and the altar came into full view. Despite the shadows and the poor lighting, he was able to make out the object on the stone surface with complete clarity, and he barely bit back the scream that launched itself toward his throat. Gasping, he took a step back and slammed his eyes closed, fighting for breath. That sight had returned his control, but it had also dropped him out of synch with the group. The image strobed in his mind like the after-image of a lightning strike.

On the altar sat a human head. It was not attached to any body, but the eyes were open wide. Staring. He knew that they had been staring straight at him. The mouth had been open, as well, and the voice of that shriveled caricature of humanity had imbedded itself in the intricate cadence of the chant.

Slowly the sound died away until only one voice rang out through the chamber. Le Duc had managed to get his lips moving again, though he'd lost whatever connection had given him the sound, and he ceased all movement, thankful for the moment of control that allowed him to devote his attention to what was happening at the front of the room. Lost as he'd been in the emotion of the ritual, he might have remembered nothing useful to report to Montrovant.

Santos was dancing about beside the altar. His expression was one of complete rapture, and his eyes were backlit by an unholy light. He grinned down at the gathered monks, striking a leering, arrogant pose. It did not seem like the same man at all as he who had prayed so devoutly only moments before. It was as if some other spoke through his lips and controlled the features of his face. The energy that rippled through those limbs was uncanny.

"He has come," Santos gloated. "He is here with us now, and he will speak. He who holds the future in his mind like the pages of the books of our history. He who binds us to the darkness and gives us direction. He will speak, and you will listen. So has it been written, so must it be done."

Santos danced toward the altar, waving his hand at the head that sat there grinning out at them through a rictus of death and something more. The eyes watched him approach with dark intelligence.

"There are questions, and there are answers...both are as one to him. He will guide us to our future, and there will be no turning back. We will protect that which is ours..."

As the priest's voice died away, Le Duc saw the head's features ripple, and the expressions that rode so oddly upon Santos's own countenance transferred to the head. Santos seemed himself again, but the head had been transformed. It twisted and writhed for a moment, as though grasping the strands of control that would work its features, then it slowly spun to leer at the gathered monks. The jaws opened wide, exposing sharp, gleaming teeth, and it began laughing maniacally. Long, greyish wisps of hair drifted back and away from the shriveled skin of its scalp, and flames leaped madly about in the sunken pits that should have been eye-sockets. The mouth was so wrinkled at the edges that it seemed to have been sewn shut, or it had seemed so until the jaws had flown open.

Its skin was dry—brown and weathered. When the laughter died away, its lips remained slightly parted. Madness slipped from the face, and the expression it wore became more calculating and predatory.

"Flight is upon you!" the head screeched suddenly. "Darkness and flight, flee the light. He is here. He is near. He will find what you hold precious—that which is old and binds you to the shadows. He is old, as well. All will be revealed and the future sealed. You must be ready to flee. You must be ready to fight."

Le Duc managed to tear his gaze from the apparition on the altar long enough to sweep the room. Each set of eyes was locked firmly onto the apparition that glared back at them from the altar. There was so little movement among the gathered monks that it was difficult to tell if they were breathing. The thrill of power beyond anything he'd ever encountered seared through Le Duc's mind, but he held fast. It was not for him—it was not his power.

"Give us his name!" Santos chanted, beginning a mincing dance step about the altar. "Name the one who would bring us down, and we will put an end to him. Give us a name, that we may make him our own, that we may destroy him."

"Montrovant," the head said quickly. "His name is Montrovant...this I have told you."

"His true name," Santos insisted. "There is more. He is no man, and his name is something more. What is his name?"

The head began to chuckle, then, and Le Duc felt his skin growing clammy and colder. Those dead, empty sockets were staring directly at him. The ancient lips parted to speak once more, and suddenly it was very important that the next words not be heard. He didn't know where the knowledge came from, but it burst in upon his thoughts like a raging tide. This moment would win or lose the battle. For reasons unknown, Le Duc found that he did not want the true name of Montrovant spoken here. He was as surprised as anyone when a cry burst free of his throat—

"No!"

The sound of his voice cracking through the silence was so sudden and unexpected that the others in the room were unable to register exactly where it had come from. The head grew suddenly rigid, losing both animation and the sense of dread that had radiated from it since it had begun to move. The chanting ceased, but there was no immediate rush toward where Le Duc stood. His heart was hammering in his chest, and he knew there was no way out, but he had to try. Inching his way toward the door, he milled about as stupidly as possible, trying to mix in with the confusion of the crowd surrounding him. He had almost made it to the door when a hand fell roughly on his shoulder.

Spinning, he found himself staring directly into the red pits of Santos's eyes.

"You have made a grave error, my friend," the priest whispered softly. "Very grave indeed. Welcome to my world."

FOURTEEN

Montrovant did not pause until he reached the desert, and then only because he felt the call of Kli Kodesh drifting to him across the sands. He did not hesitate. Too much was happening at once for him to ignore the only one who might hold the answers he required. Besides, he'd had just about enough of the old one's games to last him his second lifetime.

He spun to his left and sped across the sand in the direction of the old one's call. Questions whirled through Montrovant's mind, and mad or sane, Kli Kodesh was the answer who presented himself. He would have to suffice.

Kli Kodesh stood as he had the first night he'd called to Montrovant, alone upon the hill called Golgotha, staring upward into the stars. Montrovant couldn't tell if it was posed indifference that kept the ancient from glancing his way as he approached, or if Kli Kodesh's thoughts were truly focused on those stars. Perhaps nothing in the world seemed enough of a threat, or a diversion, to interrupt his thoughts.

"It is time," the old one said, turning quickly as Montrovant approached.

There was Montrovant's first answer. He was aware, and he was paying attention. "I didn't think you'd bring things so far so fast, but it is time—tonight—to end this. It seems a waste, so much entertainment so swiftly passed, but there is no other way. Santos has been disrupted in his ritual, and the power that he summoned has left him. I felt it only moments ago."

"De Payen," Montrovant said softly.

"No," Kli Kodesh said, shaking his head quickly. "De Payen prays and cowers in his chambers. His own brush with Santos's power did not differ much from your own. It is not he, but another who has saved you—a darker one. I sense a slight taste of your own essence in his. Did you send him and forget? Could it be that you lack full control of your own resources?"

"Le Duc?" Montrovant was momentarily taken aback. He'd not sent the man to do so much. He'd only instructed him to gather information. How had that gathering become so much more without his own influence, and what would it mean to the final outcome of his plans?

"What do you mean, Santos is disrupted?" he asked at last. There was no sense in dwelling on things that were already done. He had to focus on the moments to come.

"Santos called on ancient powers this night," Kli Kodesh replied. Then he grinned. "And those powers answered. He has connections to forces neither you nor I can fully comprehend, though I can sense much of what use he is making of them. Your true name was on the lips of that force when the disruption came. I don't know when you chose this follower of yours, or how you have trained him, but it would appear that you have done well to place your trust in him. He must have sensed what was about to happen, and prevented it. It would appear that he has sacrificed himself for you."

Montrovant shook his head slowly. "I still sense him—he is not dead. Is there further danger, now that this ritual has been ended?"

"There is no time for Santos to regain the link tonight," Kli Kodesh assured him. "For the moment you are as safe as you will ever be with that one. That is why I have called you. Another such opportunity might never present itself—it is time to strike."

"How shall I strike?" Montrovant asked. "I have but one follower, and he is human. With or without their *old power*, Santos has a small army. I am not foolish enough to believe myself his equal under such circumstances."

"You must use the Knights and the Church," Kli Kodesh urged him. "Is that not why you created them in the first place? They can be powerful allies, once outraged. Go to Daimbert, bring him to the mosque. Bring him to de Payen and show him what Santos has wrought.

"They will see, and they will understand. There is enough evil in that labyrinth to convince any who doubt the presence of evil. Once they know, they will fight. Do not underestimate humans. Many I have known did so, and they have passed on."

Montrovant's mind was whirling. What would Daimbert do if he burst into the temple unannounced? Would any among his followers recognize him? If he acted so openly, chose to risk so much, would others of his kind make their presence known and stop him? He'd not bothered to contact any in the city, but now he wondered if such absence of alliance was in his best interests. His discovery would bring to light facts that were not meant for humans and would bring danger onto all the damned of the Holy City. It was not something that was likely to go unnoticed.

He hadn't been contacted, but that did not mean he wasn't being watched. As old and powerful as Kli Kodesh was, he did not have the aspect of a prince, and Jerusalem was too old and powerful a city to lack its own dark inhabitants. How much would they stand by and allow before they took a stand of their own?

He made his decision quickly. "I will go, and I will do as you say, old one, but I wish I knew what you stand to gain from all of this. I have never known anyone to take such risks for no reason."

Kli Kodesh only smiled, and there was no time left to pursue the question. Montrovant could think of no reason to trust the ancient madman, but he had no other options before him. He also had no reason *not* to trust. If Kli Kodesh had meant him harm, that harm would have been sudden and swift. He had to move, and swiftly. Midnight had passed, and the hours before dawn were far too short for Montrovant's taste. He spun away, leaving Kli Kodesh standing as he'd found him.

With his mind set on a goal, Montrovant could move very quickly, and the old familiarity of the streets was returning to him. He remembered a much different Jerusalem, a world and lifetimes away from that through which he ran, but for all the years and wars it had endured, it had changed little in its physical aspect. It was more cluttered, and there were traces of Moslem influence in the buildings and temples that had not existed in his time. He felt nothing for the loss of his past; the lifetime that had cared for it had withered to so much dust.

The palace of the Patriarch was less impressive than that of Baldwin, but it had a feel of solidity and permanence that the monarch's did not. It belonged to powers more ancient than the royalty of Jerusalem. There was something about the Catholic Church that had a way of adding security and stability to its holdings. When Baldwin and his descendants crumbled, and there was no trace that they'd ever walked these streets, Rome would still be a power. Montrovant had seen empires fall, but the Church, whatever face and function it put forward to the world at large at any given moment, had survived. It rarely seemed to understand or support the concepts it claimed as a foundation, but it understood power.

He did not try to slip in past the guards or make his way to any balconies. He wanted to get Daimbert's attention, but not by making a spectacle that would draw that attention to himself. He rushed up to the huge front doorway, grabbed the first guard he could find and slammed his own thoughts into the man's brain without hesitation. There was no cry, nor did the guard cause a disturbance. Montrovant did not allow it. Glassy-eyed, the man led Montrovant into the entrance hall of Daimbert's palace.

"Bring the Patriarch," the guard barked. "Wake him quickly, it is an emergency." There was an urgency to the man's words, but for all that, they seemed forced. The reaction was not immediate.

Those inside looked at the first man as though he'd lost his mind. Then they spotted Montrovant's huge form at the guard's side. They took in the set of his jaw and the glitter in his eyes, and without further debate they complied. Better the wrath of Daimbert, with whom they were familiar, than this huge shadow of a man. The Church, at least, purported to be forgiving.

It took longer than Montrovant would have cared to spend to get Daimbert roused and dressed. Another few moments and he would have lost control, tearing through the palace himself to drag them all from their beds and speed things along. With an effort, he stood silent and still, holding his frustration in check.

Guards appeared first, scrambling about with armor

half-fastened and confusion ruling their eyes. Behind them followed a flustered Daimbert, his robes askew and his eyes wild. He stumbled into the room looking as though he'd been awakened from a deep and troubling nightmare.

"What is the meaning of this?" he cried, eyes bright with a combination of outrage and fear. "Who is this man, and why has he been allowed here at such an hour?"

Montrovant strode forward, ignoring the threatening gestures of the guards, to confront Daimbert directly. "I stand before you, Daimbert, and you will address me with the respect I am due, rather than speaking of me as if I were a statue. I will accord you that same respect. I have been 'allowed' nowhere. I go where and when I please."

The room grew suddenly silent. The guards had never heard anyone but Baldwin address the Patriarch in such a manner and live. There was tolerance in the Church, but this was an outrage that would not easily be forgiven. Hands on their weapons, they stood ready to cut Montrovant down if Daimbert gave the order. He did not.

Instead the Patriarch huffed slightly, as though he would rebuff his arrogant visitor, then grew silent. Something in what he saw caught his attention, and at the last moment he thought better of whatever words he'd been about to speak.

Montrovant continued. "I have come to you with a matter more urgent than any you've encountered in all the years of your life. There is an evil afoot in the city, beneath your very nose and under the cloak of Rome's protection. You must move now—this very night—to put an end to it. You must come with me. You are the most powerful of God's servants in the Holy City. The protection of that city from evil is your responsibility."

Daimbert was backing away now. Courage was not his strong suit, and the mention of evil under the protection of Rome had put a bad taste in his mouth. That, coupled with the notion of responsibility on his part was more than he was willing to accept before he was fully awake. Still, he hesitated. Montrovant's words painted a brave portrait that it was difficult to find fault with.

"You are mistaken," he muttered. "You must bring your

complaint during the daylight—there are proper forms of address. I am a busy man, and this is most improper. You..."

"I am here now!" Montrovant thundered. "You are a man of God, are you not? I tell you, there are followers of the devil himself beneath the halls of the mosque of al Aqsa. They have begun to draw upon ancient powers and great darkness. They have made themselves known to de Payen, and he needs your support."

Daimbert's expression showed that he was thinking hard, possibly harder than he had in years. He ceased his backpedaling and began to listen with more interest.

"De Payen? The Knight of the Temple?"

"He has faced the evil of which I speak," Montrovant grated. "You know him to be a man of great faith, and yet he has retreated in fear. If you are the power of the Church in Jerusalem, now is the time to assert that power. Now is the time to prove your faith."

Daimbert's men were beginning to look askance at their leader. Many of them knew de Payen, and the thought of that man retreating from anyone in fear was news of the darkest sort. It was also an interesting thing to see their leader put on the spot over his faith. Faith was not addressed that often by their Patriarch.

"De Payen?" Daimbert repeated, blustering. "De Payen is in trouble? Why didn't you say so?"

It was obvious that the man was, if anything, more reluctant than before to lend his aid, but he was backed into a corner. Something else was happening, as well. Montrovant saw Daimbert's jaw stiffen slightly, and his shoulders drew back so that the Patriarch stood a bit straighter. Frightened and unwilling as he might be, it appeared that the decision had been made to answer Montrovant's call.

"Quickly," Montrovant urged. "They will escape, and it will be too late. You must move now."

"Muster the guards," Daimbert cried, moving toward the door. "Those of you present, come with me."

"I will carry the news of your approach to de Payen," said Montrovant. "You have renewed my faith, Excellency." He bowed low and moved quickly toward the door. He feared that Daimbert would question him further, or request that he remain with the guards, and that would not do at all. He had to be free to act, and he had to be free to find his way to safety when the encroaching rays of the sun drove him below. He had set the wheels of the Church in motion, but he had no intention of remaining in the road to be ground beneath them.

Daimbert said nothing, and Montrovant did not hesitate to make his exit. Now that he had cast the gauntlet, Daimbert would have to show himself at the temple, and in strength. Montrovant had called the man's faith into question, and Daimbert's reputation since coming to Jerusalem had not been one of careful adherence to the scriptures. He couldn't afford to be lax openly, not in such an instance.

Besides, Montrovant believed that Santos was probably a concern of Daimbert's on many levels. Though he was the Patriarch of the city, answering only to the Holy Father in Rome in matters of the Church, Daimbert had no control over the dark priest or his small domain. Montrovant hadn't mentioned Santos by name, but he was certain that Daimbert had picked up on the reference to the lower levels. Nothing would grate on the nerves of a man like Daimbert more than secrecy and deception that he was not privy to. If the Church trusted him to oversee the holiest of cities, it would be incomprehensible to him that he was not trusted to know Santos's business, and to have a part in it, whatever it might be.

Montrovant knew that whatever force in Rome was behind Santos, it was not the Holy Father. There were powers embedded throughout the structure of the Vatican. Claudius himself held great sway there, and Montrovant wished for his sire's aid in that moment. Claudius would have been able to find out who, or what, Father Santos was, and that knowledge, or the lack of it, might prove all the difference in the end.

What remained was to reach de Payen and get him prepared, as well. Montrovant strode through the front doors of the mosque once more, ignoring the servants and guards completely as he made his way up toward de Payen's quarters. They would recognize him, and he had no time to bother with their curiosity.

Reaching de Payen's door, he slammed it open violently. De Payen raised his head, turning to stare at his unexpected visitor in startled fear.

Montrovant saw a different man kneeling before him than the one he'd left scant hours before. He hesitated, then slammed the door shut behind him and moved to de Payen's side.

"Get up, Hugues. Stand and face your fear."

De Payen did rise, but his confidence had not returned. He was trembling, and his voice betrayed him as he found himself unable to speak. Something desperately wrong had happened this night, and Montrovant cursed himself for sending the knight into that darkness alone. He should have known it would not be enough.

"Daimbert is on his way," he said quickly, "along with his guards. You have to pull yourself together and rally your men. Now is the time. Santos has failed in his plans tonight, and one of your men, Le Duc, is in his clutches even as we speak. For that man's soul, and for your faith, Hugues de Payen, you must act."

Montrovant saw that his words were having the desired effect, though not as quickly as he would have liked. Moments earlier, de Payen had been alone, trapped within his mind by shadows and his failing faith. His heart must have nearly stopped its beating when Montrovant had slammed through the door.

Now he would have something to place his faith in—the presence of the Patriarch and Montrovant himself. He would also have his knights, and a chance to fight. Sneaking through the passageways like a thief in the night had not set well with him, but the notion of a head-on assault worked almost instantaneous wonders on his state of mind. He straightened his shoulders, and the fire returned suddenly to his eyes.

"I...I have failed," he said, regaining control of his voice. "I have fallen to my knees in the face of the evil that lies below, like a coward."

"You could not have known what you would face," Montrovant said soothingly. "It is enough that the events of this night have brought new light. With Daimbert's support, Santos will not be long at his dark practices. You should be proud."

"I will not be proud until this is at an end," Hugues replied, his fear melting to a grim determination.

His features were setting themselves into a mask of growing anger, and Montrovant fought back the urge to smile. De Payen's emotions were so mercurial as to be refreshing. He almost wished he had more time to spend here.

"Go then. Go and wake your men. Ready them for what is to come, but reveal as little as possible. There is no way to know what you will face below, and there is no reason to undermine their confidence."

De Payen nodded. He moved to the door, then hesitated. "You will join us, will you not, Lord?"

Montrovant met his gaze steadily, then shook his head. "I told you before, Hugues, this is not my fight. This is your moment, and you must trust me when I say that all you need for victory is in your heart, mind, and the strength of your body. God has given you the answers: listen to them."

De Payen did not answer, turning instead and leaving Montrovant alone in the room. The sounds of shouting voices, slamming doors and the clatter of weapons rang through the walls moments later. Montrovant could hear the excited voices of the servants announcing the arrival of Daimbert and his men.

For just an instant, he considered joining them after all. He had a score to settle for his own experiences with Santos, and he wondered how that might change were he to get the opportunity to drain a bit of the good "father's" blood. What would blood that ancient be like? Did Santos even *have* blood? There was no warmth to give it away, if he did.

The notion passed as quickly as it had risen. He had a mission, and this was the moment he'd been waiting for, however premature it might seem. He needed to get below, but not with de Payen, or with Daimbert. Whatever the outcome of that confrontation, he needed to find his way to the vaults in the confusion, and he needed to find his way back out past who- or whatever might stand in his way. The others could fight among themselves until they were all dead for all he cared, as long as they stayed clear long enough for him to find his way clear.

The window beckoned, and he stuck his head out into the darkness, scanning the walls above and the ground beneath. No one was in sight. The activity was all in the front of the temple, and the moon wasn't bright enough for its illumination to put him in particular danger. Besides, after this night, it would matter little who knew of him. He took a last glance over his shoulder to be certain no one was in the doorway, then leaped into the night, gliding to the ground in a graceful arc. He was already running when he hit the ground.

Pale figures watched Montrovant's exit from de Payen's window in silence. As he passed them, rounding the building and making his way toward the stable entrance, they melted into the darkness. A shrill, eerie cry broke through the silence, echoed once in the distance.

On the hillside at Golgotha, standing still as if he'd not moved an inch since Montrovant left him, Kli Kodesh heard the cries, and his smile widened. It was an interesting night, and he hadn't been able to say that in many, many years.

FIFTEEN

Le Duc had a thousand questions he'd have liked answered, but he found himself unable to reply to Santos's words. His throat had constricted from the sudden and overpowering sense of dread that was creeping over his flesh and invading his mind. It went beyond anything he'd ever experienced. Santos stood before him, swaying back and forth like a snake preparing to strike. His motion still mimicked the rhythm of the chant, as though not yet ready to release that power. His eyes blazed in anger, and something else. Hunger?

"You have caused me a great deal of—inconvenience," he said at last. "You have no idea of the powers you have stumbled upon, but you will know before you cease your miserable existence. You have disrupted my work of several days, and I take such offenses—personally. I will make it my personal goal to instruct you."

Santos hesitated, cocking his head to one side, and Le Duc would have sworn that the man was sniffing the air. He'd seen dogs and wolves do the same when something at the edge of their senses caught their attention. There was something odd about Santos's skin, the stiff way in which he moved, but Le Duc was in no position to give these facts any consideration.

"You have come from him, from this dark one, Montrovant." Santos moved closer, sliding his face in close to Jeanne's, his eyes glittering. "I sense his essence within you. You are bound to him."

Le Duc shook his head, finding his voice at last. "I am bound to no man," he croaked. "I follow whom I choose."

Santos smiled. "You do not even know the situation of your

own soul. Interesting. Pathetic, but interesting. It would appear that I have at least one more lesson I can gift you with before I end your life. Perhaps, if you listen carefully and learn well, I will allow you to remain as my servant. You seem well-suited to the task, though you will certainly prove his downfall, now that you are mine."

Le Duc lurched forward then. His anger overrode his common sense, and he lunged for Santos's throat. Better to die quickly than to suffer this man's insults.

Santos never moved, or it seemed that he did not, but somehow Le Duc missed. He clutched at the air where Santos's throat had been, but there was nothing, and he felt himself falling off balance and careening toward the wall. His arms were grabbed from both sides before he could make contact with the stone, and as he was jerked upright he saw that he was held tightly by two of Santos's shambling, robed followers. Their grips were as icy and strong as manacles of iron. He couldn't move, even if he'd had anywhere to go.

"He will come," Jeanne said at last. He didn't know if there were any truth to his words, but he had no other weapons close at hand. "Montrovant might not care about me, but he will not take an insult lightly. He will come, and we will see who becomes the servant."

Santos laughed then, and the sound that emerged from his throat was as dry and humorless as wind across a barren desert. It was the sound of bones clattering on dusty stone and fingers clawing outward from the inside of graves. Jeanne could hear the his own death knell in that sound.

"He will come." Santos agreed. "I do not doubt that he will come, but he has no more idea than you what he will face when he does. His is a dark power, and he is old, but I am older still. There are forces at work here that he can't begin to comprehend. I think he will find me more than a match."

Le Duc didn't comment further. He didn't know if what Santos said was true or not, but he knew that the man believed it to be so. There was something ancient in Santos's eyes, an icy darkness in the tones of his voice. One could believe almost anything about such a man, if man he was.

Le Duc let his eyes stray to the altar and the head, sitting motionless as if it had been carved from stone. Lifeless as it now was, it had the the appearance of something stolen from a grave. Le Duc was outraged at the blasphemy, but he couldn't help being curious at the same time. He'd seen that thing *move*!

Santos followed his glance, and the dark priest's smile deepened.

"You saw, then. You know that the head is more than it seems. That is the first of your lessons. You will find that there are many things in this world that are more than they seem. Never take anything at face value. That head is no head, but a window—an oracle. There is no secret it cannot ferret from the vaults of history, given the proper preparation and ritual."

Le Duc was about to ask a question in an attempt to buy time, but at that moment Santos stiffened and turned toward the door. The odd, faraway look returned momentarily to his face, as if he was listening to a voice from within his mind; then it passed, and the fire blazed even more brightly in his eyes. Le Duc would have given a lot to have known what Santos had seen, or thought, during those few short moments.

"Bring him," the priest said, gesturing at Le Duc. "We must make our escape more quickly than planned. It is as we were warned—flight is once more upon us."

Le Duc was bundled quickly out the door, and though he kept his eyes roving and his mind working constantly, no chance at escape presented itself. He didn't plan to allow himself to be taken away and enslaved without a fight, but for the moment his best move seemed compliance. He needed them to forget about him as completely as possible so that he might find a moment when their concentration had slacked.

Santos paid no more attention to him than he might have a bothersome gnat. Whatever plans had been going through the priest's mind had changed drastically in the past few minutes. Something big was happening, something unexpected. All Le Duc could do was to hope that, whatever it was, it provided a distraction that would give him a chance at freedom.

The robed monks were rushing about madly. Weapons clattered, and they had formed a chain of men leading off into the depths of one of the storerooms to pass the contents out into the passage.

When they were satisfied, or when Santos ordered it—there was no way to tell—the door was sealed once more, and they turned away from the stables. Their arms laden, a few hauling small wagons behind them, the entire entourage began to move in a line that led steadily deeper into the tunnels. Santos paced up and down the passageway, barking commands and waving his arms in hurried, impatient gestures. Whoever was coming for them was not far behind, and for all the priest's blustering about ancient powers and servitude, he seemed in no hurry to meet with his enemies.

Other sounds were reaching Le Duc now, cries from behind and above him, and the clatter of boot heels on stone. Santos's efforts became more frantic. Jeanne saw a monk flash past with the head cradled in his arms, and behind him a small group had gathered to add speed to the movement of a particularly heavy cart. Their *treasure*, whatever it might entail, was slowing them down considerably. It might give those pursuing a chance to catch up.

Santos and his men had apparently been prepared to flee, just not on such short notice. He wondered why they would go deeper into the tunnels when freedom, if it was to be had, would seem to lie in the direction of the stables. He wasn't entirely certain he wanted to know the answer.

Despite his fear, that answer wasn't long in coming. He was dragged along in the center of the pack at a stumbling run. The torches lining the walls became fewer, but it didn't seem to matter to the monks. A different sort of light had begun to permeate the air, and though there was no obvious source of illumination, it was enough by which to see. It surrounded them as they moved, clinging to the fleeing band and breaking the impenetrable darkness apart just long enough for them to slip through, then fading behind as if they had never passed.

The darkness would be much more of a hindrance to those who followed. Jeanne wondered fleetingly if Montrovant would be with them. Somehow he doubted that his dark master would have any trouble with the shadows, and Jeanne wanted very desperately for someone, anyone, to catch up with them.

He quit trying to count the sudden twists and turns as the futility of it became obvious. There was no way he could have recreated their course, not in total darkness. After what seemed an eternity of being buffeted along by the guards who still clung to his arms, he noticed that the floor beneath them had begun to slope upward once more. He could still make out faint sounds of pursuit, but they were fading steadily.

Feeling the need for positive action, he began to drag his feet. He moved more slowly, purposely tripping and trying to slow progress as much as possible. It seemed to be working, and he was about to drop to his knees once more when Santos appeared suddenly at his side.

He reached out quickly and laid one clammy hand on Le Duc's shoulder. The passageway whirled beneath his feet. There was a strange sensation of dislocation, and suddenly his mind was no longer his own. He was aware of what he did, but he was unable to exert any control over his limbs. His body straightened, and he began to move forward again.

A single word had imbedded itself in his mind, and he acted upon it. *Come.*

Moments later, all sound save the slap of their feet on the stone and the creaking of the carts they dragged behind was swallowed by the darkness.

De Payen led the way back down the winding stone stairs to the lower level of the mosque. He knew the way better than the Patriarch, and he had a burning desire to redeem his honor, even though none present knew the circumstances of his last visit.

Daimbert and his personal guard followed a bit more slowly. They descended cautiously, surrounded on all sides by de Payen's men. Almost as soon as they'd begun their descent, they heard the sounds emanating from below. There was crashing and the sound of rushing feet. They were expected, it seemed.

Whatever it was, de Payen knew it could only mean that the time remaining to him was becoming even more limited. If Santos and his minions were to escape, there would be too many questions left unanswered. It would also put de Payen in the unenviable position of explaining himself to Daimbert with no evidence to support his claims. He could allow neither scenario to become reality. Santos had to be stopped, and it had to happen now.

There was none of the shadowy dread hanging in the air this time to cling to him or drag him down. None of the dark fear clutched at his heart, as it had before. The air was damp and cool, and they made their way down quickly, weapons drawn.

"We must hurry," de Payen grated. "Do you hear?" He turned to Daimbert, who nodded, grim-faced. It was obvious that the Patriarch was not accustomed to such late-night antics, and his pallor suggested somewhat less courage than he was putting forth. De Payen could not blame him. This was a matter for warriors, not priests, and he was almost sorry that Daimbert had insisted on accompanying him. He was burdened now by the necessity of seeing to the Patriarch's safety.

"It sounds as though they are fleeing," Daimbert cried, fighting to keep pace with the guards and knights. "Is it possible that they already know we are coming?"

"It must be so, Excellency," Hugues replied. "We must not let them leave the tunnels." He gestured to Cardin, who ran at his side, and the man moved a bit closer. "Take three others and seal off the passageway between here and the stables."

Cardin nodded, and as they reached the bottom of the stair, he diverted a few of the knights to the right, moving cautiously toward the sound of the animals, who appeared to have been spooked. Frightened whinnies and the crashing of hooves against the wood of the stalls echoed through the tunnels. Pierre doubted that the horses' fright had been caused by the sounds of Santos's flight. Something else was happening.

He met the eyes of the knight directly at his side, a young French noble names Louis de Moyer, and he saw his own confusion and fear mirrored. Doubling his pace, he gestured for the others to follow. The small group flew down the passage toward the stables, their hearts slamming wildly in their chests and their eyes wide. Pierre wished, just for a moment, that de Payen had sent more than four men.

Meanwhile, de Payen and the Patriarch had moved inward, slowing their pace as they searched the deeper shadows for signs of Santos. Despite the sounds of retreat, they couldn't risk the chance of an ambush. The tunnels were made to order for treachery.

They could hear the retreating monks clearly now, and de Payen pressed ahead urgently. Darkness and familiarity with the passages would give Santos an advantage, and he didn't want to add too much distance to that imbalance. His knights pressed around him, and, bolstered by their energy, he began to run into the darkness.

Daimbert was in less of a hurry, taking time to search each alcove and room as they went. When they reached the large entrance that led to the room where Le Duc had infiltrated the ceremony, he stopped entirely, staring.

Candles still burned in niches around the walls in a mockery of a temple of the Church. The trappings of the dark ceremony that had been interrupted earlier were still clearly evident. There was a chill that still hung in the room, dropping the temperature several degrees from that of the passageway beyond. It was like a painting conceived by a madman, or a living nightmare. Daimbert moved through the room, sweeping his gaze from side to side to take it all in. Two of his guards flanked him nervously, but he paid no attention to them at all.

He moved to the altar, noting the odd symbols etched into the wooden surface and the dark velvet covering that was spread across the center. In the middle of that cloth was a small indentation. There was no way to tell what had been placed there, but somehow the sight of that empty space filled Daimbert's heart with an inexplicable dread. He reached out to run his fingers across the cloth, but at the last second, he pulled back. A sensation of unclean power clung to the surface, and he could not bring himself to let it contact his skin.

"Excellency?" one of the guards asked, confused.

"I don't know. I truly do not know. Whoever, or whatever filled this room was evil. We must follow. What happened here must not be allowed to make its way back to Rome."

There was a strength behind Daimbert's voice that the

guards were unaccustomed to. He moved more resolutely, his steps sure and firm. Whatever he was thinking, he seemed to have found a purpose in the last few moments, and his men found themselves suddenly pressed to keep the Patriarch's pace. De Payen and his men had continued down the passageway, moving as quickly as the poor lighting would allow. Their run had slowed to a trot, then to a stumbling, cursing high-speed walk. Torches had been torn from the walls to light the way, but it was slow going, and it soon became obvious that they had lost their quarry. The question became, where had they gone?

The tunnels were much more extensive than de Payen would have ever believed, and the deeper he went into those labyrinthine depths, the less certain he was that the only way out was through the tunnels near the stable. It was becoming obvious that the underground system extended beneath a wide section of the city, possibly into the desert beyond. It was also apparent that Santos knew exactly where he was going. One of the worst tactical blunders possible was to let the enemy know the terrain better than you, and to have it happen beneath the very structure you purported to be leader of was inexcusable to Hugues's way of thinking.

There was also the growing fear that they were becoming lost. Each turn and twist they followed loosened de Payen's grip on his surroundings. There were niches and crevices lining the walls, and more than once he had the sensation that someone— some *thing*—was watching him, waiting for him either to make the wrong decision on their route, or to hesitate and try to figure it all out.

Cursing, he tried to drive his men to greater speed, but it was hopeless. He couldn't be certain that they were following the same track that Santos had taken, and he was not going to catch up. If he continued to wind deeper and deeper into the maze of passageways, it was possible he would find himself, and his followers, lost for their trouble, and a worse fate was difficult to imagine.

Finally he called for a halt, and stood very still, staring into the darkness and trying to decide what was the best course of action. It occurred to him that this was the second time in a single night when he would very much have liked to have seen some divine intervention. A sign, anything he could follow, would have been enough. There was nothing.

He had just decided to turn back and rejoin the Patriarch, sparing his men the darkness, when the silence was shattered by an ear-splitting scream.

De Payen hesitated for only a second, then turned into the shadows once more and cried out to his men to move onward again. The going dragged on more slowly now that they had something to follow, but with more purpose. The sounds of a battle raged ahead, and after his experience earlier that night, de Payen wanted a good look at just what kind of battle it might be before he plunged his small band into the center of it. The blade in his hand had never seemed quite so inadequate.

Le Duc didn't see the first of the dark ones slip from the shadows, but he felt the sudden release of the power that held him. One moment the small band of refugees was rushing headlong, the next they were surrounded and infiltrated from all sides by grinning, pale creatures with burning eyes and the fangs of some nightmare beast. He was reminded for a moment of Montrovant, and his hand went quickly to his throat, then dropped again.

He continued to run, following the last command that Santos had planted in his mind, but those around him came to a startled halt, bunching toward the center of the passage and surrounding the carts protectively. With a snap, Santos released Le Duc's mind, and Jeanne stumbled, nearly crashing headlong into the stone wall of the tunnel. Scrambling for his balance, he caromed off the wall and managed to remain upright. Though the temptation was nearly too much to resist, he didn't look back. He could hear Santos's voice crackling through the air like lightning, could hear cackling, demonic laughter and muffled screams. No way to tell what came from the warriors of which side. The attackers had outnumbered the priest and his minions considerably, and the short glimpse Le Duc had gotten had seemed more a lingering bit of nightmare than any sort of reality. Nothing in his world made sense any longer.

They'd forgotten him, and that was all that mattered beyond placing one foot in front of the other as rapidly as possible and following the upward slant of the floor. He was forced to slow to a staggering walk after only a few hundred feet. All light had died around him, and he was only able to continue ahead by dragging one hand along the wall to his right.

He had no way of knowing how long he'd been moving, but at last a dim radiance broke the blackness ahead and he began to be able to make out the contours of the passage. Soon that light grew brighter, and he saw an opening ahead. It was the first traces of the sunrise, and he stumbled into the sand of the desert beyond the city.

Le Duc almost allowed himself to laugh. So much danger, and here he stood—alone and free. He took a deep breath of the fresh night air and leaned against the stone to catch his wind.

He didn't notice when the tall, dark figure emerged from a hidden pocket in the stone outcropping to his left. A stone shifted beneath the newcomer's foot, and Jeanne whirled, ready to strike out. He was too weary to move swiftly, and a strong hand clamped easily over his mouth. Before he could mount any counter-move, he was dragged back into the tunnel and out of the growing light.

"Be silent, you fool," Montrovant hissed. "They will return at any moment. Are you in that much of a hurry to die?"

Recognizing the voice, Le Duc breathed a sigh of relief and allowed Montrovant to draw him back into the shadows. He didn't know if Montrovant meant that Santos would return, or whatever had attacked the priest in the tunnels, but neither was a good option. He didn't want to be caught in the open if they made it to the desert and attempted to make their escape.

The two waited, Montrovant brooding and silent, and Le Duc feeling the sudden fatigue of the night's adventure. No one came. The sunlight began to leak into the passage, and Montrovant moved suddenly, drawing Le Duc behind him.

"I must get farther in," he said tersely. "We will find a safe place inside and wait this out. In the evening, we will follow."

Le Duc didn't bother to respond. He tripped and stumbled along behind as quickly as he could, as Montrovant ducked into the tunnels and took the first twisting turn that they encountered. It was not the way he had come, but Jeanne didn't mention it. Montrovant seemed to know where he was going, and though there was no light, the dark man was having no trouble finding his way. For the moment it was enough to Le Duc that his life did not seem in danger of ending in the next few minutes.

Montrovant stopped, at last, in a small alcove off of one of the side passages. Le Duc couldn't see what was taking place, but it sounded as though a massive piece of stone were being rolled across the floor. Then he heard the scrape of boots, and Montrovant was at his side again.

"We must rest," the tall man said softly, "but first, come, Jeanne Le Duc. I would have what is mine."

Jeanne felt himself drawn forward, felt Montrovant's strong arms closing about him, and then the pain at his throat— suddenly and achingly familiar. He remembered the faces of those who'd attacked Santos's party in the tunnels, and he shuddered. Surely Montrovant was not of their ilk—so tall, so strong. As Le Duc passed from consciousness, Santos's words floated hazily into his thoughts.

"You do not even know the state of your own soul."

SIXTEEN

De Payen rounded yet another twist in the dark tunnel and found himself face to face with insanity. The creature lunged from the shadows, eyes alight with hunger, and skeletal, claw-like hands reaching out to rip Hugues's throat. The thing was wickedly quick, and only instinct kept de Payen's life from ending in that second. He dropped to one knee on the stone floor and brought his blade straight up into the thing's torso. The sharp metal sliced straight through its paper-thin frame and out the other side. It twisted its gaunt face toward him and grinned, lunging yet again.

De Payen yanked his blade free, but it was too late. The thing had his sword arm in an icy grip, and it was yanking him forward. He could see its jaws opening wide, and he knew it would be only seconds before those impossibly long teeth sank into the flesh of his throat.

Then a second blade sliced through the air, narrowly missing de Payen's head, and that grinning monstrosity of a face was falling away, bouncing into the darkness. Its body, now headless, jerked about for a few moments longer as if uncertain in which direction it should flee. Then it fell and lay still.

The thing had still gripped de Payen's shoulder, and that grip held for a moment as it fell. It seemed that it was unwilling to admit defeat, despite the loss of its head. Hugues wrenched it from him and the thing crumbled away. Free of its clutches, de Payen staggered to the side. Ahead, the passage was a confusion of brown robes, blood, and screeching, hideous creatures like the one he'd just faced. It was unclear which side was actually winning the battle, but there were fallen monks littering the passageway, and de Payen could see Santos, drawn up to what seemed twice his actual height, calling out commands and curses in some twisted, ancient tongue. A few of the priest's followers held attackers aloft in their hands with surprising strength. Where their hands met that cold, pale skin, it burned and flaked away. As they burned, the creatures snapped and lunged at their captors, fighting with an insanely focused sense of purpose.

Where Santos turned, their monstrous attackers burst into flame, or fell back in fear. The power the priest wielded was astonishing, but there were too many for him. He couldn't encompass the entire passage with his gaze, or his concentration, and the monks themselves were falling swiftly under the attack. They seemed more than a match for their attackers one-on-one, but each was plagued by at least three.

Hugues drew back against the wall, mesmerized.

"Wait," he cried to his men, holding one arm out, palm flat to halt their progress. "What in God's name…"

It was madness, and there was no way that he could sort it out in his mind. Santos and his followers appeared human, at least, and yet it would seem that these nightmare—things—were fighting the battle that Hugues had planned for himself. Which side should he join, or would both turn on him if he and his men interfered?

Santos drew a small group of his men into a tighter circle around a small wagon and a couple of wooden cases which two of his monks held between them. The small party began to edge toward the tunnel on the opposite side of the battle from the knights, and for the moment Santos was actually making headway. The remaining monks fought with renewed fervor, driving the pale creatures back in a sudden surge of effort.

Before de Payen could decide what to do, Santos turned and ran. He was gone down the tunnel, followed by the small group of his followers who pulled the cart and carried the crates. Behind him the battle raged on. For the moment, the attackers had lost sight of their goal, if they'd ever had a goal. Santos was getting away! That was all that it took to galvanize Hugues into action. If he were to die in these passageways, it would at least be for a reason.

"We must find a way past this and follow," he whispered harshly. His voice carried too loudly, he thought, but there was nothing to be done about it. "If we can slip around the right side, maybe we can flank them and win through to the tunnel beyond. I don't know where Santos is going, but I don't want him getting away."

His men nodded grimly, though he read his own uncertainty mirrored in their eyes. Hugues leaped from the shadows with a cry and launched himself forward. In seconds he was abreast of the monstrous things threatening to overrun the monks. He slanted past them at an angle and aimed his blade at the first throat that presented itself. He'd not calculated for the creature's swiftness, and it nearly dodged his blow. He sliced flesh, but its head was not cleanly severed. It lolled to one side grotesquely, but the creature didn't fall. Instead it turned, howling in pain and outrage and raked its claws in a slashing attack. Hugues only just managed to slip beneath the blow and dive forward.

They were into it now, and there was no way out but through. De Payen heard the gurgling scream of one of his men from behind him, accompanied by the outraged cries of another, and he risked a glance over his shoulder. One of the things had grabbed Louis Le Chance, one of his oldest and most loyal knights, and had dragged him down, latching onto his throat like an animal. Blood coursed out of a gaping hole where the thing had torn le Chance's throat with its teeth, and that blood ran down the sides of its face as it glared at de Payen in hatred.

"Leave them," he thundered. It was all he could do to turn his back on that sight and not launch himself at the creature's back. It would have been his last act, and as much as his heart cried out to him that it was the right thing to do, he had a responsibility to the rest of his men, and to the Church. Turning, he drove onward again.

Behind him one of the monks had taken advantage of the moment to pounce on the creature who'd turned on Le Chance, and when Santos's follower grabbed the thing, its flesh began to sizzle and pop. The brown-robed assailant screeched, its voice a hideous parody of human speech, and though there were no words recognizable, de Payen knew it for the same dark tongue Santos had used earlier. What in heaven had he gotten himself into now? And what were these things, if not men?

The ghoul, or whatever it was, dropped Le Chance and reached with all its dying strength for the monk, but it was too late. The distraction of feeding on the knight's blood had cost it precious time. It withered and cracked away, flesh flaying from bone and dissolving to the floor as the monk turned, dropping it and launching back into the last of the battle.

De Payen was more concerned with breaking through without losing any more men, and the monk had left an opening he'd been waiting for. As it moved aside, he launched himself through. At the death of their comrade, the pale creatures redoubled their assault on the remaining monks, and the knights dove after de Payen into the shadows beyond. They had lost their torches, but they moved ahead blindly. Even total darkness was better than what they'd just faced. None of them wanted to become the victory feast for the winners. Somewhere ahead of them their quarry was fleeing. That meant there had to be another way out.

"I can feel a breeze," de Payen called back to them. "It is fresh air, and it is coming from the right."

He groped his way along the wall until he came to an opening, and without hesitation he slipped through, grasping the arm of the man behind him and ordering the knight to do the same for the man behind him. They moved steadily along the wall, the sounds of the battle behind them drifting away until they moved in a silence broken only by their own heavy breathing and the scrape of their boots on the floor of the tunnel. Their breath echoed loudly through the shadows, so loudly that de Payen had the irrational fear that the sound would give them away to their enemies.

If Santos's followers had powers like he'd just witnessed, Hugues was beginning to have serious doubts, faith or no faith, in his ability to face down their leader. Even so, he knew he had to try. He'd run from this man once, and those few moments he'd cowered in fear had been the worst of his existence. He would not bow down so easily a second time.

Montrovant had said that he had all that he needed to succeed within him. If this were true, then it was time he made use of it. Santos would not have fled if there were no chance of his destruction, and Hugues kept that thought foremost in his mind.

Ahead, a dim light had begun to seep through the shadows, and he hurried his pace. There was no sign of movement, no sound from the shadows, but he did not relax his vigilance. He moved warily, ready for attack from any side. The swiftness of the earlier attack from the creature in the tunnels had proven enough to keep him attentive.

Behind him, pressed into an alcove on the far side of the passage where de Payen had taken a right toward the surface, Santos stood, huddled with a small band of his faithful. They remained as still as statues as Hugues and his men inched past. He stood so close, in fact, that he could sense their fear, and their determination.

He smiled. The mortals had taken the path to the surface, as he'd known they would, and he was free to continue on his way to freedom. Darkness and tunnels were second nature to him, as comfortable as they were terrifying to those who pursued him. It would never occur to them to follow him deeper, only that he would seek the surface and escape.

There were many byways beneath the city of Jerusalem, and he knew them all. They would not easily follow his escape, now that he had slipped free of their sight. He would disappear into the night and be gone before they even realized they'd missed him. It was refreshing to see that the new crop of fools was as easily duped as the last hundred.

He spun, whispering commands to those around him, and they slipped on down the larger main passage, moving deeper into the bowels of the city.

When it became clear that he would never catch up with de Payen, Daimbert turned resolutely back toward the chambers that Father Santos had fled. He would need to know as much as was possible about this place—this evil—before he made his report to Rome. They might have sanctioned this man's actions, but Daimbert could not believe, if this was the case, that they'd understood them. It was a chance to redeem himself in the eyes of the Holy Father, and Daimbert suddenly found that he wanted that very much.

He himself had met Father Santos only twice, and the man, while dark, had not struck him as being anything beyond a very mysterious and perhaps overly arrogant priest. There had been no indication of otherworldly activities, and even with the evidence staring him straight in the face it was difficult to grasp. It bothered the Patriarch that after so many years in the service of the Church, albeit not entirely faithful years, he could so easily be duped by evil.

What his eyes and mind had not seen before, his heart and soul could now sense. He returned to the room where the ceremony had been held and began a more thorough investigation. He found the curtained alcove behind which Santos had meditated. The chill was deepest in that darkened corner, and intricately embroidered tapestries covered the walls.

The man had left in great haste, and there were a number of objects left behind—leather-bound tomes of a sort Daimbert had never seen, scrolls that appeared to have been penned in Egyptian hieroglyphics. He knew he would have to take each of them to the Temple and have them deciphered by his scholars. He might have to send some of them to Rome to make sense of them.

He kicked aside a blanket, and a small box was revealed. He picked it up and carried it into the main chamber, calling for one of his guards to bring a light closer. Setting it on the altar, he examined it for a long moment. It was gold, that was obvious, very heavy and inlaid with precious stones. The workmanship was exquisite. On the top of the box was a finial in the form of a scarab beetle. He had to calm his nerves before he could find the courage to flip open the lid. He backed away a step as it popped open, but nothing assaulted either his person or his soul, and he moved in close again to inspect what had come to light.

There were two things in the box. One was a pendant, strung on a leather thong. It was in the shape of a cat, and the two eyes were inlaid emeralds. The body was formed of gold, and, just as the box that held it, the detail of the work was incredible. He lifted it free, letting it dangle for a moment. Remaining in the box was a small pouch. He gazed at it for a long moment, then, very carefully, he lifted it free as well and handed it to the guard nearest his side.

"Open it," he commanded. The man stared at him, obviously terrified by the situation and the object resting in the palm of his hand. Daimbert glared at him, and the strings of the pouch were loosened. The guard pulled the pouch open wider, and looked inside. Confused, he tipped the bag, holding his free hand beneath it.

What poured free appeared to be nothing more than dust. It piled in the palm of his hand, forming small drifts like a tiny desert, and he turned his eyes back to meet those of the Patriarch.

"Ash." Daimbert didn't know exactly how he knew this, but he did. It was ash, and his heart told him he didn't want to know of what.

"Carefully now," he instructed. "Put it all back into the bag. Be very careful to spill none of it."

When the operation was completed he beckoned the guard to draw near. "Bring us water," he commanded.

One of the others nearby complied hastily, and Daimbert took the cup that was offered, blessed it quickly, and splashed the water over the man's hands. He said a swift prayer, then raised his head so that his eyes met the those of the guard.

"I don't know what it was that you held in your hand, or who, but the Lord is with you. Go in peace, and do not fear. We shall cleanse this place, and God will grant it his light."

Turning to the doors once more, Daimbert called his men about him. "Let us find de Payen and set about the cleansing," he cried. "There must be no trace of Santos or his evil left. Nothing. I want this place scoured and blessed. I will send word to the Holy Father in Rome myself, telling of the deeds of each and every one of you this night."

His men, happy to set about any task that didn't involve confronting the demons their imaginations had already created from the rumors of Santos and his followers, moved quickly to obey the Patriarch's orders. None had seen Daimbert so full of purpose. None had seen him full of anything except himself and wine, and that in itself was close on to miraculous.

Daimbert moved among them in a steady circuit, calling out encouragement and granting blessings where they were desired, or required. Everything that was found was being hauled to the center of the passage, and Daimbert had sent two of his men toward the stable after Cardin to fetch some sort of wagon or cart to carry it all in. Daimbert didn't know exactly what they had found, or what more might be uncovered, but one thing was certain—what was deemed important would go to Rome, but the rest he would burn. All of it. Every trace that Santos had walked these halls would be eradicated.

He watched as his men disappeared down the corridor, not turning from them until their forms had melted into the distance. Outwardly, he was the man of God he'd always been meant to be. In his eyes, however, swam only questions.

Pierre and Louis had reached the stables without incident. The disturbance among the animals, whatever it had been, had ended, and they found each and every horse in the place it had been left, resting easily. Pierre was ready to turn back toward the tunnels and find a suitable place from which to protect the entrance, when Louis cursed and dropped suddenly to one knee.

"What is it?" Cardin asked quickly, kneeling beside his companion.

"This," de Moyer replied. He held up a shiny silver pendant. It was an ankh—Pierre recognized it from tales of Egypt. De Moyer had seen it flickering in the scattered dirt of the stable floor. As his eyes neared the floor, Pierre saw that there were footprints leading away from where the pendant had lain. He followed them with his eyes, and they led straight at one of the stone walls.

Staring at one another in consternation, they followed quickly. The trail was joined by the twin tracks of a small cart, or wagon, and they hurried their steps. Pierre kept a close watch over his shoulder to prevent ambush, and Louis, who had been a skilled tracker as a youth, was bent low, scanning the ground and the surrounding shadows.

They came to the wall, and the tracks ran straight into it. De Moyer pointed to the ground on one side, and Pierre cursed softly. There was a long, sweeping scrape in the earth, as though a door had swung open across it.

He pressed his hands against the wall, groping among the nooks and crevices until he found what seemed to be a man-made indentation. His fingers slid into it easily, and he pulled. Nothing happened. He slid his hand upward a bit, and his thumb brushed something thin and cold. He gingerly took hold of it, and found that it was a lever. Flipping it up, he stepped back and a large section of wall slid to one side easily.

"That stone must weigh more than twenty horses," Louis said, awestruck. "And yet it moves as easily as the door to my chamber."

Pierre didn't reply. He'd heard of such things. His father had traveled to Egypt, and there were architectural marvels there that still set his mind reeling. This was the first time he'd witnessed such—magic—in his lifetime.

"Someone has taken this path," he grated, "and not long ago. Whoever it was stole one of the feed carts."

"Should we follow it?" Louis wondered out loud.

"We cannot," Pierre answered. "We must guard the passage, as ordered. I will hold that entrance," he pointed to the main tunnel, "and I will keep an eye out for any who might pass this way. You return to de Payen, or Daimbert, and tell them what we've found. I will place the others around the stables, watching from different angles. Quickly—success could depend on your speed."

De Moyer nodded and turned away, racing off down the passage. Pierre hesitated, then grabbed the recess in the stone door once more and pulled it to. It slipped back into place as easily as it had opened, leaving no trace of its existence. Pierre had to mark the spot by tying a small scrap of cloth they'd found around the lever to be certain he could find it easily when de Moyer returned.

This accomplished, he moved back across the stables,

never letting his eyes cease their constant scan of the shadows surrounding him. He quickly dispersed the other two knights, one to the back of the stables, in case there was more than one secret opening, and the other toward the exit leading to the streets above. If whoever had taken that cart was to return, he would probably not be alone. Pierre was in no mood to face Father Santos or his men with only two others to aid him. It would be better to follow, and to see where they might disappear to.

He found a niche just inside the entrance that shielded him from view in either direction, but that allowed a clear view of the wall that held the secret passage. It seemed, already, that de Moyer had been gone for hours.

Santos pressed on through the shadows, his followers gathered closely about him. The only sound was the creaking of the cart's wheels. He'd lost quite a bit in this encounter, but nothing of true consequence. Those who had been destroyed he could replace, and the treasures so long buried beneath the temple, and then the mosque, had been removed safely. What they couldn't carry had been buried more deeply still in the bowels of the city, and despite his own disappearance in those catacombs, he doubted that de Payen, or that fool of a Patriarch Daimbert would venture in too deeply to search them out.

He thought with regret of the amulet—the cat had been powerful, and he'd not wanted to leave it, but time had been more important. He thought as well of the ashes. He wondered what de Payen, or Daimbert, would do if they had any idea whose remains those actually were. Some things could be replaced, others were eternal. He stole a quick glance at the cart being dragged behind them.

So many years he'd had this burden. There were few beings, alive, undead, or otherwise, who could remember a time when he had not guarded the secrets. His purpose had always been clear. He was very good at what he did, and each passing year brought more power, more understanding. His flesh was not what it had once been, but his mind, his essence, these were infinitely more. A small price to pay.

He smiled as he thought of the mortals left behind, dashing about the tunnels in shock, finding the tidbits he'd left behind and realizing that it had all been there from the start. Under the noses of the Patriarch and Baldwin, and more recently de Payen, he'd flouted their faith and drawn the curtains across their eyes so perfectly that they hadn't even suspected. If it hadn't been for Montrovant, curse his thrice-damned soul, Santos would *still* be leading them astray.

Now it was undone, for the moment. He would have to find a new place, a new haven for that which he guarded. He would need time to regroup and build up his forces. It was a game he'd played countless times. The one thing that itched at the back of his mind was the attack he'd just escaped.

He had followed Montrovant's actions as closely as his situation allowed, and the Nosferatu who'd attacked did not fit into the picture well at all. Montrovant was old, and dark, but he was not Nosferatu, nor was he ancient enough to command any allegiance beyond his own family. That meant that there was a third party to be considered, and thus far that party had not made their presence known. Whatever the meaning behind that attack had been had not yet come to light.

Santos searched his memories, seeking any who might know of him, or carry some sort of grudge, but he came up blank. Many knew he existed, but most were content to leave him to his task. Others knew enough to fear him, and left him alone. No matter. The Nosferatu had failed. He'd escaped, and that was the end of the issue.

Not far ahead they would make the ascent to the surface, well clear of any holding of the Church, or Montrovant. Once clear of the city, they could make good time, and he knew the Dark One could not follow him by day. Such a limitation on a powerful spirit like Montrovant widened Santos's grin. It was good to have a challenge, an enemy worthy of more than passing thought. It had been too long—centuries.

He felt the slope of the floor shifting gently upwards, and he hurried his pace. Time to be free of these caverns once and for all, and on the open road. They rounded a bend in the tunnel, and from the shadows a calm, lilting voice called out to him, stopping him as though he'd slammed into a wall.

"So good to see you, Astrokhen," Kli Kodesh greeted him. "Such a shame it has to end this way."

As the pale, thin creatures dropped upon them once again, Santos cursed. Within moments they were buried in the onslaught, and he had no time to think of anything except clawing his way through the pile to where the ancient madman grinned at him.

"Kli Kodesh," he grated. "I should have known."

"That is true," the slender vampire replied, still grinning. "But then, where would the fun have been in that?"

Santos began to feel fuzzy, and he shifted his thoughts to fight off the sudden inner attack—too late. Darkness engulfed him, and he cried out in dismay. The last thing he heard before oblivion claimed him was Kli Kodesh's wild laughter ringing from the walls and driving him farther and farther into darkness.

SEVENTEEN

Le Duc had watched over Montrovant's prone form until he could no longer keep the lids of his eyes open. At last exhaustion stole his final strength, and he'd begun to nod off, his chin dropping to his chest and his prone form slumping against the wall. He didn't know what he would have done, had Santos or any other enemy confronted them in that tiny space. In fact, he did not believe that there was anything he could have done against a being powerful enough to move aside the stone that Montrovant had used to seal them away, especially not in his own weakened condition. Somehow he still felt the need to be vigilant. Montrovant showed no signs of life at the moment, and it appeared that he would not be rising any time soon. He'd mentioned sunset.

It was a lot to take in all at once, particularly on the far side of the last couple of days' events. Le Duc had remained conscious during Montrovant's feeding this time—and the full memory of the previous instance had returned as well. He'd known the tall, dark man had been something more than what he appeared to be on the surface, and he'd suspected the truth, though he'd cloaked it in every form of reality but the obvious. Even Le Duc's dark mind wasn't quite ready for the truth. Vampyr. He was the servant of a dark spirit, the spirit of a man gone to the grave and returned to tell the tale, and for the life of him he could not be upset by the knowledge.

It was one thing to be attached to the Temple, to de Payen and his unwavering faith and Pierre Cardin with his deep-set compassion. These were men that, while Jeanne could respect them for their strength, he could also understand all too well.

There was nothing about them that commanded his emotions in the way that Montrovant had so accomplished so effortlessly.

It was quite a different matter to know that the one you served was more powerful than any of them could imagine, and that you were closer to his thoughts—and his actions—than any of them might hope to be. It was a position of power, despite the servitude involved, and Le Duc was determined to ride it out for all it was worth. The prime rule of royalty and power was that you got as close as you could to the top, so that when the time was right, you could be there to take it for yourself.

He tried a final time to force his eyes open, but it was pointless. There was no real reason to keep watch. If something found them, then it was over, and it had been a grand ride. Otherwise, the night would bring a chance to explore his options, and those options were looking more and more appealing.

Darkness swallowed him before the sounds in the passage beyond the stone grew near, then faded once more. He did not note Santos's passing, nor that of de Payen and his knights. He slept, and he dreamed.

De Payen saw the light ahead, and he drove his men onward. He didn't know what they might face when they reached the surface, but he knew that they needed to get out of the tunnels, to feel the fresh air surrounding them and to see the stars, or the sun, or whatever filled the sky at the moment, beckoning from above. The darkness was suffocating, and the terrors they'd witnessed continued to occupy his mind.

Besides, the creatures they'd faced would surely shun the sunlight. By day, nightmares grew dim and powerless, and the light shining at the end of the passage was the brightest and purest that Hugues had ever seen.

Not for the first time since beginning their trek through the tunnels, he wished that Montrovant was by his side. Somehow, he believed that all the strangeness, all the visions of hell on earth he'd witnessed that night would not have thrown the man, or angel, or spirit. Whatever he was, Montrovant was more than met the eye, and in a world that had suddenly proven to match that, de Payen was willing to admit he didn't have all the answers. It pained him to feel dependent on any power but that of his God, but situations changed. It was becoming painfully obvious that faith alone would not sustain him through all that he was to face. He'd founded his order in the hopes of one day facing great challenges. Even after reading the great epics of the Bible and hearing the tales of the first Crusade, he'd not been prepared for Santos, or what the man stood for. He'd thought he understood evil, but it had been a vain notion. He'd had no idea of the scope of what had stood before him, nor the depth of his own inadequacy in the face of it. Humility, it seemed, was the first lesson he was to be taught.

He moved toward the daylight more quickly, his men crowding in behind him. He heard muttered prayers, and he wished them godspeed. If they were to overtake their quarry, it would be in the next few moments. He didn't know exactly what lay ahead, or where they would win free of the tunnels, but he knew that the long chase was at an end. That alone was enough to lift his spirits. When he realized that the light was that of the sun, he nearly fell to his knees to give thanks on the spot.

A week, maybe even a day earlier, he would have. The changes that were being wrought on his mind and soul were permanent, and he felt his purity scarred beyond redemption. The urgency of the moment drove him onward. Santos had not been overtaken in the passageway by whatever those fiends had been. That mean he'd made a bid for freedom, and since that freedom beckoned in the form of the open desert, de Payen had to believe he was on the right track. What other course could the dark priest have taken? Surely not farther into the tunnels.

The sunlight was too brilliant at first, attuned as their vision was to the dim half-light of the end of the tunnel. De Payen and his men staggered blindly into the desert, and it was long moments before they could focus on their surroundings. He cupped a hand over his eyes and stared across the desert in every direction, but there was nothing to see. Wavering drafts of heat rose from the desert floor to warp his vision, and the damp chill of the tunnels was giving way to a sheen of perspiration that stung his eyes and brought a sudden chill to his bones. *Nothing*. He turned back to the door of the tunnel and began to examine the ground at the tunnel's mouth. There was a jumble of footprints outside the entrance, most of them belonging to himself and his men. There were two other sets, though, leading to one side of the entrance, then back inside. He stared at them for a long moment, trying to rationalize a return to the shadows, even on the part of Santos. He could not, and yet the evidence stared him in the face.

"I don't believe the tracks belong to Santos." The words came from Antoine le Puy Doc, a knight who'd served de Payen all his life, sharing his goals and later his oath to the Church. "These tracks were made by a very tall man. Look at the length of the stride and the size of the boot. Santos is not so large, and his followers all seem about the same height and build. This track was left by another."

De Payen considered the man's words carefully. If it were true, then there were others who knew of this entrance to the temple. How could he have ever believed his defenses were adequate? How could he have felt secure? The place seemed riddled with secrets, and Hugues had been privy to none of them.

Even as his mind worked out plans to continue the search for Father Santos and to set things right with the Patriarch, de Payen made a resolution to himself. From that moment on, he would trust no man but himself, and no spirit but God himself. The Church he'd sworn allegiance to had been fooled by Santos and his evil, and that meant that any who came in contact with such evil could be corrupted. It did not mean that the Church was part of the evil, only that it needed protecting. Faced with this, the only person one could trust was one's self.

This changed his entire perspective on life. He'd trusted his faith, but he'd also trusted other men of faith. He'd trusted them, and they'd failed him. He'd failed them as well, but he had the advantage that he now knew his enemy. He had no intention of letting that failure repeat itself.

"Let's get back to the city," he growled at last. "I don't have any desire to return through there. I'm not even certain we could find our way back. We need to regroup, count our losses, and mount a further search of these tunnels.

"With Santos gone, we will establish our own perimeters. There cannot be secret passages and entrances to our halls unless we control them. I will dispatch a detail to close off any tunnels we do not have sufficient men to guard. I want this underground mapped and secure."

None of his men seemed eager to return to the shadows, even with the threat removed. If Santos hadn't been enough, the strange, pale creatures had driven the courage straight out of them. Hugues knew it was going to be more of a challenge than ever to maintain their support and their belief in his own strength as a leader. He'd failed them more than once this day. Worse yet, he'd failed himself.

They began the weary trek across the sands of the desert surrounding Jerusalem with heavy hearts. Despite all they'd been through, they were no closer to their enemy than when they'd begun. Off to the right, de Payen spied the hill of Golgotha, and he paused for a moment, turning and letting his imagination roam back to a day when there had been three men crucified there. Crosses still stood as an example to him, a symbol of sacrifice and endurance. He silently thanked Daimbert for whatever inspiration had made him erect them.

The images he'd conjured blurred slightly, and for a moment it seemed that all he saw was a lone figure standing atop the mount. The man was slender, white wisps of hair flowing out behind him and dancing lightly in the breeze. Hugues had the sudden and insistent impression that his eyes had locked for an instant with those of the lone man on the hill—and then he was gone. Shaking his head, de Payen looked again, and there was nothing to see but the hill and the three empty crosses.

"For our sins," he muttered.

"What?" Antoine asked, half-turning to face de Payen.

"Nothing, nothing at all. We must hurry."

As he turned his back on Golgotha and his vision, de Payen was certain that he heard a voice in his head. There were no words, and he was neither frightened nor comforted by what he heard. The mocking laughter followed him through the city gates and on to his temple, feeding the fire of his resolve to put an end to the devilish strangeness that had engulfed his life.

For the moment he pushed it all aside. There were too many questions, too few hours in a day—and he'd had too little sleep. He pushed the invading mirth aside and stepped ahead more resolutely than before.

They entered the mosque just as Daimbert and his men were making their exit. The Patriarch stopped on the stone steps, staring at de Payen in obvious amazement.

"We thought you lost, Hugues," he said quickly. "It is good that you have made it through. Tell me, have you found Santos?"

The expression on de Payen's face should have been enough, but he gathered his failing strength about him and replied. "No trace of him, Excellency. We did find some tracks near a hidden entrance to the tunnels beyond the city. It was there that we won free to the desert. It appears that our mosque is anything but secure."

"Who else has dared to invade?" Daimbert demanded, suddenly passionate.

"There is no way to know," de Payen said tiredly. "They have come and gone, and all they left were their tracks. It is Santos that concerns me. While we found tracks, none of them belonged to the 'good father,' and I would like very much to know in which direction he was headed. If he didn't come back toward you, and he didn't take the exit in the desert, where is he?"

"Was there only one track he might have taken?" Daimbert asked.

"I truly do not know," de Payen said, considering. "We followed the tunnels that led upward, and that is how we made our way back to the surface. We moved in total darkness, and I could not tell you how many passages or rooms we might have passed unknowing. It is possible that he is still beneath the city, or that there are countless entrances to those tunnels. In any case, we have lost him, for now."

"I will set up a perimeter around the city," Daimbert said, his brow furrowed in thought. "Baldwin will support me in this. I will cover every avenue of escape and await their departure from whatever hole they've crawled into."

"We will assist you, of course," de Payen replied quickly, though weariness blurred both sight and thought.

"Rest, Hugues," the Patriarch smiled. It was the first honest emotion that de Payen could ever remember seeing on that face, and he returned the smile with a weak grin of his own. "You have done well this night, and I will see to it that the Church knows of your deeds."

"I will rest, then," Hugues replied. "When the sun sets, if Santos is not ours, I will lead my men back into the desert and we will begin the search anew. We have a lot to learn about this mosque, and the ruins of the ancient temples it stands upon, it would seem."

"We all have a great deal to learn," Daimbert said, laughing. "That is what makes it all so very interesting."

With this, Daimbert turned, beckoning to his men to follow, and made his way back to the streets. Hugues watched until they were out of sight, then he turned toward the doors to the mosque and made his way inside. The sun was rising higher in the sky, and the heat was beginning to beat down against the base of his skull, bringing a dull ache. He needed sleep more than he could remember needing it on any other day of his life, and yet he desired it less.

He wondered where Montrovant had gotten himself to, and what part he might have played in all the evening's adventure. One thing was certain. Montrovant had told Hugues that he had everything he needed to see it through to the end, and he'd been correct. Perhaps the dark one was a prophet.

He slipped inside the mosque, his men following slowly, and made his way to his quarters. For the first time since they'd come to the Holy City, no prayers were heard in the chapel, and no meal was served in the dining hall. It was a time of deep thought, deeper exhaustion, and silence. Within the hour they all slept. Of them all, only de Payen dreamed.

In his dream, Hugues walked across the desert toward Golgotha, and the thin, willowy figure he'd imagined there upon his return to the city awaited him. The man's eyes were endless and his lips were turned up in a smile at once full of mirth and ancient tragedy.

De Payen approached, and the man held out a hand, beckoning him to come closer.

"I am Kli Kodesh," he intoned, "and you will heed my warnings. You play in a game where you do not know the rules. You must be careful whom you trust, Hugues de Payen. Leave no stones unturned in your search for the truth. Even the familiar may prove far different than you've imagined."

"Who are you," Hugues asked, "and why would you help me? Why should I trust a dream?"

There was no answer, and suddenly the hill he faced was bare. There was no trace of the man, Kli Kodesh, or any other, and the three crosses, stark against a backdrop of jet black, glowing softly with an inner light, filled his sight.

"For our sins," he repeated his prayer of earlier that day. "For our sins." He was still repeating it when he felt himself drawing back toward the mosque—away from the hill—back to his own world. With a shiver, he released himself. The darkness released him as well, and, rolling over once, he fell to deep, uninterrupted sleep.

When Montrovant awoke he found Le Duc sitting across from him, wide awake and studying him carefully. The man did not have a weapon drawn, but there was a definite tension in the air. It appeared that a great deal had been going through the knight's mind.

Stretching casually, Montrovant rose, giving himself the advantage of looking down from the full extent of his six-foot-plus frame before speaking.

"Much has changed since I first spoke to you," he said quietly.

"Nothing has changed," Le Duc replied. "Nothing, except that we stand, facing one another, in a cavern with no torch, and I can see you plainly. There is no light here. Perhaps you could explain this to me?"

"You will find," Montrovant replied, his smile widening, "that your acquaintance with me will not be *totally* to my advantage."

"I am not certain that seeing in the dark is a thing I have dreamed of," Le Duc replied, rising swiftly. "This is especially true, my friend, if this is the only advantage offered."

Montrovant moved so swiftly that Le Duc was only aware of the sudden pressure cutting off his windpipe. He had seen no motion, and yet Montrovant was so close that the scent of him filled Jeanne's nostrils and his cold flesh gripped the knight's throat. Montrovant flexed his fingers, then eased back a bit. He waited for Le Duc to finish choking and coughing before continuing to speak.

"You will also find," he grated, "that I am not long of temper. I do not need you so badly, my friend, that I cannot cast you aside if you annoy me. Keep that foremost in your mind, and our relationship could be—endless."

Le Duc glared at him still, though fear warred with anger in his eyes. At last the man nodded, and Montrovant released him, turning away and moving toward the stone that blocked their exit from the small cavern.

He hadn't moved two steps when he stopped cold. He ignored Le Duc for the moment, his eyes faraway. There was a long moment when the control of his emotions slipped, and he cursed. Le Duc would have seen that flicker of uncertainty, and Montrovant knew that the smaller man would be considering the option of slitting his throat. The moment passed, and Montrovant returned to himself.

Cursing, he crashed against the stone that sealed them in, and it rolled aside as though made of smoke. Le Duc stared at the opening that loomed before them for a long moment. Seeing that Montrovant had not hesitated, and that the tall man was moving swiftly toward the tunnel that led to the desert entrance once again, he leaped to his feet and followed quickly. Though he could now see his own way out, he had no intention of being left behind.

Montrovant paid no more attention to Le Duc than he might have a gnat. He'd felt a summoning, and though it had not been directed at him, he knew the source well enough. The worst of it was, he knew the one summoned, as well. De Payen would be no match for Kli Kodesh, and there was no way of knowing what the ancient madman might say, or do.

There was nothing to protect the knight from what might come, and Montrovant would have given much to have known exactly what it *was*. Kli Kodesh was no more predictable than the weather, and quite a bit more dangerous. Would he give away Montrovant's secret, or would he kill de Payen himself? Perhaps he only found the huge knight "entertaining."

With Le Duc in his wake, he burst from the tunnels into the desert sands and made for Golgotha. Though he moved far too quickly for his follower to match his pace, there was a trail—a bond between them—that could not be denied. Given time, Le Duc would find him. The important thing—and Montrovant didn't even know why it seemed so important—was to catch Kli Kodesh before he left Golgotha. Somehow he knew there were answers to be found if he could only get the opportunity to ask the proper questions.

The laughter that had ushered de Payen back into restful sleep died away, and Montrovant screamed his curse to the night. The summons was ended, and Kli Kodesh had vanished without a trace. When he reached Golgotha, it was bare. The crosses stood in a row, mocking him, and behind him he could hear Le Duc cursing.

"Kli Kodesh!" he cried. "Kli Kodesh, you owe me an answer. Where is he? Where has he taken it?"

There was no answer. The wind carried away the dying echo of a madman's laughter, and Montrovant dropped to his knees, paralyzed momentarily by his own anger and frustration. Then he rose.

From the desert, he heard Le Duc crying out to him, and he managed a smile. "Interesting." he muttered. "You wanted it interesting, old one. It shall be as you wish."

He turned to the shadows, and he did not look back.

EIGHTEEN

When Santos came to his senses he was sprawled out on the stone floor of the tunnel. As he lurched groggily to his feet, the image of Kli Kodesh's face rose to mock him. His followers cowered against the walls, watching and waiting. It seemed that the ancient vampire had allowed them their freedom once he'd gotten what he'd come for. There was no sign of the Nosferatu. Santos ignored his followers. He searched the shadows for the cart they'd pulled behind them from the caverns, but as he'd feared it would be, it was gone.

"Damn you," he cursed, spinning quickly. "Did you see him? How could he just take it?"

Though he fumed, pacing back and forth in barely controlled rage, Santos knew the answer. If Kli Kodesh could best their master, these would never have stood before him. It was a wonder, under the circumstances, that they'd not volunteered to pull the cart for the undead one. One thing was certain. The vampire's love of entertainment would be his downfall. He should not have left Santos alive.

There was no way to know how big a lead Kli Kodesh had on him, but Santos knew with certainty that he had to follow. He'd been charged with the care of certain artifacts and talismans, and the trust that had been placed in him could not be betrayed. Not if it meant following to the ends of the desert, or the world itself. One thing he and Kli Kodesh had in common was time. Following would not be a problem, either. The aeons had linked him to those treasures in ways even Kli Kodesh would not be aware of. They would draw Santos like a magnet.

He strode purposefully to the tunnel's end and stood, the

night wind blowing gently against his face as he raised his eyes to the stars. He let his thoughts drift away and blanked his mind, reaching out to grasp at the strings of essence that would lead him to his attacker and return what was his to guard, his to care for and protect. The summoning was as comfortable as a second skin, and he felt his anger cooling into steely resolve.

Kli Kodesh was old, and he was wise in many ways, but he was mad, as well. The objects he'd taken, if they reached the wrong hands in human society, could spread havoc; the repercussions of which might never cease to rock the cornerstones of reality. Not that Santos cared much about reality, but the thought that he had fallen short of his responsibility, that was another thing entirely. He was always amused by the notion that men—in particular Christian men—believed him to be evil. He served a purpose that was in the best interests of all. If his service did not fall within the guidelines of their accepted reality, that was a problem they would have to deal with among themselves. If he didn't find and retrieve those artifacts soon, it was likely that all the world would find out first hand what they'd owed him for so long.

He could sense traces, faint and fading fast, but traces that he could follow. He thought back to the things he'd left beneath the mosque, and for a second time he wished he'd not forgotten the pendant. He'd had it for many years, and it would have served him well in this instance, as it had so many times before. It was linked even more solidly to that which he'd guarded than he himself.

There was no way to return for it. Either that fool de Payen or the pompous Patriarch had taken it for his own, and he had no time to trifle with either. They could go about their petty business and meaningless lives, never realizing the safety and protection his existence had brought to them, and to their faith. He would go after what was his to keep.

Not all of the secrets Santos had guarded were Christian, but there were enough to have made a difference. There was history, and there was truth. When you have lived too long with history, sometimes it is best to let truth remain buried. Santos had studied artifacts that the Patriarch, or even the Holy Father in Rome had only read about, or heard tales of around late-night fires. He had held in his hands relics that would pale the most powerful in the coffers of the Vatican, and he'd walked the sands and times of their savior.

His studies, and his knowledge, had been sufficient to protect that with which he'd been charged for so long that the sensation of worry and the possibility that he might actually fail were as alien as the humanity he'd forsaken in the Rite of Rebirth had become to him. His studies had taken him into darkness his mortal self would have never comprehended, and yet he'd risen from that, even from a time spent in the Underworld itself. He knew the secrets of true names, and his time with the Cappadocians had given him a means to release that potential. His time in the lands of Egypt had given him the secrets of amulets, and relics. He had been perfectly molded to the role of guardian. Now the perfection of that mold had been challenged, and broken.

There were endless secrets to be uncovered by one with the combination of endless time and infinite patience. Even after so many years of study, he craved more. There was an underlying essence to all power that Santos could sense, but never quite grasp. Others believed in specific paths to that essence of power; Santos believed he would have to find his own. For the moment, his path led after Kli Kodesh.

He returned to the passageway. "He took everything?" It was more of a statement than a question, but one of the robed monks stepped forward eagerly.

"No, not everything."

From beneath his robes, the man produced a wrapped bundle which he held forth reverently, his arms shaking so violently in fear that he was scarcely able to maintain his grip.

Santos reached for the proffered package, but he knew before he touched it what it was. The head. Somehow they had kept it from the mad one, the one object that mattered most of all in the struggles that were to come. He held it at arm's length for a long moment, letting the aura of its magic seep through his bones and revitalize his mind. Turning to his followers, he even managed a quick, emotionless smile. The trail would be easier to follow than he'd imagined.

"We must leave this place immediately," he said. "If we give them time, they will hem us in, and we will never break through. I have no time to play games with them in the tunnels. Every moment counts."

They gathered around him wordlessly, and he handed the head back to the monk who'd brought it forward. "You will guard this," he said, his voice barely a whisper, "and you will guard it with your life, and your soul. I tell you now, if you allow another to touch it, I will take both for my own and transcendence will be denied you. Do you understand?"

The man nodded and quickly tucked the head back beneath his robes. Santos dismissed the issue from his mind. Kli Kodesh wouldn't be returning for the head, or for anything else. He had everything that he'd come for and was long gone, trying to put as much space between himself and Santos as possible before the chase began. He knew as well as Santos that the chase would end, sooner or later, and how; but for Kli Kodesh the amusement of the intrigue that would bring that end was everything.

For Santos, the question was how much damage could be done in the interim. As Kli Kodesh worked to see how much entertainment could be wrung from the experience, Santos would have to worry about the rest of the world. Kli Kodesh would also be wondering if he would make it through the coming encounter safely. Santos knew the answer, and he shivered.

Kli Kodesh suffered under the weight of a curse of his own, and it was a magic beyond Santos's ability to counteract. Nothing that he did would end the existence of that one—it was foreordained that he walk the earth as long as there was an earth. Even Santos didn't expect to last beyond that.

For the moment, flight was the only thing that mattered. He had sensed another in that darkness—the dark one, Montrovant. That one figured into it all somewhere, as well, though he was hardly old or powerful enough to pose a real threat. Santos didn't want to underestimate another enemy, so he left the Dark One alone. Everything in his heart and mind cried out the necessity for speed and distance. There would be plenty of time to sort out the facts and develop a plan for chasing Kli Kodesh.

They moved out of the tunnels and into the lesser darkness of the desert swiftly, crossing a small patch of sand and rounding the corner of a low-slung building that loomed from the shadows. It was a stable. Santos had planned well for this moment. With their lost cargo, they would have been pushing their luck, but unhindered by burdens, and with the cover of darkness and Santos's abilities, they could easily slip past any guards Daimbert or Baldwin could have mustered. Once free of the city, there were innumerable places they could find refuge.

Within moments of entering the stables, the group rode out again. Santos rode at the lead, and the five followers who remained to him closed in about him protectively. The moon washed the landscape with silvery brightness, but none rose to bar their passage.

Santos rode with his eyes closed. He concentrated on the desert surrounding them with one part of his mind, scanning for any who might spot their flight or attempt to attack. De Payen and Daimbert were not the only ones with men on the roads. There were bandits littering the desert as well, and though they were no danger to Santos or his followers, the disturbance such an encounter might create could bring others down upon them.

He also concentrated on the fading tendrils of the essence of his lost treasures. In his hands he held a stone ankh that dangled from a leather thong about his neck. The flesh that had formed that leather had belonged to a lesser Egyptian sorcerer with big dreams. Santos had taken it when he'd caught the man searching for his name.

And that was a good question in itself. How had Kli Kodesh learned so much? The name he'd spoken, *Astrokhen*, was one Santos hadn't heard in over a century. It was known to one other living being, besides himself, and now apparently Kli Kodesh, and it was a cause for more concern than even the loss of that which he'd protected. It gave the old one a defense. That name, in the wrong hands, could even be Santos's undoing.

He wouldn't be taken by such a ruse twice, but to lose half his true name to one such as Kli Kodesh was a nightmare from the depths of the Underworld itself. Not since he'd held the tattered pages of the ancient writings of the Egyptian mage Cabiri had he heard any other use that name. He'd expected that condition to last an eternity, since he'd destroyed all who had known him, save the one who had helped create him. Somehow Kli Kodesh had managed to draw back the veil that covered Santos's past. His own power was so closely related to that which Kli Kodesh had used on him that it grated on his nerves to have been bested. His was the mastery of true names, *Ren*, as the ancient writings called them. To find the ability to use such a power in the hands of one of the Undead was a sign of changing times, and different rules. Already Kli Kodesh was protected from destruction by his curse; now he was doubly dangerous by the knowledge he'd gained.

Perhaps too many years in hiding, alone with his own followers and the treasures that had been entrusted to him had made him soft. His edge was fading, and he'd not learned anything new in more years than any mortal man on the planet had lived. The night air felt soothing against his skin, and the steady rhythm of the horse's gait relaxed him further.

He gripped the reins tightly and allowed his mount to carry him forward with the others. Willing his hands to remain fixed in their grip, he released his Ka to the Shadowlands, floating free of the physical restraints of body and form. Those around him were still visible, but their pallor had changed. One of his followers' head lolled to one side, nearly touching his shoulder and bouncing erratically as he rode.

Santos ignored the death sight, concentrating on covering ground as quickly as possible beyond the Shroud and scanning the terrain ahead. He was able to travel more swiftly with his spirit form released from his body, but it was a risk. There were many things that could harm the part of him he'd left behind.

He passed over a rise and into a small village. There was an inn, the doors hanging loosely from broken, rusted hinges. Outside, the bones of a horse were still tied to the post as they'd been in life. Dust rose from the stone lip that was the establishment's well. Santos ignored it all, concentrating. He knew the horse lived, and he knew that what he sought could be found inside. He needed to get himself and his followers out of sight as quickly as possible, and this appeared to be an opportunity to do so. He let his spirit form slide through the walls of the inn and made his way directly to the kitchen, where the innkeeper, a huge, burly man with a red face and bulbous nose that spoke of too many pints of ale stood stirring a huge kettle of stew.

Concentrating, Santos willed his form to materialize as a glowing, floating spirit, directly over the man's pot. He blended his form with the smoke that already rose from whatever vile concoction was simmering, and it took a moment for the man to realize that his situation had changed.

Choking back a scream, the innkeeper took a step backward, ripping the ladle free of his stew and sending droplets of the foul, thick fluid flying in sparkling arcs to every corner of the room. The man looked as though he stared into the face of Death himself, and Santos did nothing to correct this notion.

Reaching out with his mind, he implanted his words carefully.

"You will open your cellar door in one hour," he directed, "and when you are certain that the party I shall send to you has entered, you will close that door once more. If any come to search, you have seen nothing. They will require food and drink, and they will remain in the cellars until I visit you once again—let none intrude."

If Santos had not kept an iron grip on the man's mind, he would have fallen to the floor, gibbering. As it was, he stood, mouth agape, quivering like a large mound of animal fat. Santos released him slowly, letting his image disperse into the smoke over the pot and returning to the Shadowlands. The innkeeper's slack jaw did not give him great confidence, but the suggestion he'd planted was a strong one. He did not doubt that he would find that cellar open when he arrived in his true form. If he did not, well, there would be one less stupid innkeeper watching over the hunger and thirst of this particular stretch of road. Santos was still in a foul mood, and his patience was worn as thin as possible without snapping.

The return to his body was a quicker journey than the descent to the Shadowlands had been. He felt the pull of his own form, the two halves that made the whole drawing one to the other, and he allowed that pull to take control. There was no time to waste.

He sat up suddenly on his mount, eyes wide and seeking, and it was in that moment that the patrol struck. He saw them coming out of the corner of his eye and cursed. They wore the white of the Knights of de Payen's temple, and they bore down on Santos's party like a thundering herd of cattle.

Barking a command to his men, he reined in to face the onslaught. The monks continued away at a mad dash, as he'd instructed, and Santos sat astride his mount calmly, facing the small army with contempt splashed across his features.

He raised one hand and muttered a quick incantation under his breath. The names of his attacker's mounts came clearly to his mind. Acting instinctively, he called out in a commanding voice, demanding that the animals halt. The sudden cessation of motion threw all but two of the startled knights to the ground violently. The two who remained mounted righted themselves, but it was a short-lived victory. Santos called out a second command, and the horses reared in fright, dropping the remaining riders on the ground beside their fallen companions.

Santos released his hold on the animals' minds, and they fled into the desert, ignoring the dismayed cries of their fallen riders. Santos rode forward a few paces, smiling down at them. He still wore the collar and vestments of a priest.

"You do not show the proper respect," he spat. "I would hear your confessions, each and every one of you, and exact penance, but I fear that my time here is limited. Go back to your weak, pathetic leader and your insipid, mindless church. Tell them to leave me, and I will trouble them no further. Follow me, and it will be the dying act of your bodies and the beginning of the torture of your souls."

With a theatrical gesture he couldn't resist, Santos made the sign of the cross flamboyantly, then turned his mount and rode hard after the retreating monks. He needed to throw the men behind him off the trail. He believed he'd made an impression on them, but mortals were prone to foolish acts of heroism, and he was in no mood to deal with them. They also tended to forget the supernatural as soon as the natural reasserted itself.

As soon as he'd drawn abreast of the first of his followers, he diverted their course toward the village. Rather than riding hard, he planned to lay low, waiting for the search to slip past them. Before the next wave appeared, they would be out of the basement and on the road again, traveling in an entirely different direction. The chase was an age-old game, and Santos knew it well, though he'd not had to involve himself in it for quite some time.

The past few years had been eye-opening. First the Holy City had fallen to the Turks, and he alone had remained to keep them from the objects in his care. His followers had been taken, one by one, and tortured. None had, of course, revealed anything, but each loss had been a blow to Santos's eternal confidence.

He'd been forced to seal the treasures, those he could not carry easily, into the vault beneath the temple as the mosque of al Aqsa was built on the bones of the ancient structure. It had been the only way to ensure that the Moslem dogs would be unable to claim them.

In the months and years that had followed, he'd been forced away. He'd spent that time in Rome, following the mincing steps of the priesthood and recreating his following among the ranks of the Christian "faithful." All that time, studying in the vast libraries of the Vatican and building his power to new heights, he'd yearned to return to his post—his mission. The talismans had cried out to him, and he'd feared that those who'd created him might return, unhappy with the way he'd carried out his assignment.

There had been no reappearance of ancient powers, and eventually the Church had ventured back to the Holy Land, reclaiming that which had been lost. Santos had wormed his way into the front lines of that first Crusade, and he'd remained behind when his "brethren" returned from the Holy Land, sending a few agents of his own along to Rome.

Rumors had been spread, rumors that linked "Father Santos" and those who followed him to great secrets, secrets the Church desired to keep concealed. The rumors were false, in most cases, but they'd served their purpose. Santos had been granted his haven in the bowels of the mosque.

The Church had turned away, ignoring his actions and protecting his rights, even as he'd deceived them. Plans had been in place to remove the treasures, at last, and to transport them to a safer location. That was before Montrovant, de Payen, and their damned knights.

Kli Kodesh, Santos knew. The ancient's obsessions were documented to the depth of legend. Montrovant was a different sort of challenge. The arrogance dripped from him, and his purpose appeared as single-minded as Santos's own. The only question was, which of the treasures did the vampire seek?

His musing was cut short as they passed within the confines of the village. There were none about at such a late hour, and Santos led them unerringly to the inn. He slipped from his mount, and his followers did the same, leading the horses to the stable and inside. A groom staggered from the shadows, rubbing his eyes to free them from the stupor of sleep and too much wine.

Santos moved forward and laid his hand quickly on the man's shoulder. The stablehand stiffened, his eyes bulging suddenly, then he slumped forward. Santos slid him to the side, into the arms of one of the monks, and the man was deposited to one side and was propped against one of the wooden walls.

Working quickly, the monks stabled and fed their mounts. This done, Santos led them into the night once more and they made their way to the inn's cellar. The door stood wide, just as he'd ordered, and they slipped inside, pulling it shut behind them.

As his men attacked the food and wine hungrily, Santos pulled off to one side and seated himself on the ground. He let his mind go blank, and he rested. There was much to do, but as always, he had nothing if he did not have time. None disturbed him.

NINETEEN

It was nearly midnight, and the city slept quietly. Regardless of the scale of the battle that had been joined, the city itself was oblivious. No warnings had been sounded: what would they have said? *There are ancient evils crawling through tunnels beneath your homes. Your souls are in danger.* It would have caused a mass panic, and neither Daimbert nor Baldwin was prepared to handle something on that scale.

De Payen had slept like the dead, rising just before dusk to rejoin the search. His men had already joined the patrols by the time he'd made his way to the streets, and Daimbert was there to greet him, harried, but alert.

The leader of the last of Daimbert's patrols rode forward and dismounted, climbing the steps slowly to where his lord and de Payen stood, side by side, waiting for some word that their quarry had not eluded them. The set of this man's shoulders did not lend them confidence, and his words confirmed it.

"There is no sign of him, Excellency," the guard said, dropping to one knee and lowering his eyes to the ground at Daimbert's feet. De Payen gnashed his teeth. This was the third such report in less than an hour. There was only one more patrol out—his own—and if they came in without word of Santos he would have to concede defeat. It galled him that, after causing so much grief, the man, or demon, had slipped between their fingers and was lost to them. Hugues hated to leave any business unfinished.

He had to admit that the absence of Santos's darkness wasn't such a bad thing, but the failure to capture, or destroy evil that had been within his grasp ate his heart. His own faith had come into question, his courage had been mocked. These were not insults he would lightly forgive or easily forget. His entire world had been changed, and who was to say for better, or for worse?

Daimbert had been surprisingly strong and efficient throughout the entire process. Word in France had made the Patriarch to be a greedy, self-indulgent oaf. If that had been true at one time, life in the Holy Land seemed to have purged it from his soul. Daimbert had disdained sleep and eaten only lightly since he'd been awakened by Montrovant. His desire to find Santos seemed as strong, or stronger, than Hugues's own, and his followers had reacted in kind. De Payen was glad to have the Patriarch's support, and their combined forces had been able to comb the area surrounding the city with surprising efficiency. A mutual respect was growing between the two, and de Payen knew that this would be a good thing when he returned to France, and then to Rome. It also couldn't harm his status with Baldwin.

He stood on the steps of the mosque, watching the street that led toward the desert beyond, and waiting. It shouldn't be long before his men returned. They'd been the last patrol to go out, having taken a few hours for sleep and refreshment, but they hadn't been so far behind Daimbert's guards. The perimeter of the city had been divided equally between each patrol. He expected their report to be in within the hour.

The sudden thunder of hoofbeats echoed through the streets, and all eyes turned to follow the direction of Hugues's gaze. A single animal, riderless, rounded the corner, several guards in pursuit. None of the men chasing the animal were his own. The horse's eyes were crazed, and foam flew from its flanks as it turned toward the mosque, heading directly for the steps where the small party stood, watching in shock.

At the last moment, the animal veered to the side, heading toward the entrance to the stables beneath the temple. De Payen turned to Daimbert, already moving toward the doors. "It is one of mine. I will take the remainder of my men and see what has happened. I only pray that it is not too late."

"I will send men, as well," Daimbert called after him. "The

more you have, the more quickly you can cover the ground. Godspeed, Hugues de Payen."

Phillip met Hugues at the door with his gear, and de Payen nodded at the young servant, allowing himself a grim smile. One day this one would make a knight himself, he thought. That was assuming Hugues ever came back from the ride he was about to embark on. It seemed that he was too often thinking such thoughts these past days. The confidence that had driven him through so many hard years of life was failing, and he didn't know anything to do about it but dive ahead and win it back.

Phillip's eyes were bright, and he watched Hugues with a respect that bordered on adoration. The tall, broad-shouldered knight was used to such reactions, but for the first time in his life he began to wonder how deserving he was of another's respect. Had he not run, cringing, to his quarters the first time he'd descended to Santos's lair, might things have ended differently? He didn't believe so, but he had to wonder. Surely he would have died, but might he not have raised enough of a disturbance that others could have made their way below in time to be of assistance? Might Santos be in chains, or dead, even now? There was no way to be certain, but it was the uncertainty that goaded him onward.

Those who'd not been on the first patrol joined him now, and their numbers were alarmingly few. He noted that the new man, Cardin, was among them. He wondered briefly where Le Duc had gotten himself to. The man was difficult, but in a battle he was a formidable ally to have by one's side.

Then, in shock, he remembered Montrovant's words. Le Duc had been the one to disrupt the ceremony. He'd been in those tunnels, and he'd not come back. His features growing grim, Hugues added another mark to the tally of debts Santos owed him.

Shrugging all other thought from his mind with an effort, Hugues hurried his steps, making his way to the lower levels where his mount was being readied. He would find his own answers, or he would die in the attempt. One way or the other, this was the night he would see his heart calmed once again. As he moved, he began to pray under his breath, and the weight on his shoulders lifted slightly. It was a grand night to die.

He entered the stables lost in thought, and thus he did not immediately recognize the two mounted figures who awaited him there. Stopping in shock, he raised his eyes to meet those of Montrovant. Those eyes blazed brightly in the deep shadows, and the torchlight flickering in the background gave Montrovant the aspect of a great, predatory shadow, seated as he was on a magnificent, prancing war horse.

At his side rode Le Duc, and that man had changed in some subtle way that de Payen could not immediately recognize. He seemed taller, or darker, and the set of his shoulders was, if anything, more arrogant than before. Still, it was good to see him. It was a very good time to see them both.

"Come, Hugues," Montrovant urged. "It is time that we rode together. This is a night upon which many things will be decided, and there is no time to waste."

De Payen didn't hesitate. He called to Phillip, who'd been paralyzed by the sudden intrusion of these unexpected knights. The boy shook himself free of his momentary paralysis and ran forward to bring de Payen's mount. The others filed in behind him, taking note of Le Duc and their new, dark ally, but keeping their silence. Too many things beyond the ordinary had taken place in the past day and half for them to be too surprised at any development. If Hugues wanted this dark stranger riding at their sides, then they wanted it as well. None knew if their tall leader could bring them through this time of darkness, but they knew that if he couldn't, there was none among them who could.

In moments the entire party was mounted, and they spurred their horses up the slanting passage to the streets above. The moonlight was nearly as bright as day after the shadows of the stables, and they turned in front of the mosque and made their way toward the desert without looking back.

The city, unaware of the darkness that had passed from their midst, or the struggle that continued, slept on. Larger buildings, white stone that caught and glistened in the moon's glow, faded to smaller, stouter homes and smaller businesses.

The scents and sounds of animals, restless in the darkness, came to them through the stillness of the night air. It was as if the beasts sensed what was happening.

They passed a small group of young men who were making their way from the Temple. Ignoring the comments and whispered laughter, they moved on. Daimbert watched them ride away, noting Montrovant's presence with keen interest. He remembered the dark one well enough from his bold entrance into the temple. De Payen would have to explain that one when they returned.

When they had passed from sight, the weariness overtook him suddenly, and he turned toward his own temple. His guards fell in around him, but he spoke to no one.

The road was empty and barren, and the moonlight lent an air of ominous surreality to the landscape. De Payen thundered along, matching the pace that Montrovant set, wondering briefly how the man knew which way to go. He didn't question him, but after the dark powers he'd witnessed in the past few hours, any hint of the supernatural made him nervous. It would have been better had the dark knight taken him into confidence, but he did not.

Words that had come to him in a dream resurfaced, and Hugues worried over them as the road flew by beneath his mount's hooves. "You must be careful whom you trust, Hugues de Payen. Even the familiar may turn out to be far different than you imagine."

Everything had turned out to be different. That was the problem. Hugues was a man of faith, and that faith, along with the strength of his sword arm, had been enough to bring him safely through every situation life had presented to him. Now that had changed, and the longer he rode at Montrovant's side, the more he wondered who, and what, this dark stranger was, and why he'd intruded himself into the life of a simple knight. Too many questions, and no time to seek their answers. He wasn't certain at this point that he wanted those answers, or that they would make any difference. His path was set.

Ahead the silence was broken by a sudden shout, and they

came abreast of a group of knights walking. Hugues counted heads quickly and found that all of his men were accounted for, but none was mounted.

"What has happened here?" he thundered. "Where are your mounts?"

Robert de Craon, a young man who'd shown extreme zeal in following de Payen's orders in the past, moved forward to speak. He lowered his eyes, as though shamed, then raised them again in an almost defiant gesture.

"We had them, Lord," he gasped, tired and thirsty from a long trek. "They fled before us, and we were about to move in when the thin one—the priest—stopped his mount in the center of the road. The others continued to flee, but he just sat there—staring at us. I swear by God's own word that he was smiling!"

"He waited for you, and you did not take him?" Hugues asked incredulously.

"He began to speak, Lord, a tongue I've never heard, nor hope to hear again. He cried out, and I swear our horses fell under his spell. We rode at him at a full gallop, but when he spoke, the horses stopped. It was as though they'd come up against a fence of stone, but there was nothing there. Most of us were thrown when the horses stopped, the rest when he spoke again and they all reared up in fear. Before we could act, he'd sent them running into the darkness, and he'd turned away again, following his men."

Hugues sat still as stone. The man was mocking them. He could have fought, perhaps they all would have died, but instead he'd chosen to humiliate them. Man, demon, or whatever he might be, this creature had no honor. De Payen didn't look again toward the men on the ground. He turned instead to Montrovant.

"What manner of man, or devil, do we follow?" he asked. "I have seen much, but I have never seen a man who could speak to animals. I have never seen a man who could escape an army of knights and the guards of the Patriarch himself so easily. I have never felt the fear his words brought to my heart."

"Do not despair, Hugues," Montrovant replied grimly. "He can be killed, like any man. Santos is but one name he has gone by. He has many. He is no priest, rest easy on that count. He is ancient, older than the earliest ancestor you remember. When Jerusalem fell to the Turks, he was old then."

"Then he must be a demon," de Payen asserted.

"There are other powers, Hugues, than your God with his angels and demons. Do not be too quick to apply his mark to every strange thing you encounter."

"And you, then," Hugues asked quietly, fully expecting Montrovant to remove his head in anger at the question, "are you of our Lord, or some other?"

"We walk the same road," Montrovant replied, spinning his mount away once more. "Let that suffice, for the moment. We must move now, or we will lose him."

"Lord," de Payen called out, still hesitating, "Who is Kli Kodesh?"

Montrovant drew in his mount once more, turning quickly. "Kli Kodesh is a madman," he said softly. "He is one who prefers games to reality. He, also, is of an older time, though he is most certainly enmeshed in the affairs of your Church. Why do you ask? Have you seen him?"

"Only in my dreams, Lord. He warned me to be careful whom I trusted."

Montrovant's features grew suddenly cold and distant, and de Payen would have sworn that the temperature of the air dropped several degrees in that instant. Perhaps this had not been the time for such a question. He hadn't meant to raise doubts of his own loyalty.

"Whom *do* you trust, then, Hugues? Be careful how you answer, because my temper is short these days. I have given you a purpose, given you these brave men to fight at your side and Bernard to support you. You have no reason to doubt my motives, and yet I see in your eyes that you do."

"After what I have seen these past days, Lord, I doubt my own mind."

"Do not doubt this," Montrovant said, his gaze driving spikes of ice into de Payen's heart. "You will live, or die, by the decision you make this moment. There are powers at work here that you do not comprehend, and there is no time for me to explain them. We move now, or I move alone. That is your choice. Santos must be stopped."

He spun away and spurred his mount, plunging along the road at breakneck speed. Le Duc gave de Payen a quick glance, then followed. After only a second's hesitation, Hugues raised his arm and led the others in pursuit. Montrovant no longer appeared as the angel he'd once seemed, and that was a discrepancy that Hugues would have to work out for himself when time permitted. Nothing else had changed, though, and if Montrovant was going after Santos, Hugues would follow. If it cost him his soul, then he'd probably relinquished that long ago, when he'd begun his journey from France.

As Hugues felt the wind begin to grip his hair and drive the tears from his eyes, he blinked once. It was a sobering concept. Montrovant offered him choices, but it appeared that the true choice had been offered when they first met, and Hugues had made it, for better or for worse.

The dismounted knights watched them tear off into the distance, then turned disconsolately back toward Jerusalem and resumed their journey. It would take the rest of the night to reach the city, and none of them wanted to be on the road when de Payen returned.

Montrovant had pulled ahead, and de Payen spurred his mount onward, bringing himself nearly abreast of his dark companion. The man rode with no regard to terrain or the animal beneath him, as though once he reached his goal he would just cast it aside and take another. De Payen wondered if that weren't the truth of it. Nothing seemed to matter to Montrovant beyond the dark secrets he kept and pursued. He wondered briefly how far and hard he'd have to run before he, too, was cast aside for another more suited to the moment.

Many things would have to be revised in Hugues's own heart and mind. His faith was unshaken, but his notion of what that faith meant, and how he would act upon it, were beginning to shift in focus. There were obviously many powers abroad in the land that he'd been unaware of, and many secrets that, if the Church knew of them, were not spread beyond the priesthood. A week, even a day before and he would have considered his own train of thought blasphemous. Now that notion seemed absurd, and it was the earlier level of awareness that took on the semblance of lunacy. How could he have ever hoped to be a "strong arm" for the Lord if he couldn't even make a decision for himself? While he understood that priests were closer to their Lord, he did not understand subversion, trickery, or lies. If that had been the fare the Church had offered for so long, then he would seek the answers to those secrets himself.

Everything in his world had become suspect, and that meant that if he were to find any safety, it would have to be of his own creation. He would find those secrets. He would share what he learned with those who followed him, and he would build his knights into a power that could reckon with whatever it came across. These and other resolutions evolved during that midnight ride, but all of it was forgotten when the village loomed on the horizon.

Montrovant reined in suddenly, dropping back to a trot and gesturing for de Payen and the others to follow suit. None stirred among the homes or businesses, and the silence gave the impression of a large community tomb. Hugues shook off this vision and concentrated. He didn't know what Montrovant was seeking, but he figured that, whatever it was, he'd know if he saw it.

Montrovant was swinging his gaze from side to side, and his movements were slow and cautious. He seemed to be scanning their surroundings, though what method he might be using beyond sight Hugues could only imagine. Suddenly, Montrovant stiffened.

"What is it, Lord?" de Payen asked quickly, moving up to Montrovant's side.

Montrovant didn't answer, but he pointed to one side of the road where an inn stood, dark and silent. The place was closed down for the night. A thin wisp of smoke wound its way up and out of the chimney from a dying fire. Only a single dim candle burned in the interior, and there was no movement at all.

"They stopped at an inn?" De Payen's voice must have given away his incredulity, for Montrovant turned to him crossly.

"Of course not. The basement, Hugues. They have secreted

themselves in the basement. Santos is a creature of tunnels and darkness. If he could have found a suitable tomb, you can bet we would have found him there."

"Shall I ask the innkeeper to open it?" de Payen asked, chastised and inwardly cursing himself.

"No," Montrovant replied. "If we have any chance to take them, it is in a direct assault. Make no mistake, Hugues, Santos is not an ordinary man. If he knows he is in danger, he may destroy us all. Surprise is our only weapon."

De Payen did not miss Montrovant's self-inclusion in that last statement, and he shivered.

They dismounted, securing their horses to a railing on the far side of the road, and moved into positions surrounding the cellar door as quickly and silently as possible. Montrovant and de Payen moved directly to the doorway itself, and Montrovant directed Le Duc, silently, to take the handle of those doors and prepare to open it.

Gathering his courage, de Payen watched, and waited. The last time he'd faced the man they sought, he'd run in fear. This time he would face that fear, or he would die in the attempt. The silence was so heavy that it dragged at Hugues's senses. None of it seemed real but appeared to be taking place in a slow-motion blur.

In the distance a dog howled. As the sound echoed through the streets, Montrovant gave the signal, and under the screen of sound that the animals provided, the doors were flung wide. De Payen dove into the darkness on the heels of his dark companion, praying silently for their souls.

Montrovant prayed for nothing.

Santos heard the sound of the doors being flung wide, and he was up and moving before the first foot hit the stairs. He'd been seeking Kessel, his spirit turned away, and he'd been a fool to ignore the other threats that surrounded him. Somehow he'd not thought that Montrovant would make such an open show of his own power. De Payen and his men would never have found the wine-cellar on their own.

His followers were floundering about in the darkness,

reaching for weapons and scrabbling across the floor like animals. They were lost. He saw it in that moment, and he made the only decision remaining to him. Turning, he moved to the side of the man who had carried the head.

Reaching down, he slammed the monk's head sideways into the wall, killing him instantly. As dark forms materialized about him, striking out at his remaining men, Santos pulled the head free from the man's robes and tucked it under one arm. He had to get out, and he could not lose the only thing left to him to such as these.

He sensed Montrovant instantly, and he knew the vampire knew him as well. There was no time to think. At his back a small tunnel loomed, a drain to help keep the room dry. He reached out with his mind for the proper name, and he willed the transformation. Moments later, as the battle raged about him, he shrank to the form of a large rat. Grasping the wispy hair of the head between strong jaws, he began to back into the tunnel, dragging his prize behind him.

He knew that Montrovant would detect the energy dispersed by the magic, but he was counting on an unfamiliarity with his abilities to grant him the few moments he needed. The action would likely be perceived as an attack of some sort, rather than a retreat. Already he was planning the days and weeks to come. He would travel more swiftly without his followers, and perhaps they could buy him the time to escape. It would be easier to set up in a new place without having to find reasons and excuses for his entourage.

He ascended slowly but steadily and he could feel the cool air of the street beyond the inn ruffling the fur on his back. He backed out and dragged the head through the hole after him, rising swiftly to his own form once more. He called out another word, more elegant than the last. It dredged forth a name in the true language.

At that moment, Montrovant burst free of the cellar once more, moving swiftly toward him. Their eyes locked for just an instant, and Santos saw the hunger in his opponent's gaze, the fury at being tricked once again. He smiled. Perhaps Kli Kodesh had something in his pursuit of entertainment after all. Santos hadn't felt so energized in centuries.

Crying out the name he'd discovered, he transformed once again, taking the form of a vulture. With the head grasped in his talons, he took off in a flurry of wings. Montrovant watched for one long moment, a moment of hesitation that cost him his prey. Santos was moving with the swiftness of the wind.

Montrovant leaped to the air himself, but it was too little too late. Though he shifted form himself, cloaking his actions to those below with a flicker of mental energy, it was no use. Santos's powerful wings carried him away far too swiftly for Montrovant to match, and the first glimmers of the dawn were beginning to send feelers of light over the horizon. Even if he could have changed to a swifter, more powerful form, he had no time left. Santos flew into the light of the sun.

Cursing, Montrovant dropped back to the earth in an alley beyond the inn and made his way hurriedly back to where he'd left de Payen and the others. The innkeeper had awakened, and many other inhabitants of the village were making their way into the streets to find out what the disturbance was. Montrovant pressed his way through them roughly, and they fell aside at his approach.

None of Santos's men had survived. Hugues was dragging the last corpse from the cellar when Montrovant arrived. The knight looked up, and it was obvious that he read the fact of Santos's escape in Montrovant's slumped shoulders.

"We have taken them," de Payen said quietly.

"And yet the one we sought has escaped us," Montrovant replied. "It is a great victory for you, Hugues de Payen, and it should serve to return your faith in your own strength. I will depart now, for I must continue to seek the one we have lost. We will meet again."

De Payen rose to his feet, as though he would say something more, but Montrovant had no time to listen. He moved so swiftly that none present, except Le Duc, who remained with de Payen for the moment, noticed the motion. He was there, then he simply was not, and Hugues was left to stare into the darkness, his mind more in turmoil than ever.

Montrovant streaked across the sands, crossing the miles

as though they were inches. He slipped beneath an old church, long gone to the wind and sand, and pulled open the door to the tomb he knew lay beneath. He'd spent more than one night in the bowels of that house of God, though the last time he'd seen it, it had stood whole and filled with light. So many things he'd known were gone. So many years piled on his shoulders.

He pushed aside the bones of the saint who'd originally been buried there and stretched out, dragging the tomb's door closed behind him. Santos was gone, but he did not have the Grail. Montrovant had seen the eerie, grinning skull-face that the ancient one had carried, but that had been all. Nothing had been dragged free of the cellar. It could mean only one thing.

Santos had escaped, but not with his treasures. That left only one loose end untied—Kli Kodesh. Whatever else the man might be, mad or otherwise, Montrovant would have to find and face him once more. For reasons Montrovant could only wonder at, he'd been duped into putting Santos on the run.

He could only suppose that he was not expected to have survived the ordeal. That would be one surprise he could spring on the elusive Kli Kodesh when next they met. For the moment, he released himself to the silence and to the darkness. Above him the sun rose, bright and hot, and he rested.

TWENTY

Two days' ride from Jerusalem, a party of knights made their weary way down the road in silence. They were led by a thin, wiry knight by the name of Gustav Monterey, and they were bound for the Holy City to enter the service of Hugues de Payen and the Church. Their heads swam with visions brought to life by the words of Father Bernard, visions that had drawn them from home and hearth and beckoned them to a new life. They were the first wave of dedicated knights to attempt that journey since de Payen himself had departed France.

There had been little trouble on the road, one passing band of Turks who'd swung clear when they saw how well the band was armed. Pilgrims were one thing, but no bandit in his right mind would attack an armed party of knights. This party wasn't quite as eager to fight as de Payen's had been, and did not pursue. Gustav was a man of deep thought, and it was the vows and lifestyle of de Payen's knights that drew him to the Order.

It had been hours since they'd last rested, and they were readying themselves to camp. It would be their last such camp before reaching Jerusalem, and Gustav had planned it as a special moment. As he reined in his mount his attention was captured by a pale, slender figure moving toward them across the desert.

At first he thought his mind, and the heat, might be playing tricks on him. The image wavered like that of a mirage, and the man wore only robes and sandals—no protection against the light of the day. There was no way to properly judge the man's age, but his hair flowed back over his slender shoulders in waves of purest white, and his eyes were bright and intense.

Those eyes glittered across the distance that separated them.

Gustav raised his arm and the line of mounted knights paused in the road. All eyes had turned to the desert, and they waited for the old one to reach the side of the road where he could be hailed. It would not be the first traveler they'd encountered on their long journey, but he was certainly the oddest.

As the man approached, a strange lethargy fell over Gustav. What he'd thought were hallucinations brought on by the heat intensified into waves of dizziness that threatened to topple him from the saddle. He reached for the reins of his mount, trying to drive his heels into the beast's sides. He fell short. His legs would not move as he bid them, and suddenly—with the old man so near and those wondrous eyes locked onto Gustav's own, the reason for flight was slipping away. He couldn't understand why he'd wanted to leave. There was nothing to fear.

Gustav didn't know where that thought had come from, but he knew it had not been not his own. He slumped against the neck of his mount, sliding to the side and unable to right himself. Though he could not lift his head to see, he sensed that those about him were suffering the same fate. He heard a crash, as if from a long distance, and a clatter of weapons as one of the knights behind him fell from his mount.

Gustav could see that the old one was still moving closer, but his thoughts were failing him. He knew that there were things he should do, things he should say, but he couldn't form a coherent sound. He fought to keep his eyes open and his mind aware, but he failed. Darkness claimed him, and he saw nothing at all.

Kli Kodesh stood over Gustav's slumped form for a moment longer, then smiled. Grabbing the horses' reins he led them off the road and out across the desert. He wasn't really in any hurry. They would not awaken until the darkness, and that darkness would be the last thing they would see through mortal eyes. Kli Kodesh had a plan of his own, spawned by Montrovant's use of de Payen and his knights. New entertainment.

Darkness would have to come first, though. Kli Kodesh's followers were old, but not as old as he. They could not walk in the daylight, nor did they desire to. They shunned society, and they were not...attractive in bright light. The very nature of the Nosferatu made them inappropriate for the type of service he would set for these. His followers would aid him in the embrace, but it would be Kli Kodesh's own blood that supplied the conversion. That was the beauty of the plan.

The sun blazed away, but he ignored it, taking for granted what other damned only dreamed of. Nothing on the earth was a true threat to him, and the blood that sang through his veins was old and powerful beyond comparison. Some others he'd known had considered this invulnerability the greatest of powers. Kli Kodesh knew it only as a curse. He had no need to feed, nor did he need to seek the shadows during the light of day. These factors had allowed him the opportunity to ensure that he never grew too bored with the world around him. He could involve himself in any intrigue, and doors that were shut to others of his kindred opened wide at his approach. In truth, it was more cruel a mockery of human life than that of other undead. He was only a mockery of what they were, as well. Alone.

It was not enough, of course. It never would be. He needed to find new purpose each day, new reasons not to fall to the ground and howl the pain of his torture to the heavens. He could not bear the notion of defeat, even at the hands of time. He knew that his madness could no more destroy him than the knights on the horses he led, or Montrovant, or even Santos. He could be harmed, controlled, changed, but never destroyed. Eventually, he would defeat any enemy, save boredom, by entropy if that were the method he chose. It tended to take the sting from day to day challenges.

Kli Kodesh was far from the oldest entity to walk the earth, but if he were any judge of things, he was in danger of becoming the eldest as the others dropped away around him. He would be here when the last days came—waiting. He would wait for the only being who'd ever mattered to him to return with answers that could be had in no other way. Until that time, entertainment would have to serve to keep him sane.

He crested a large dune and led the horses into a small valley. Below was a cavern, and within, the Nosferatu slept. They had served him for so long that their individuality had melted away, leaving them almost extensions of his being. He'd never shared his blood with them, but the scent of it kept them near, and their minds were easily enough controlled by one such as he. He longed for more interesting companionship, but at the same time he knew the folly of allowing any other to grow too close. They would die, leaving him alone once again, and another piece of what had been his soul would wither. He had far too little of himself remaining as it was.

In a way it was refreshing to know that beings of Santos's ilk still shared eternity with him. Santos was older than he, and the Egyptian was one of the only creatures living who knew of Kli Kodesh's curse. They had met on more than one occasion— Santos had had the advantage during most of those encounters. This time Kli Kodesh had found a way to come out on top. Such amusement was had only at great cost. He didn't want to think of the price he'd paid his Shadowlands spy for the information on Santos's name, incomplete as it had been. Half a name had been plenty for his purposes.

He tied the horses carefully to the short, gnarled trees that surrounded the small clearing, and he entered the cavern to lie back against the stone. He didn't require rest, not in any real sense, but it was good to slip away from his thoughts. As he drifted off, he wondered what had become of Santos, and of Montrovant. He would need to steer them away once more—a task that should not prove too difficult. Both were so single-minded and filled with grand purpose that they had allowed themselves to be predictable.

Further into the cave, two large crates sat astride a wooden cart. He'd helped to get the treasures this far, and this night he would put one of them to use, but it would be up to others to transport them to safety. He would have to cover their tracks and lay down the intrigue that would lead those any who followed astray.

He was looking forward to the moment, facing Montrovant again, reading the frustrated anger in the young vampire's eyes and knowing that the hatred burning there was directed at himself—a gesture of futility that would enrage Montrovant all the more. Such an excitable boy.

Beyond the cavern's entrance, Gustav Monterey and his men slept, still astride their horses. The sun transited the afternoon sky, and dusk was beginning to fall before the first man stirred.

On the road where Kli Kodesh had waylaid the group of knights, Pasqual, the young man who'd fallen from his mount, awoke to a pounding headache and a parched throat. The sun was falling beyond the horizon, and he was alone on the road. Shaking his head groggily, he stumbled to his feet. His skin was burned where he'd been scorched by the surface of the road, and he felt as though every drop of moisture had been drained into the sand. But he was alive.

He scanned the desert in all directions, but there was nothing to see. He found the tracks of the horses, leading off into the desert, but he did not follow them. There was no way of knowing what had befallen his companions, but if twelve mounted knights hadn't been enough to overcome it, one fallen knight dying of thirst and without his mount would be of no use whatsoever. His one hope of living, and of saving his companions, lay in continuing along the road they'd been traveling until he found help.

It occurred to him that neither end was likely, and that he would probably end up feeding the buzzards, but he pressed on. He'd left his home in the hope of adventure and service to the Church. If God were looking out for him, he would make it to safety; and if not, then it was his time. Either way, he had no intention of sliding easily into the next world.

If this were the adventure he could expect from the Holy Land, he was already beginning to wish for a peaceful existence. There had never been such heat near his home, and he'd never gone more than a few hours without prospect of food or drink. These were lessons, Gustav would have told him. The lessons were for a purpose, and that purpose was known only to God himself. Gustav was full of spiritual guidance. Pasqual found that he missed the older knight greatly.

Though the sun had dropped beyond the horizon, the heat still seeped up from the ground at his feet, soaking through his boots and blistering his feet. He pushed the pain aside, gritted his teeth, and moved onward. He walked through a surreal landscape of twilight until the moon rose, lighting his way, and finally the heat began to dissipate. It was not long before he saw the low walls of several homes lining the road ahead. He hurried his steps as much as he could, trying to keep his sight from blurring and his feet from faltering.

There was no movement in the small village, but he didn't hesitate. If they would help him, let them do so, and if he were to die, then let that happen swiftly. He fell against the first door he came to, banging his fist weakly on the wood and crying out in a dry, rasping voice for water. Moments later the door swung wide and he collapsed across the threshold. He never felt the arms that circled his chest, dragging him inside, or the cool water that was poured past his parched lips. He didn't even know that he'd lived.

Kli Kodesh awoke before the others, as he always did, and made his way from the tunnel. The knights were still unconscious, and he began to drag them from their mounts, seating them in a circle around a small fire he'd laid out before he'd brought them to the valley.

He worked quickly, securing each man's hands behind his back before moving on to the next. He had no fear of their strength, and there was no possibility of their escaping him, but he needed to be certain he could get their undivided attention for what he had to relay to them. They'd sought a mission, a Holy Quest. He would provide it. It was important that no detail of that quest slip past them.

The Nosferatu were beginning to stir, and the first of them slipped from the tunnel just as Kli Kodesh finished placing the last of his captives in the circle. The vampire circled the bound men, gazing at each in turn from beneath hooded eyes. Kli Kodesh paid no attention to him, or to the others that flooded out behind the first like a swarm of insects. The Nosferatu had their own reasons for following Kli Kodesh, and whatever those might be, the ancient did not care. They served a purpose, and they were reliable. It was more than could be said for most beings, alive and undead alike. He trusted them no more than

was wise, but much more than most creatures he'd encountered
in his life.

There was no physical beauty to the Nosferatu. There was
only the strength of their convictions, and the power of their
spirits. Kli Kodesh had long since given up the search for
material pleasure, and so their partnership, such as it was, had
been a good one. He knew he'd be leaving them behind soon.
They knew it as well. Should he return to the Holy Land, they
would be waiting. In its own way, it was comforting.

The last real family he'd had had turned on him bitterly.
Those days were the nightmares plaguing his soul. No matter
how hard he worked at distraction, there were mirrors of his
actions on all sides of him, hemming him in. His true name
had been dropped for more reasons than simple anonymity. He
couldn't bear the burden of the knowledge of how others saw
him. He knew what they would do, what they would think, and
it was too much to be tolerated. He had been called betrayer, but
he would not live that role.

His thoughts snapped back to the present as a groan
announced the return of the first of his captives to consciousness.
He moved into the circle he'd created, seated himself in the
center beside the fire he'd yet to light, and waited. He saw
the first man's eyes flicker, then open, and he drank in the
confusion and fear that washed over the man's features as he
comprehended, bit by bit, the situation he'd awakened to.

The others were moving now, as well, and there were rounds
of curses, moans of pain, cries of anger, all of it fascinating—a
pageant of helplessness. Kli Kodesh drank it in greedily. He
got so little interaction with mortals that he'd begun to crave it
like the taste of a fine wine or a well-roasted fowl had tempted
him in life. They were so...vital. Every little detail could be so
important to them. He was handicapped in this regard by a
clear view of the reality of eternity. Nothing mattered that much
to him.

"Who are you?" a voice grated from his left. Kli Kodesh
swung his gaze to the speaker, smiling.

"I am your future," he said, speaking easily and calmly.
"You are here because I have need of your service."

"You will have no service of me after such treatment," the man spat. He put on a brave front, but behind the bravado of his words his eyes danced with fear and uncertainty. He was a brave man, but not as foolish as he let on.

"Oh, you will do as you are told," Kli Kodesh said, smiling. "It will not be so bad, you know. I have much to offer, as you will find. In fact, this is an opportunity most men go a lifetime seeking, and never find. The first order of business, though, is for you to be introduced to my companions. They are very thirsty, and it has been a long journey. I believe they want you to share in a little—drink."

The Nosferatu poured from the shadows, one for each of the captive knights, and they latched onto their prey before any more words could be spoken. Kli Kodesh watched, fascinated, but he did not rise. It had been many years since he'd sampled the blood of a living being. He no longer required it. Some of the damned would have called this a blessing, but he knew it as another part of his personal curse. The savor of blood, the taste of life—it had been the best of what had remained to him after his life had ended in shame. Now that pleasure was denied him, along with the other things he'd loved, and his closest contact with that sensation lay in watching others feed.

The deed was done swiftly, and completely. Each of the knights was drained near to the point of death, and held there. Another Nosferatu, their leader, made his way slowly from the shadows. Clasped in his hand, he carried an old metal goblet. He moved slowly, his gaze locked on the object in his hands in reverent awe. Kli Kodesh smiled.

The goblet was handed to him, and without hesitation he raised one wrist, slashing it with the elongated nail of his right index finger. He held the goblet beneath the tear he'd made in his own skin, and blood poured forth. The wound was healing, but the goblet was nearly full before the skin had knit itself fully back together. He'd known it would work that way—it had done so years before when he himself had last fed. It was the same cup, as well.

The Nosferatu stared longingly at the blood, but none was foolish enough to make a move to try to take it for his own.

They wouldn't have made a full step before he'd struck them down, and they knew it only too well. Kli Kodesh might have been mad, but he was old, and he was strong. Those gathered had never known one so strong, and likely never would again. There were others, but they spent little time among mortals, and even less with their kindred.

Kli Kodesh rose, holding the goblet before him, and he made his way to the knight who'd awakened first, he of the strong will. The man's glazed eyes stared up at him from the arms of the vampire who held him, and Kli Kodesh smiled down at him in return. He tilted the goblet over the man's open mouth and let a few drops of the blood fall to trickle between his lips.

Gustav, for it was the leader of the knights who'd proven the strongest, swallowed convulsively as the rich, coppery liquid slid over his lips, and the glazed expression of his eyes became a passionate plea for more. Kli Kodesh complied. He dribbled a small stream of the blood into Gustav's mouth, then moved around the circle. Each of them got his fair share, gulping greedily at what was offered. When they had all been fed an equal amount, Kli Kodesh turned to Mordecai, the leader of the Nosferatu.

"You have served me well, and I would have you continue that service."

He offered what remained of the cup's contents, and the old vampire took it reverently. There was a moment's hesitation in which Kli Kodesh believed he might have misjudged his servant, but it passed swiftly. It had seemed that his offer might be refused. He should not have worried. The vampire drained the cup in a single gulp, his head falling back and his eyes gazing in rapture at the skies overhead. Falling to his knees, the cup dropping forgotten by his side, he lowered his head at Kli Kodesh's feet as the ancient blood coursed through his veins.

"I will need a leader for these," Kli Kodesh said, gesturing toward the newly embraced knights. "They are too young and too weak to survive without guidance, and their mission, their survival, is imperative. You will be that guide."

Mordecai did not nod, nor did he acknowledge the new responsibility that had been thrust upon him. His emotions were perfectly controlled, even through the rapture that the blood had brought. Kli Kodesh knew that the blood Mordecai had swallowed was pure and strong, stronger than any draught he'd tasted since his death, and he was fascinated as he watched the old Nosferatu pull himself together, holding his ground in the face of the sensual onslaught. The ancient smiled.

Mordecai turned to his own followers, and he took a step forward. They retreated, but he held up his hands, and they stopped, watching him warily. He had distanced himself from them in that instant, and nothing between them would ever be the same, though he was their prince.

"I leave you now, but you will always be a part of me. My blood lives within you, and my spirit gives you strength." He turned to the next in the line of power, a thin, emaciated creature with a skull for a head and the face of one centuries dead. "Samuel," he said softly. "You have stood by my side through all that I have faced, save he who brought me to this existence, and it is to you that I leave what there is of my inheritance. You will care for the others, leading them to safety and keeping the trust of our secrecy. You will wait for my return. I promise you that I will not remain free of the Holy Land forever. Watch for me in the shadows."

Samuel returned his sire's gaze with mixed emotion and desire warring in his eyes. He'd smelled the blood that Kli Kodesh had offered, and he knew the perfection of the sensation that blood could bring. He knew, also, that his own situation had improved. He would lead, and the others would follow. He would be eldest in the blood. It was a great responsibility, but there were rewards that accompanied that responsibility. There was eternity to await the next opportunity for growth.

Mordecai stared at his protégé for what seemed an eternity, gauging the response to his words and his charge of leadership. He might have waited longer, but Kli Kodesh's hand dropped lightly on his shoulder, and the ancient's voice whispered in his ear.

"We must continue the instruction. There is no time to wait."

Mordecai nodded once, then turned to Kli Kodesh. "You may tell me now what you require, and it will be done. These," he gestured at the knights, "will not be ready for travel before tomorrow, maybe longer."

Kli Kodesh smiled. "You may find them a bit more— resilient—than you believe. You will find the same of yourself. In any case, it is you who must understand my charge.

"You will take the treasures I entrust to you, and you will travel far and fast, stopping only when you find a defensible stronghold. You will spread rumors as you go—rumors that speak of your new order, but speak only in half truths. I don't want anyone to understand exactly what has happened here today, but I want them to 'believe' that they understand. I want what they believe to amaze them. In this I have no doubt you will succeed."

Mordecai's eyes glittered, and his smile nearly matched Kli Kodesh's own enjoyment of the moment. "It will be as you say, Lord," he replied. "There will be none to match our pace, and when we stop we will find ways to protect that which is yours."

"These treasures are not mine," Kli Kodesh said softly. "They belong to humanity. I only wish to ensure that, eventually, when they figure us out and begin to hunt us as the evil we represent, there will be secrets for them to divine—powers for them to unlock.

"I lived in a magical time, Mordecai. I walked this earth with those who are nothing but legend and myth, and they called me by my true name. I would not have that be the last such time before the end of the world, and this is my part in seeing that it will not be so. Do you understand?"

"Not completely," Mordecai replied, "but there is time, I believe, to learn almost anything."

"That is the understatement of several lifetimes, my friend," Kli Kodesh replied, laying a thin, bony hand on the old Nosferatu's shoulder. "There is nothing *but* time, and you will find that there is so much of it that it threatens to drive you mad. Do not fall under that spell. Keep things interesting."

"As always," Mordecai replied. "As always."

Kli Kodesh looked around the circle a last time, then he beckoned to Samuel, who nodded quickly. He and the Nosferatu, all but Mordecai, made their way from the valley. The knights were stirring again, but to a different world than that which they'd left behind.

"So young," Mordecai muttered to himself. "So young to awake to such power." He went among them, laying his hands on each of their shoulders and loosening their bonds. It was going to be a long night, but for the first time in a century, he would awaken to the light of a new day. Kli Kodesh's blood would assure it.

TWENTY-ONE

When Montrovant awoke he wasted no time in climbing free of the debris and making his way into the ruined church. There were too many things happening at once for him to risk sitting still for any length of time. If he missed Kli Kodesh now, he might not find the elusive ancient again for a century—if ever. He stopped short as he stepped free of the debris and ruins. Le Duc sat waiting for him, carving a piece of olive wood with the blade of his dagger and staring into the night sky.

"You found me," Montrovant stated unnecessarily. Le Duc merely regarded him, watching to see how Montrovant would react to his presence.

"It is not so hard," Le Duc answered finally. "In fact, to ignore the ache you have placed in my heart would be an impossibility, but I suspect that you know this. It is my hope that you have not done so with the thought of leaving me behind to suffer it alone."

Montrovant shook his head. "I feel the bond as well, but of course not as powerfully. I would have come for you eventually."

"Of course," Le Duc replied, rising easily. "I think," he added, "that I would like to know more about what is happening to me. I was not consulted, after all—it would seem only fair that I understand fully the conditions of my service."

"Your service is unconditional," Montrovant spat. "I will tell you what you are becoming, but it would make no difference if I did not. You will do as I bid you, and there is nothing you can do to prevent that. You can make the best of the situation. That is what I advise."

"I am dead, then," Le Duc said softly.

"You are not. Not yet. You will live until I deem it is time for you to do otherwise. You have a part of me within you, and you may become as I am, eventually, if it is my will. That is, you will do so should I will it. For the moment, you live. You are of more use to me as a being of flesh and blood, even half-changed, than you would be as another such as I."

Le Duc nodded slowly, as if he were beginning to put together the pieces of some difficult puzzle. Montrovant strode from the ruins, leaving his servant to follow as he might.

"There is no time for this now." he said. "There is an ancient one, Kli Kodesh, who has stolen the treasure I desire from beneath our very noses. Everything we have done is at risk of failure. De Payen and his knights seek Santos, as does Daimbert, but they have no chance against such as he. Even if they did, he lost the treasure as surely as we. Kli Kodesh has made us to appear as fools, and it is up to us to find him and make a final attempt to set things right."

"And you have a plan for how to handle this ancient one?" Le Duc was following, his features alert and attentive. There was a hint of challenge in the question.

"That remains to be seen," Montrovant answered. "I am no match in a straight test of will or strength, but these are not the only available avenues of attack. I need to find out where he has taken certain objects. You will find that I am not easily discouraged, once my mind is set."

"Perhaps de Payen is more resourceful than you believe," Le Duc said softly. "Might it not be a good idea to return and see what he may have uncovered? The man may be too pious, and he is certainly a fool of the highest magnitude, but he is not without certain abilities."

"That he is not," Montrovant agreed. "That is why I chose him to lead the knights in the first place. If Kli Kodesh is still near, then he will call to me, and the most likely place to find him is near the city. Do you have your horse?"

"Better yet," Le Duc grinned, "I have yours as well. You took off in such a hurry, it made things a bit—difficult—for a few moments in that village. I told de Payen that I would remain behind, wait for you and bring you your mount. He didn't want to let me stay. I don't believe he entirely trusts me anymore."

Montrovant nearly grinned. Le Duc was proving a surprising ally in all that was happening. Montrovant knew he could make much better time without the horse, or Le Duc, but he held his emotions in check. There was no real reason to hurry. If Kli Kodesh were near the city, he'd soon know it, and if not, well, then the quest would begin anew. If that were the case, Le Duc would prove an invaluable aide in crossing the country and obtaining shelter.

Caution was what was called for. Attention to detail might mean the difference between success and failure—even between a continuation of his existence, or total destruction. He knew the powers he dealt with were immense. Only a fool would plunge into a whirlpool without some scrap of wood to cling to as he went down, and Kli Kodesh made a whirlpool seem tame.

They mounted up, and within moments the ruined church faded behind them in a cloud of dust, returning to its solitary vigil over the encroaching desert. Neither man nor vampire looked back.

Staggering to his feet at the sound of hoofbeats, Pasqual lurched toward the door of the hovel. His hosts started from their seats at his sudden motion. They'd been seated at a small wooden table, and they hurried to the door in time to support him as he flung it wide and stared into the street beyond. He would have fallen without their aid as a sudden wave of vertigo swept through him. Surely the sounds he'd heard would be his companions returning. If he sat still, they would pass him by, and he'd be left on his own. He had to let them know he was here, that he had survived.

He saw two war horses approach, then thunder past without hesitation. Astride the first was a tall, pale rider with long ebony hair sweeping out behind him and the glint of ice in his eyes. Pasqual met that gaze for an instant, and the eternity that he saw there nearly froze him in place, despite the weakness of his knees.

Behind the first rider came a second, smaller and more slender, but with sharp, wary eyes and the appearance of steel in his wiry frame. This one looked neither right nor left, but stared intently after the first, ignoring Pasqual as if he were so much landscape.

Neither of them was familiar, and the disappointment robbed the young knight of his strength. The stablemaster and his wife, who still held him by his arms, barely managed to lever him back onto the bed he'd leapt from moments before. The woman clucked her tongue and tucked the single coarse blanket around his frame. The man watched at the door until the two strangers had ridden out of sight.

"Who were they?" the knight managed.

"I do not know," the stablemaster replied. "I have never seen them, nor their mounts, before. Perhaps they are of de Payen's knights."

Pasqual's eyes grew far away. De Payen. His goal. He let his head fall back against the softness of the bed, and his eyes closed almost instantly upon its contact with the crude pillow. It felt like heaven to his ravaged body.

"I will go to him tomorrow, or whenever I've regained my strength," he vowed.

The two who'd taken him in smiled, nodding their heads and sharing a quick glance. Their young guest wouldn't be moving for at least another day, but they kept their silence. No sense in upsetting him unnecessarily. There would be time enough to talk once he was more coherent.

Darkness engulfed Pasqual, and he drifted into a world of castles and battle where he wore a bright red cross and rode to war in the name of the Lord. He knew, somehow, that he'd reached a new home—a new fellowship.

De Payen stalked the halls of the mosque in a horrible fit of temper. Santos had escaped, half of his knights had been dismounted and forced to walk back to Jerusalem, and the shame of this had driven three of them to leave his service permanently to return to their homes in France. He and his men had been humiliated, and Montrovant was nowhere to be found. He'd searched the city, even kept his knights actively patrolling the perimeters of the city, but to no avail. The tall, dark knight had left them in the village and disappeared. Every time things got out of hand, Montrovant departed. De Payen was beginning to wonder just what sort of patron he'd given his loyalty to.

There had also been no word from Le Duc, who'd gone after the dark one. De Payen hadn't wanted to allow this, and the fact that neither Montrovant or the knight had returned only served to anger him further at his stupidity. He should have gone himself. He should have demanded answers. Montrovant had all but promised him victory, and yet it had eluded him. In the face of that, rather than offering answers, Montrovant had fled himself, leaving de Payen to explain this second failure to Daimbert, and to Baldwin, and to bear the shame alone. It was small consolation that all of the strange monks had been killed and dragged back to the city. Daimbert had had them burned.

Now the Patriarch sought Montrovant. Daimbert had not asked after the dark knight in so many words, but it was obvious in the tone of his other queries that he was fishing for information. Montrovant had that dual effect on people. He was imposing on a deep, primal level that seemed always to limit conversations involving him to whispered, secretive tones; but at the same time, he inspired a curiosity that would not be stilled. The longer he remained absent, the more of Hugues's curiosity melted to anger.

His journey to France had been delayed. He knew he couldn't wait much longer, but he wanted to see this through to its end, whatever that might be. Bernard would be paving the way, and his letter might be arriving at the Vatican even as he stood thinking about it. He had to get there while sentiments were in his favor.

There was also the matter of the three new pilgrims who'd arrived at his door during the night. They refused to leave without speaking to him, and from the expressions on the faces of his servants, there was little doubt they would remain where they were until he *did* see them. They wanted to join the order—and they claimed to have been sent by Bernard. More mysteries. Bernard had been strangely silent throughout the entire odd business. At least he would end it all with the same number of followers with which he'd begun.

He knew it would be a new beginning for them all. There was too much that had changed.

He was nearly ready to head for the stables and go out himself to search when Phillip burst into his chambers, breathless. The boy's eyes shone, and he could barely contain his excitement.

"He has come, Lord," the servant blurted quickly. "The dark one, Montrovant, he is riding through the city as we speak, and Le Duc is with him."

De Payen barely acknowledged Phillip's presence, but he'd reacted instantly to his words. Before the young man could elaborate further, Hugues was out the door and making his way swiftly down the passageway toward the stairs. Santos's trail would be cold, if indeed Montrovant were still on that trail. It had been too long since they'd last spoken, and if there was new information to be had, then Hugues wanted to be there to receive it in person. If not, he wanted to know why.

Montrovant was dismounting as Hugues burst through the temple door, and Le Duc was already on the ground, taking the reins of the larger man's horse.

Montrovant spun and headed straight for de Payen. He moved with an odd, liquid intensity that nearly drove Hugues to back off a step. He brushed the notion aside and stood his ground.

"He is gone," Montrovant said flatly. He made no apology for his disappearance, nor did he appear alarmed by, or even interested, in Hugues's anger. He stated Santos's escape in such matter-of-fact tones that de Payen nearly screamed in frustration. Did no one but himself care that such an evil man had gone free?

"You let him go?" he said icily.

"I let him do nothing, Hugues de Payen. I have told you before, there are forces at work here that you do not understand. Everything is not the cut and dried truth of your faith. He has slipped through our grasp, but without that which he sought. Santos is a very powerful being, and he has not lived to such an age by being a fool."

"How do you know this?" de Payen asked. "Has he left something more behind?"

Montrovant shook his head. "No, but I saw him in his final flight. He carried only what appeared to be a single human head. The carts that he dragged through the tunnels were nowhere to be seen."

"None of his men made it out of that room alive," de Payen said. "There were no carts there, no treasures."

"Then there is but one answer," Montrovant said shortly. "Someone else got to him before we did."

"You will pardon my bluntness, Lord," de Payen grated, "but if one such as yourself could not stop him, who else—*what* else—could have done so?"

Montrovant didn't answer. He turned back toward his mount, and de Payen, pushing himself forward with every ounce of courage granted him by a long life and strong faith, laid a hand on Montrovant's shoulder, stopping him.

"What shall I do now?" he asked earnestly. "We have failed, and the first great enemy that we have faced has fled."

"You will continue with your mission," Montrovant replied, suffering the knight's touch for the moment, and turning back to face him. "You have not failed, Hugues de Payen. You have driven the enemy forth, and he has lost everything but his life. You should be content, and you should carry out your plans. They are good plans, great plans, even, and they will help to shape much of the history that is to come. Be content with this. Go to Bernard."

"But..." Hugues could think of no question likely to elicit a better answer. He wanted to believe that what Montrovant said was true, but his faith was founded on shakier and shakier ground the more often the dark one appeared to him.

"We will meet again, Hugues," Montrovant said softly. "I am going to need the services of one of your knights." He nodded at Le Duc, whose eyes had taken on a strange glint since de Payen had last seen him. The man seemed taller, somehow, more forbidding. He grinned down with a defiant tilt to his head as if waiting for Hugues to refuse.

Hugues nodded. He'd never trusted Le Duc fully. Let him follow whom he wished. There was no room in de Payen's order for those divided in their loyalty.

Montrovant turned to mount up again, and Hugues merely watched. Just as Le Duc launched himself into his own saddle, Hugues spoke again.

"I don't know who you are, and I have come to doubt who you appear to be. I don't know from whence you've come, or from whom. Despite this, I feel honored to have known you. Go with God, the both of you. May you find whatever it is you seek."

"And you as well, Hugues de Payen," Montrovant called over his shoulder. The two riders thundered into the distance, leaving de Payen to stand, to watch, and to wonder. Nothing, it seemed, was as it seemed.

As Montrovant rode away, he heard a young man rush up to Hugues, out of breath. He heard the words that followed, and he smiled. De Payen would do fine.

"Sir—Lord," the boy babbled, trembling in fear and with the effort of his flight, "there is a report that a band of pilgrims— three hundred strong—has been slaughtered on the road. The Patriarch has asked that you come to him."

Montrovant could almost see the big man's curt nod. Entertaining indeed.

As Montrovant turned toward the desert once more, he felt a now-familiar call reaching out to him. He didn't hesitate but urged his horse toward Golgotha. Le Duc rode at his side and a little bit behind, scanning the desert as they moved through it. He could sense something, as well, though he had no idea what it was they sought.

The ground melted away beneath the flying hooves of their mounts, and what seemed only seconds later, though it must have been longer, Montrovant saw the three crosses on Golgotha silhouetted against the light of the waning moon. There was no one standing on the hill, but he did not change his course. He made straight for the edifice, jumping from his mount as they approached more closely, and leaping to the summit in a single bound.

Kli Kodesh was nowhere to be seen, and Montrovant sent his senses questing in every direction at once, calling out for the old one to appear. There was no sign that his call had been heard, but a hint of mocking laughter floated across the desert.

He saw Le Duc whirl, first one way, then the next, trying to pinpoint the sound. Ignoring his servant, he reached out again. Closing his eyes, he pressed the limits of his ability, reaching further and finding nothing.

The light, gentle touch of a hand on his shoulder nearly sent him leaping from the hill in shock. His eyes flashed open, and Kli Kodesh stood before him, smiling serenely, as though he'd been there all along.

"Hello, Solomon," the ancient greeted him. "You certainly took your time coming back."

Montrovant shook his head, trying to clear the cobwebs the other was weaving in his mind. "Where is it?" he grated, taking a step toward the older vampire. "Where did you take it?"

Kli Kodesh only smiled at first, and it nearly drove Montrovant over the edge. Attacking such as Kli Kodesh could have but one end, but anything would have been better than that silent, mocking face.

Then the old one spoke.

"I have taken nothing," he replied. "The secrets and treasures of that temple do not belong to me, or to you, but to the world. What I have done is to release them back into that world. Without the magic of the ages it has been much too boring for my tastes."

"You have given them away?"

"Not exactly," Kli Kodesh smiled. "I have raised a new group of guardians from the ashes of your Father Santos's failed efforts. They hold the treasures of ten generations, but they cannot use them. They are as you and I, walking, not alive, and not quite dead...not quite undead."

"Not quite undead? What sort of gibberish is that?"

"Haven't you wondered, Solomon," Kli Kodesh asked, "why I have been so hard to find? Why, in fact, my kills have not been noticed? Why none have sought me?"

"I have never questioned the ways of my elders," Montrovant replied. "I always assumed that when I was meant to understand, I would."

"Understand this, then, Solomon," Kli Kodesh went on.

"I have not needed the blood for over a hundred years. I have not needed the touch of the earth for twice that long. I am as comfortable by day as by night. My followers will share many of those traits.

"The secret you seek is cryptic in nature, as are all great secrets. You seek the Holy Grail, but how do you know it does not stand before you, even now? When my savior said, 'Take, drink, this is my blood,' do you truly believe he was pouring wine into a goblet? Do you believe, even for a moment, that my kiss in the garden at Gethsemane was merely a kiss, and nothing more, and that that kiss has damned me for eternity?"

"I have only the scripture, and my memory, to guide me," Montrovant replied. "I have no answers. I did not walk those roads."

"And yet, you seek," Kli Kodesh mused, his smile widening. "May you find what you wish for," he added, "and may it truly *be* worth wishing for, when you find it."

Montrovant was staring straight at Kli Kodesh, but suddenly he stared at only empty air.

"Wait," he cried. "Your followers, where are they? How will I find them?"

"Seek the Order of the Bitter Ash," Kli Kodesh replied, his voice floating across the sand as if from far away. "You will find all that you seek there, and more."

Then there was nothing. Montrovant turned to where Le Duc was watching him, still mounted, confusion masking his features.

"Who did you speak to?" the knight asked.

Montrovant stared at him, then turned back to the empty desert. He almost smiled.

"No one. I spoke to no one. Come, we must ride. There are many things to tell you before dawn arrives, and we must be long gone from this place by then."

Without a backward glance, Montrovant strode down from Golgotha. He leaped into the saddle and kicked the animal's flanks, sending it speeding across the sand. Le Duc turned to follow, but he allowed himself one last glance at the crosses on the hill above him.

Hanging from the cross-bar of the central cross, a frail, pale figure smiled down at him. The light of madness was in those eyes, and wild laughter was bubbling forth from between ancient lips.

Le Duc whirled his mount and followed his new master into the darkness. The laughter surrounded him as he rode. He caught Montrovant after a mile or so, and they rode on in silence. The shadows beckoned with endless promise as the laughter chilled his heart.

EPILOGUE

Pasqual had risen early and started on the road before his hosts could protest. He knew he wasn't at full strength yet, but he felt a burning need to get to Hugues de Payen, and to report the loss of his companions. He felt that, had he remained bedridden for another second, he would have gone insane, despite the wonderful treatment and the food, which, while simple, had been the best he'd had in weeks.

He'd left a short note, written on a scrap of the paper he'd brought along on the journey. Pasqual had wanted to chronicle his adventures. Eventually he'd thought to gather the notes of his journey together and make a book of them. There was something magical in the permanence of written words. Though he knew it had always galled his father, he'd felt more inclined to the life of a scribe than that of a warrior.

Now he felt as though he'd be lucky if those adventures ever made it past their beginnings. He'd been walking since morning, and though he could see dim lights from Jerusalem over the skyline, he knew he was still a long way from reaching his goal. He'd not brought much water or food, not wanting to further inconvenience the stablemaster, and what he'd had was long gone.

The heat was melting into the chill of the desert night, and the weariness in the young knight's bones threatened to drive him to his knees and leave him lying in the road for the buzzards. It was then that he heard the thunder of approaching hoofbeats, and he stopped, waiting. He didn't know if it would be a patrol, bandits, or passing travelers, but he hoped that, whoever it was, would have water to spare. The food he didn't miss so much, but for water he would have killed.

He stepped to the side of the road, just as two dark shapes flashed out of the shadows astride war horses. He started to call out to them, then hesitated. There was something about the lead rider, the way his cloak billowed behind him like the wings of a gigantic bat, and the way his eyes blazed from the darkness as though lit from within. The two were familiar in some way, but he couldn't place them in his mind.

The horses reined in suddenly, and the tall man stared down at him. Pasqual's knees nearly buckled at the expression of hunger masking the man's otherwise handsome features, and he backed away a step before freezing in his tracks.

Montrovant saw the young man alongside the road, and something within him snapped. Kli Kodesh's cryptic words and the frustration of having everything he'd worked for slip through his hands was too much for him, and he threw caution to the wind. Baldwin, de Payen, and all their patrols be damned, he was going to feed.

He would have been fine had there been some clue, some source he might have wrung answers from, but there was nothing. He'd tried to make sense of Kli Kodesh's words, but he'd found nothing but more questions, and the growing impression that he'd appeared a fool ate at him like acid.

He didn't even bother to reach out to the boy or savor the moment. He leaped from his mount as it came to a halt, rearing and whinnying in fear, and he drove the boy's heat-weakened body to the road mercilessly. Without thought he latched onto the flesh of his victim's throat and drank in deep, heaving gulps.

It was over in moments. Le Duc, who had never witnessed his new master in such an act, sat immobile and shocked on his horse, unable to tear his eyes from the scene before him, and unable to get the scent of the blood from his mind. He retched at the thought of drinking another man's blood, but at the same time it called to his soul.

Montrovant dropped the boy in the road, but as he did so, the last dying thoughts seeped from the broken, wilted body, and Montrovant drank it in without hesitation. As the images formed in his mind, a group of knights—an old man beside the road. The disappearance. He lifted his arms to the moon and screamed his anger.

Kneeling quickly, he tried to bring the boy back, but he was gone. Dead, never to return, and his secrets dead as well.

Montrovant remained kneeling, closed his eyes, and concentrated, pushing aside the taste of the blood, fresh upon his lips. There had been twelve of them—thirteen with this boy. They were gone, but not that far away.

As suddenly as his anger had come, it passed. He didn't have all of the answers yet, but he had something to follow, and that was enough. Time was always on the side of he who had the most.

Without a glance at Le Duc, who fought a new hunger of his own within the depths of his mind, Montrovant remounted and sped off down the road. It was just possible that things were about to become...entertaining.

About the Author

DAVID NIALL WILSON has been writing and publishing horror, dark fantasy, and science fiction since the mid-eighties. An ordained minister, once President of the Horror Writers Association and multiple recipient of the Bram Stoker Award, his novels include *Maelstrom, The Mote in Andrea's Eye, Deep Blue,* the Grails Covenant Trilogy, *Star Trek Voyager: Chrysalis, Except You Go Through Shadow, This is My Blood, Ancient Eyes, On the Third Day, The Orffyreus Wheel,* The DeChance Chronicles, including *Heart of a Dragon, Vintage Soul, My Soul to Keep, Kali's Tale* and the stand-alone spinoff *Nevermore – A Novel of Love, Loss & Edgar Allan Poe.* His novels in the O.C.L.T. series include *The Parting, Crockatiel,* and the novella *The Temple of Camazotz* He is also the author of the memoir / cookbook *American Pies: Baking with Dave the Pie Guy.* David can be found at http://www.davidniallwilson.com and can be reached by e-mail at david@davidniallwilson.com.

Curious about other Crossroad Press books?
Stop by our site:
http://store.crossroadpress.com
We offer quality writing
in digital, audio, and print formats.

www.ingramcontent.com/pod-product-compliance
Lightning Source LLC
Chambersburg PA
CBHW060413180626
46817CB00007B/2570